CATRIONA
THE SCOTTISH LIONS

ANNE GREGOR

All rights reserved.

No part of this publication may be sold, copied, distributed, reproduced or transmitted in any form or by any means, mechanical or digital, including photocopying and recording or by any information storage and retrieval system without the prior written permission of both the publisher, Oliver Heber Books and the author, Anne Gregor, except in the case of brief quotations embodied in critical articles and reviews.

PUBLISHER'S NOTE: This is a work of fiction. Names, characters, places, and incidents either are the product of the author's imagination or are used fictitiously. Any resemblance to actual persons, living or dead, business establishments, events, or locales is entirely coincidental.

Catriona Copyright 2025 © Anne Gregor

Cover art by Dar Albert at Wicked Smart Designs

Published by Oliver-Heber Books

0 9 8 7 6 5 4 3 2 1

CATRIONA

Long looks. Long sighs.
   Daydreams and sleepless nights.
   Smiles and laughter.
   Irritations and frowns.
   Heated glances to cold shoulders.
   Love given and rebuffed.
   Secrets. Secrets. Secrets.
   Long looks. Long sighs.

1

FOUR YEARS AGO, SENIOR HIGH SCHOOL PROM —BUNCHREW, SCOTLAND

Catriona could feel her pale skin prickling with heat under the shapeless emerald slip dress—her mother swore the color made her green eyes greener. Her mom was more kind than honest.

No doubt her cheeks and chest were crimson, a perfectly unfortunate match to her crazy red curls, which she attempted to tame in a loose bun, but was afraid the result leaned less toward sophistication and more toward Raggedy Ann.

Thank God, Duncan, her prom date, was bent over a monstrously large plate of spaghetti and meatballs, shoveling and slurping noodles at an alarming rate, and didn't notice her embarrassment. He would tease her mercilessly. They could rib one another twenty-four-seven, and no feelings were crushed by the jibes. This was not the case with many of their fellow schoolmates.

While Dunc was not necessarily a friend, he was a comrade in years of shared school taunting. Duncan, because he was overweight, had no filter, and his face was spotty. Her, because she was the size of a garden pixie with the curves of a cattail plant. To add insult to injury, her curveless body was topped with miles of red waves and spirals–think Merida in *Brave* but ... more.

The thing was, Catriona loved her hair, which was why she didn't cut it often. She considered it her best ... her *only* good feature. Coll, her older brother's best friend, had told her once when she was a girl of eleven or twelve that her hair was nice. He hadn't exactly dipped his toe into poetic prose waters with that compliment, but it had made butterflies take flight in her stomach. He may have been her brother's best mate, but he wasn't related to her by blood, which meant he hadn't been obligated to drum up a compliment.

That was the day she'd fallen head over heels in love. There were two huge problems with that. One, he was fifteen years her senior, and two, her brother, Thomas, would lock her away in a nunnery if he found out–if that were still a thing, but they lived in Scotland, so probably.

The current blush parade marching across her pale skin certainly wasn't caused by excitement over her senior prom, and unquestionably not by her date or dress. No. No, no, no. Her body was reacting to the devilishly handsome man—and a man he was—sitting at a table for one, watching her while he absently nibbled on a baguette crust.

Coll. Coll Bloody Alexander Barr. The man she had secretly loved for years and her current uninvited date chaperone—as if she and Duncan would do anything during that evening's festivities but decorate the Catholic hall's moldy walls.

Cat would have referred to herself as a wallflower, but flowers were beautiful. She was more of a persistent, prickly climbing vine—attractive to few, a nuisance to most.

While one part of Cat was secretly thrilled that Coll got to see his best friend's little sister grown and all dressed up, she knew his presence would not go unnoticed. Coll was as tall and muscular as her brother, but where Tommy was all golden blond menace, Coll was dark, secretive, and brooding. Perfect.

Coll was the opposite of incognito. The mean girls were already starting to peg his presence on their radars. Several promgoers had chosen the same Italian restaurant for supper before the dance. Bunchrew, the community she'd grown up in outside Inverness, was small enough that her tormentors would easily deduce who he was and, more importantly, why he was there.

Babysitter.

Catriona did have a few friends that were kind and made her school days bearable, but they tended to be quiet and somber: science fair, automotive, or math athletes. A few had tried to stand up for Catriona over the years. It never ended well for any of them, and she'd encouraged them not to try.

Francie Wheaton was the queen of Cat's bullies. She was tall, blonde, beautiful, and curvy—the definition of the 'exact opposite' of her. The thing was, Cat was a realist. She didn't care that Francie was gorgeous, and she was plain. She only wanted to be friends, but for some reason, Francie decided to be her oppressor for the past seven years. Cat barely remembered a time when the most popular girl in school wasn't hurling insults across the playground or, eventually, the science lab.

Francie had a few girls in her crowd that enjoyed mimicking the slurs, admittedly, not with the same passion but with enough verve they still stung. Catriona learned to avoid their paths as much as possible.

For the most part, boys ignored her and didn't take part in the teasing. The fact that they didn't personally make fun of Catriona meant nothing because she knew that a real man wouldn't have stood by and watched a girl's heart be crushed.

Thomas would have razed the school to the ground had he known how awful its hallowed Catholic halls had treated her.

Coll would have destroyed the tormenters, *and* their families had he known—which was why she'd never told a soul. She would endure this night as she had so many others. At least for a moment, she could pretend Coll was seeing her as a woman and not the little girl that he used to chuck under the chin.

Dinner was an eternity, and even though she knew what was coming, she still preened under Coll's scrutiny, wondering what he thought about her appearance. Did he notice her dress? It was her mom's choice, which was why it suffered with 1980s vibes. Could he tell she'd stuffed her bra? Did he think, only for a moment, that she was pretty?

Did he hear the cutting remarks start to rumble and slink through the dining room?

In Francie and friends' defense, many of the comments were accurate. For instance, she probably did look like a child playing dress up even though her thoughts were all woman. There was nothing childlike about her Coll Barr fantasies. Catriona wanted that man with every ounce of her hormone-drenched body. So ... she let the "Babydoll needs a sitter" comments wash over her. She kept a strict lockdown on her tear ducts and focused on the shrimp scampi and pilaf rice ensemble that didn't hold a candle to her grandma's.

Coll. Coll. Coll. Thirty-three years old and every woman's fantasy. This was her senior prom, but it was also just another day to pretend she wasn't dying inside.

Words. Words. Words.

Duncan finally finished eating. She didn't care a single flip about his weight or looks, but she didn't want him to hear the other promgoers whisper "human garbage disposal," and hoped to slip out of the restaurant with him none the wiser. His greatest superpower was obliviousness, but that didn't mean it didn't kill *her* to hear their peers destroy him. Thankfully, Dunc had a zero-give-a-shit policy. She really needed to learn how to do that.

In the meantime, Coll was giving her classmates more fodder for the insult mill because he wasn't just a dinner companion but a dance chaperone too.

Once they got to the 'dance hall,' Coll was dancing with her teachers, who didn't seem to mind if he never spoke to them. He drank the disgusting pink punch like he didn't have a care in the world while she was forced to maintain a stoic façade. She let the comments about her unattractive features wash over her shoulders and wrap around her ribs like she always did.

Another day, another ... day.

Insults did eventually become tight, hurtful bands. She'd never been physically beaten but wondered if fists hurt worse than words. Probably. Definitely.

But ... little boy, tiny tits, pedophile's wet dream ... words bruised too.

2

PRESENT DAY—BUNCHREW, SCOTLAND

It was a difficult thing to be a vessel for so many opposing emotions. How could she, Catriona Elizabeth MacGregor, horticulturist, and successful business owner, be such a whiner? Her family loved her, and she loved them. Why then did it feel like she was being left behind?

The family and friend's cookout was turning out to be a real self-reflecting bullshit of a trial.

Damn, Cat, she admonished herself. Her brother wasn't leaving her. He was getting engaged to the love of his life, not moving across the world—and she loved Josephine and couldn't wait to call her sister.

Sixteen years ago, Thomas had married his best friend's sister, Aileen, when she'd fallen pregnant in college by a boyfriend that had moved to the States. Her brother stepped up and became a husband, in name only, and an amazing father to Mirren, their daughter.

Thomas wore duty like a comfortable, old coat. Cat wished she could wear her own skin with even half as much ease. Alas, she had a love-hate relationship with herself.

Cat wondered if her brother would still be married to

Aileen if he hadn't met and fallen in love with Josephine O'Connor. Of course, Aileen hadn't left him a choice in the matter at the end of it. Both Aileen and Mirren loved Thomas' fiancée and wanted to see him and Jo happy as much as Cat did. They were a complicated lot but straightforward in their love.

Jo and her brother deserved every happiness, no ifs, ands, or buts about it. If she felt a pang of envy, the other emotion crowding her tiny, almost five-foot frame, she was determined to ignore it.

Catriona had walked forward with the crowd to eavesdrop on the happy couple when they'd tried to leave the party quietly —no such luck with this rowdy crew. They got to hear her brother ask Jo to marry him, and Jo's excited yes. No sooner had he slipped a ring on her finger than she informed him he would be a father again in five months. That announcement got a lot of sideline whistles and catcalls.

Feeling much more lighthearted than moments ago, she couldn't stop her giddy grin at the thought of being an auntie again. She turned to see what Coll thought of the news. He was the furthest back from the crowd. He'd gotten quite used to hovering at the edges of get-togethers, preferring the shadows over conversation. He'd lost the lower portion of one of his legs almost two years ago in the Amazon rainforest while on a job for his and Thomas' security company and was only recently beginning to make an effort to come home to visit his family.

He only used to be broody with strangers, never with family. Cat still had hope that he would smile and laugh again like he used to. She didn't think today's taciturn mood had anything to do with his leg for once and everything to do with his sister's long-lost boyfriend and birth father to Mirren showing up for the cookout. Jo had told Catriona that Coll had been furious that Aileen's ex had been invited.

She met Coll's eyes and widened her smile, deciding to set

aside her normal feelings of irritation toward the man. No one could push her cranky buttons quite like he could. She wanted him to feel included in celebrating her brother's engagement and new baby.

The grumpy bastard simply stared until her expression wilted into disappointment. Christ, but that man lived to torment her. She turned her back on him and tried to scrounge up her excitement of a moment ago. Why did she even care? A better question would be, why was she so drawn to him?

Coll Barr wasn't an ignorant man. He was quite brilliant, really, especially with computers and gadgets. She would like to believe he was unaware of the crush she'd had on him years earlier, but she hadn't been subtle, and, as mentioned before, the man wasn't dumb.

For the most part, she'd kept her mooning over him to a minimum, but there was one time she would have sworn Coll had looked at her like he would a woman he wanted to kiss ... or more. She had smiled at him constantly that night and even touched his arm a time or two. Christ, the humiliation when her blinders had been ripped off. She wished her mind could be scrubbed of the memory.

She'd come home on school break two years ago. Coll and Thomas were both home, and her parents and grandma wanted everyone together for a family meal.

Coll was flying out the following day to return to South America, where he'd been working for months on an undercover job. He'd only come home for a short break. Little did she and her family know that he would have to be medevacked back to the States a month later.

But that night, Catriona was feeling celebratory. She was doing well in college, had made some great friends, and was learning to if not love, then appreciate her body. After all, she could crouch over her garden plants for hours and never tire.

She was a beast with her green babies. She wore white exercise pants with a navy floral pattern and a matching top that was blousy and full, hiding her nonexistent bust and cropped to show off her defined abdominals.

That night, dinner had been great. Grandma made enough food to feed Inverness and everyone's favorite sweet. They'd played card games and laughed at Mirren's sassy attitude. Aileen was there, of course. She and Thomas didn't have a traditional marriage, but she was family, just like Coll.

"I heard you had a date, Cat," Aileen announced. "With a handsome teacher's assistant."

She blushed as everyone at the table started asking questions at once. Mirren squealed in delight and asked for all the details. Thomas asked their dad if he'd gotten the man's information. She didn't bother telling her brother to stay out of her business. She'd have more luck turning water into wine.

She also didn't divulge that the date was a group date and that when Norman tried to kiss her, she'd turned her head and pretended not to notice. Norman was nice and handsome, slim and fair. She preferred dark and ... big.

Coll seemed to intrude in her thoughts at the most inopportune moments. Her eyes were drawn across the dining table, and she was startled to find his dark eyes burning into hers. He looked pissed. Before she could let his bitchy attitude ruin her evening, she was about to make up some romantic drivel for Mirren to gush over when Coll spoke.

"Careful, Kitty Cat. Teachers don't tend to stick around."

Forks clattered as they dropped, and gasps sounded from shocked mouths at Coll's thoughtless comment. Coll winced when Thomas growled his name. Her parents and grandma began to discuss the weather and clear the table.

"That was a shit thing to say, Uncle Colly." Mirren said as she stood from her seat. None of the adults at the table corrected her potty mouth, too shocked to do more than blink. "I'll leave you to your apology tour." *Lord have mercy. Catriona loved her niece's smart mouth.*

For her part, Cat didn't say a word, still thrown by the unfriendly comment. Aileen scooted her chair back, about to stand and leave as well when Coll placed his broad, long-fingered hand over his sister's much smaller one.

"I'm sorry, Sis. It was a dickhead thing to say." Aileen only continued to stare. Sighing, he tried again. "The teacher-student thing is still a sore subject with me, A, and Cat is obviously a little girl in over her head, and it pissed me off."

Catriona was in the midst of a minefield, bombs detonating all around, searing her skin. Coll basically just announced that he saw her as nothing more than a child when she was a grown woman. All her old insecurities had come rushing back. She wanted to die a hundred deaths and to think, she had been considering coming on to him that night. She had hoped to prove that he wanted her like she wanted him.

She was naïve. Very fucking naïve. She should have learned her lesson well, but here she was, still trying to share a moment with the surly prick. He wanted nothing to do with her when she was eighteen, or twenty, or even now, at twenty-two. Perhaps this lesson would sink in better than the last one.

Shaking off the memory, she forced one foot in front of the other and made her way to the happy couple's side to give Thomas and Jo hugs and kisses. "Congratulations, you two! A wedding and a baby." She grabbed two of her brother's huge fingers, the perfect fit for her tiny grasp, and one of Jo's hands. "Just tell me I get to do the flowers for the wedding and the baby shower."

"There's no one we would trust more," her brother assured.

Jo lowkey squealed before pulling Catriona into her arms. "I would be honored, Cat." The tear inducer was when she bent to whisper for Cat's ears alone. "I've always wanted a true sister."

"You and me both." Cat patted Jo's back once more, grinning tearily at her brother over Jo's shoulder, who also seemed close to sniffling himself.

Thomas gently pulled Catriona from Jo's arms by her hoodie pocket and enveloped her in his snuggly embrace. "I love you, Wee Cat."

And that was the moment that broke Cat from her moody Coll blues. Life changes all the time, but her brother would always love her no matter who else he brought into his life to love. She needed to remember to count her blessings more and wallow in pity less.

And forget Coll Barr's existence.

3

Coll was inundated with a surplus of reasons to hate himself. At the moment, the number one pick was hurting Cat's feelings. Again. *Jesus* ... It was a knife to the gut to watch her gorgeous smile turn into a sad frown.

He'd done that. He'd done that on purpose.

She'd turned around to share with him the joy of her brother's announcement, his best friend's announcement, and he ruined it. His excuse was as lame as his one-legged body. Catriona MacGregor's smile had stunned him. He'd been paralyzed by the beauty of her joy. The sun had washed her body and her glorious red hair in stars and sparkles, and ... he froze.

She wasn't for him for so many reasons. He'd lost count years ago. Too young. His best friend's wee sister. Too innocent. And now ... he couldn't even bring a whole, hale body to lay at her precious feet.

He was ashamed to admit, even if it was only to himself, that he'd been attracted to the fiery-tempered hellcat since she was nineteen. It was on that birthday when she'd turned that same vibrant smile his way, and he'd lost a bit of his heart to her. Thomas would murder him for it, and rightly so.

Coll had known for years that Cat fancied herself in love with him. He ignored the soft smiles and batting eyelashes, keeping a familial wall between them. It used to be so easy.

When she was twenty, he'd made a hurtful comment during a family dinner about one of her dates, and since then, she'd given him the cold shoulder. Today had been the first time he'd received anything other than a sneer or frown from her beautiful face.

Reduced to acting like a teenage boy, he purposely poked her, riling her temper just to get a reaction. He never thought he'd miss her dreamy looks and goo-goo eyes.

A couple of days ago, he'd eaten dinner at Grandma MacGregor's. Thomas, Josephine, and Catriona were there. Everything had been fine and normal until he'd poked Cat's temper, and she left abruptly. Grandma M had read him the riot act about teasing Cat. According to the older woman, something had happened the night of her senior prom that still hurt her feelings today.

He asked if he had done something, and the stubborn woman told him to drop it. He wasn't going to drop anything. He'd followed her to dinner that night and chaperoned the dance, so if something traumatic had happened, he would have known. Thomas was clueless as well.

He couldn't get rid of the niggling feeling that his presence had caused something to happen. He ruled out her date as the cause of her upset. Duncan Jannis had been a mouthy little shit that he and Thomas disliked, but Cat and Duncan had been childhood friends.

Coll hadn't shadowed the prom because he thought Duncan might get too fresh with Cat. He'd gone because she was such a stunning young woman. He and Thomas were fearful about what the other horny teen boys would try.

She never danced once, which still gave him an uncomfortable twist in his gut. She should have danced at her senior prom. She rarely left the wall, though he'd been satisfied to see several girls stop by and speak to her. So, surely, she'd enjoyed that part.

She only went to the restroom once and looked unharmed when she'd come back out. After the dance, he'd tailed Duncan's beat up blue Peugeot, so Coll could also confirm that nothing happened untoward on the way home.

The cookout was back in full swing. Thomas was manning the grill while the guests milled about chatting. The O'Faolain men from Oklahoma and their wives and children made for a loud, rambunctious group. Coll had met everyone prior to today, having helped the family with a stalking case, and on another occasion, a kidnapping case.

He was once again standing back from the crowd. He'd forced himself to limp over and congratulate Thomas and Jo on their engagement and the baby before separating himself once again. His damn leg or, no leg rather, was a frustrating nuisance.

He'd twisted his prosthesis earlier helping his sister unload the car, and it was still giving him fits. He had to keep reminding himself how fortunate he was that he'd only lost his right leg below the knee. He still had full mobility in the joint.

He was past due to return to Johns Hopkins Limb Rehabilitation Center in Baltimore, Maryland, to have the brace adjusted and to pick up his new running blade. He and Thomas had a row about him putting off the appointment. His oldest friend had been a belligerent asshole until he agreed to set up an appointment. He would be flying out next week. Then, true to Thomas' nature, as soon as he'd capitulated, Thomas clapped him on the back with a "Good, then."

Coll had run his whole life, and working out in a gym every day was killing him. He loved being outdoors. The changing scenery and unpredictable Scottish weather were invigorating.

The running blade would be a game-changer. It was the best of limited choices.

He had to regain some of his old self back, and being able to run again would help. He knew he'd been a shit friend and a shit brother for months. *Damn it ...* He wanted his leg back. He wished for the millionth time that he'd never gone looking for a cocaine manufacturing lab in the rainforest. He wished he'd stayed behind his computer, except he knew that someone else would have taken his place that day, and they might not have fared as well as he had.

He'd felt useless for months, but finally, even he was sick of his melancholy crap. He had limitations but nothing that would keep him out of the field if he chose to go back in. MacGregor Security, the company that Thomas had imagined when they were still in the Royal Marines, and Coll had helped bring into reality was widely varied in services.

They worked behind the scenes, with the public and deep undercover. Their security teams were hired as guard detail, cyber hackers, security system checkers, and for lost person cases. They also worked closely with law enforcement to take down criminals, from traffickers to drug and arms dealers. Most of their employees were ex-military, though Thomas had been recruiting several well-known computer hackers and overall IT geniuses.

It was during an undercover mission in Bolivia, where he'd worked for endless weeks tracking, mapping, and photographing a network of cocaine manufacturing operations, that he'd run into trouble. He still woke up in remembered anguish from stepping on that buried IED.

It was a matter of choosing thankfulness. Unfortunately, he was kind of an asshole, and counting his blessings was a little too BBC Masterpiece for his taste. Between losing a limb and his sister's recent struggle with breast cancer, he understood all too clearly not to cry about what couldn't be changed.

Aileen was family but also his closest friend next to Thomas. He let his eyes search the crowd until he found her ... smiling and blushing for that bastard Charles Morrow.

The man who had impregnated his sister in college and then moved to America, forcing his best friend to marry her to keep his parents from finding out. He should have told his parents to go to hell years before, and he should have never allowed Thomas to sacrifice himself in such a way—both of those choices had been the wrong ones and should be laid squarely on his shoulders. However, no one else would have loved his niece the way Thomas had.

Aileen had reminded him a million times that she had been the one to break up with Charles because she was too afraid to leave Scotland and that he had not known she was pregnant, "And he certainly was unaware that he's had a daughter these past sixteen years, Coll. You will behave, or I'll take your leg off and beat you over your thick head with it."

As threats went, that wasn't a bad one. Aileen, so casually mentioning his prosthesis, almost made him laugh. It felt good for his fake leg not to be the elephant in the room. He knew how nervous his sister was about meeting the bastard, so of course, he would play nice. For now.

Letting his eyes track the crowd once more, it took all of a half of a second to spot flames. Catriona. *Christ* ... That woman was born to be the counter to subtlety. She was a wrecking ball to everything demure, drawing him like a moth to her flame.

She fascinated him. As a child, he'd been proud of her fiery temperament. If she wanted something, she got it. As a teenager, she'd been bossy and demanding—expecting perfection and doling out wrath when that wasn't achieved ... especially when it came to her precious plants. The thing was, she demanded more of herself than anyone else.

As a woman, a young woman, her work ethic was already paying off. Once her parents had handed over the reins to MacGregor Farm, Cat had almost doubled the farm's profits, and if the stubborn girl would let someone design a better website—electronics of any kind were not her forte—and hire a few more employees the business would explode.

As he watched her smile and laugh with friends, he regretted that she couldn't be lighthearted with him. She had been years ago. He would offer to design her a whole new website, but she'd probably tell him to fuck off.

"If you stare at that poor girl any harder, her brother is bound to notice eventually." Hugh O'Faolain quietly announced as he casually made his way over.

Coll liked Hugh. He liked Hugh's sons, Bran and Patrick too. The three men were married to sisters—Hugh to the youngest sister, Rowan. He liked Hugh, but that didn't mean Coll wanted to hear that he'd been caught staring at Catriona.

"Hugh," he greeted.

"Catriona?"

Hugh leaned against one of the wooden pillars next to Coll. He crossed his arms and looked for all the world like an angry, antisocial man who would rather be anywhere else. Thomas said it was the man's default.

Coll would like to ignore Hugh's inferred question, but he wouldn't. He deserved to be called out for being sloppy and obvious while watching her. "No."

"No?"

Coll sighed, knowing he would regret this conversation later. "No. For many reasons."

"What are the top three? Reasons," he clarified.

"Thomas would kill me. Truly. She barely tolerates my presence. Too young."

Hugh took a moment, thoughtful with his words where many were not. They both watched the group eating, drinking, and laughing. Hugh's eyes, of course, held longer on his pregnant wife. Coll's eyes were trained on Cat again. *Damn.*

Hugh's gravelly voice interrupted his eye stalking. "I've twenty-nine years on Row." He shrugged. "I couldn't live without her."

"She wouldn't *let* you live without her," Coll corrected.

Hugh's mouth twitched in amusement. "That too. As for Catriona not being able to stand you ... her eyes following you whenever you aren't watching her says something else."

He turned his attention sharply to the older man. Hugh didn't appear to be pulling his leg—the good one or the fake.

"Your third reason, though. Thomas MacGregor. You're fucked there."

Coll shook his head at the stupidity of even allowing this conversation to take place. It was little more than fantasy. He'd only become more obsessed with her because of what Grandma MacGregor had told him. It would drive him crazy until he knew what had happened the night of her prom. Something or someone had hurt her, and he would find out.

"One more thing before I go get my wife and make her sit down and put her feet up. My mother asked me once if I was a quitter. If I was a man who gave up when things were difficult. I think it's a question you might ponder yourself. Are you a quitter?"

With that bit of roundabout, unwanted sage advice, the older gentleman did exactly what he said he was going to do. He herded his very pregnant wife toward a cushioned couch and had her seated and her feet in his lap in less than thirty seconds.

The man was smooth. Coll would give him that. His wee

Irish wife was looking at her husband as if he were the only man to walk the Earth.

Was he a quitter? Hell no, he wasn't, but it wasn't quitting if he never began in the first place.

He moved his attention elsewhere, catching Thomas' eyes. His friend raised his brows in question. *How are you holding up?* Tommy knew he hated crowds since his injury. Truth be told, he had hated most things since his injury.

He gave a slight nod of his head in response. *I'll survive.* Thomas smirked and went back to flipping burgers. It was good to be home. If Thomas knew what or who, rather, he and Hugh had been discussing moments ago, he wouldn't be so satisfied with the day.

Unable to stop himself, Coll locked on Cat's location next. She was giving Josephine another hug before wrapping one of her arms around Mirren. His niece was as ornery as a teenager comes. Mir's rosy cheeks and soft smile were a dead giveaway to her happiness with today's events.

Her dad, her real dad, not the sperm donor one, was engaged and having another child, which must please his wee niece something fierce, and her mother, Coll's sister, was just as rosy-cheeked and flush with smiles herself. Mirren would have noted her mom's happiness. Coll knew that Mirren had wanted to meet her birth father, but her true motivation was to make her mom smile again.

Coll was pissed to feel his eyes mist. Damn, but he was a softy where his girls were concerned. Mirren caught him staring and grinned, the brat. She wouldn't be looking so smug when he told her father that her prom date wannabe had gotten a speeding ticket last year and had a disciplinary writeup in his school file for plagiarism on a history paper.

Coll grinned back at his niece, imagining the fireworks at her dinner table once Thomas had the information. Catriona had been watching Mirren's expressions and followed her line of sight, meeting his eyes and freezing.

Her smile faltered. *Damn it, Cat. Keep smiling, lass.* There was nothing more beautiful than Catriona MacGregor's smile.

Her lush lips faltered before falling. He wanted to walk to her side and make her smile come back. He settled for staring. Fuck his life. He really needed to remember a bit of his younger self's easy charm that used to work with the fairer sex.

Cat gave Mirren one last side squeeze before making her way to her brother's side. She was definitely about to make her exit. She was going through the motions of the long goodbye, but there was no doubt. She was about to run.

He wanted answers about what had happened to upset her four years ago. She had them, which meant he would follow. He wasn't as fast as he used to be, but by damn, he was still speedy enough to catch a tiny sprite of a woman.

4

Catriona sighed in relief when she stepped through her office door. It was her one splurge after she'd graduated. The front was full glass panes to let in natural light. She had a simple desk, shorter than the average twenty-eight to thirty inches to accommodate her short stature. Nothing irritated her more than her legs dangling above the floor.

She had a seating area that was comfortable but lovely. The couch and chairs were a rusty brown leather accented with floral throw pillows and soft cashmere throws. She loved all the colors, just like the flowers in her gardens. On occasion, some of the floral shops and event planners had customers who wanted to come to MacGregor Farm to personally look at the selection. She always accommodated them because had it been her own wedding or special event, she wouldn't trust someone else to pick her flowers.

There was a small kitchenette and half bath for clients, with a full, private bath for herself. Many times, Cat needed quick access to a shower before a meeting. That way, she wasn't bothered to walk home and change, giving her more hours with her plants.

The back of the office had a single, wide sliding barn door that led to her workshop. Her favorite place in the whole world. She enjoyed getting her hands dirty in the property's many greenhouses, communing with the farm's hundreds of varieties of plants and flowers, but her workshop made her blood fizz and sizzle with giddy anticipation.

She would lay in bed at night and imagine new formulas for her homemade tinctures, oils, medicinal liniments, and fragrant lotions. Her bread and butter still came from mass producing and selling her plants to floral shops and even lawn and garden stores, but her passion was in creating.

She'd done a few testers for some of the local shops and her folks' shop down in Wisley, England. Feedback had been good. Really good, actually. Cat's biggest problem wasn't in creating product but rather the issue of social marketing. She was the worst at promoting. This past year, she'd gotten pretty good at dealing with customers, invoicing, and ordering supplies, but the media side of things ... not so much.

Mirren had tried to get her to make videos of herself working on the farm or showing off some of the more exotic flowers in stock, but the thought of posting such things made her gut queasy. Catriona promised Mir it wasn't completely off the table, but anything featuring herself was definitely off.

There was also the question of whether or not she would keep the product line small but varied. Have limited supply and only sell locally or try to sell quantity through a website. The former was safe with moderate earnings. The latter was the high-risk high reward option. It would also require an outside production facility.

However, that was a worry for another day. She smiled, realizing there was still plenty of daylight left to get some work done on one of her latest essential oils before she met Jo, Aileen, and the Byrne sisters, Raven, River, and Rowan. Since Jo had come into her life, Cat felt like her friend group had expanded tenfold. She grinned at their earlier conversation about going out to a pub tonight.

"No boys allowed," River decreed. "They only try to herd the women into a corral in the corner where it's easier to," and here she used air quotes, "keep an eye on us. Like they're cowboys, and we're the cows."

"Just get us a table with low chairs, guys. I think hopping my ungainly ass up on a barstool is beyond me until baby girl comes out. But bitchface over there," Rowan nodded toward Josephine, "probably wants to go somewhere that has a mechanical bull."

Clearly, Rowan was still salty over Jo's barely there bump. There was no reasoning with the youngest sister that she was months ahead of Jo in the baby growing department.

Her brother only grinned—he hadn't stopped grinning since the announcements—and placed his big hand over Jo's stomach. "I'm down for going out tonight. I've got a bit of work to do once I leave here, but I'll be ready by eight."

"You'll be ready to get ready by seven," Raven informed her. "You, Jo, and Aileen are meeting us at our hotel to get ready. It's going to be so much fun. Aileen has a new, sexy blonde lob wig to model for us."

Cat watched Aileen's cheeks flush as she smiled at Charles, who hadn't done much but look at Aileen with stars in his eyes. "I can't wait to see you in it." Charles admitted, touching her hand briefly and wearing a matching blush.

"Hey, no boys, remember?" River threw her hands up in the air in fake exasperation.

"I won't stay out long, Charles. If you would pick me up and bring me home after an hour or so, I would appreciate it." Aileen was still recovering from her cancer treatments and wasn't quite back to her old self yet, but Catriona imagined the early pick-up was due more about the man driving her home and less to do with exhaustion.

"I would like that. Very much." Charles touched Aileen's hand again. It seemed he couldn't stop.

Cat felt her eyes mist and quickly blinked and looked away. Her ex-sister-in-law deserved to find love after all these years. Or find it again, rather.

Mirren moaned beside her mother. "What do you mean you're coming home early? I thought Operation Bring OG Dad Back into the Picture was supposed to keep you occupied. I planned on having some friends over tonight while you were out."

"You can still have friends over, sweetheart." Aileen offered while attempting to hold back amusement.

"Yeah, right! As if I want Stefen to know I have a chaperone. Mortifying." The teenager shuddered. Mirren's eyes grew round as she realized her slip up in front of her dad. Cat's brother took a step toward Mirren, about to Hulk out as Mirren liked to describe his morphing into scary dad-mode.

"Stefen is your prom date, not your boyfriend, right, Mir?"

It only took her niece thirty seconds to rally. "Of course, he isn't. Yet. I mean, he's smoking hot, and so am I. We would be precious together."

There wasn't a single adult at the party that wasn't riveted to the tableau currently playing out. Cat looked at Jo with wide eyes. Intervention was needed.

Jo stepped forward. "You *would* look presh on anyone's arm, Mir, but your mom and I were talking the other day, and we thought it would be nice to actually be around Stefen a few times so that your family can meet him and your dad—dads could meet him," she quickly corrected. "If your mom wants to make an early night of it, you could always have friends meet you here. Right Thomas?"

Before her brother could unbend enough to answer yay or nay, Mirren, unfortunately, had more to say. "Oh my God, no way! Like I want my friends to listen to you and Dad go at it. I've read that women are especially horny during pregnancy. River said it's true as well." Then she turned to poor Charles. "You really let Mom down there, didn't you," she smirked.

Aileen gasped. "Mirren Mòr MacGregor!"

Deciding to break up the circus that Mirren had singlehandedly performed, she changed the subject. "I better get going since you guys are giving me one less hour to work. I can't wait to have a tall glass of Guinness tonight."

Raven jumped on the distraction. "Perfect, and just wear comfy clothes over. My sisters and I are going to have a few dresses delivered to the hotel room for us to choose from."

Now, it was Cat's turn to blush. She rarely wore cute dresses and never to a pub. She didn't have the figure for them, certainly not like the Byrnes with their lush figures and Jo with her long, gorgeous legs. "Thank you for thinking of me, but I was just planning on wearing jeans."

"Oh, come on." Rowan wheedled while sitting on the couch having her feet rubbed by her husband.

"This might be the last time we get to go out for a while since Baby O girl is almost here. It'll be fun. You'll see." River grinned at her, knowing she was going to capitulate.

"Ugh, fine. See you ladies at seven." Before Cat left, she leaned down to whisper in Mirren's ear. "You're a little shithead. You know that, right?"

With a few flutters of her eyelashes, she responded. "Dad didn't have an opportunity to question me more about Stefen, though, did he?"

"Like I said. Shithead." She grinned. Cat left the outdoor cooking space, taking special care not to look for Coll ... the ultimate King of the Shitheads.

She slid open the barn-style door of her workshop and happily breathed in all the earthy and sweet smells. She looked at her phone. She had three hours before she'd need to clean up, so she set an alarm for six-thirty.

She was about to grab one of her dirty aprons from the wall pegs when she remembered she still had on one of her favorite long sleeved spring dresses from the cookout. Easily remedied. She pulled the dress over her head and exchanged it for an apron.

It wasn't like anyone would bother her in her workshop, and she was wearing tiny compression shorts and a soft sports bra instead of a cutesy bra and panty set. Her undergarments of choice were more about functionality over sensuality. She'd seen women wearing less at the market. Twisting her hair up in a messy … a very messy bun, she got to work.

Cat wasn't sure how much time had passed while she'd been bent over her worktable, mashing eucalyptus leaves to extract its healing oil, when she felt goosebumps rise on her arms. It felt like … she wasn't sure … like she wasn't alone. Like someone was watching.

It wasn't the first time during the past few weeks that she'd felt the same.

She turned down *I'm Gonna Be* by The Proclaimers on her small, portable speaker. She liked to sing, badly, and dance, badly, to music while she worked. She slowly raised her head and scanned the rows of tables, plants, bowls, and all matter of paraphernalia when her body froze at the sight of Coll casually leaning against the sliding door.

He didn't say a damn word, just watched her with his intense, brooding stare. His dark hair was longer than he usually kept it and nowhere near his preferred military cut. The top was long enough, he was continually fussing with it, running his fingers through the longer bits and sweeping them to the side.

She had wondered more than once what it would feel like to replace his fingers with hers.

He wore a plain navy T-shirt loosely tucked into a pair of North Face hiking pants. She'd noticed he'd stopped wearing jeans after the accident. At least fitted jeans. Denim was probably a lot less forgiving with a prosthesis. She had dreamed of getting her hands on his leg. She wasn't blind. She'd seen him limping more than once. She knew one of her liniments would do wonders for his soreness and inflammation, and she knew her massages would. Getting him to let her near the part of him that he now considered imperfect would be the feat. A million times since he'd returned from the States, she'd wished to tell him that he was no less than he ever was. *Stubborn, grouchy man.*

His muscular arms were crossed over his broad chest. Truly, the man had no business looking so gorgeous or comfortable while invading her space.

She turned and leaned her hip against the rough wood of the table, crossing her arms to mimic his irritating power pose. "Did you need something, Colly?" She loved calling him by Mirren's nickname. The wince of irritation that flashed across his face was satisfying.

"What upset you the night of your senior prom?"

The absolute hell? Of all the things that she might have imagined coming out of his mouth, her prom was not one of them. "Are you drunk?"

"No. Answer me."

"I don't have to answer shit. Prom was four flipping years ago. What is going on with you?" She was transfixed when she saw his jaw clench and his hands drop by his sides, tugging his shirt and pinching the fabric of his pants between his fingers.

Coll Barr was fidgeting.

He pushed away from the wall, feet apart, and hands clasped behind his back. Once a Royal Marine ...

"Grandma MacGregor," he stopped to clear his throat. Her anxiety shot through the roof at the mention of her grandma. She would never ... "Grace, Grandma, that is," he floundered, not willing to call her anything but Grandma and risk hurting her feelings even when the old woman wasn't in hearing, "mentioned my presence might have caused you some problem." He looked up at the ceiling as if he were in pain. Looking at her once more, he finished with, "The infernal woman wouldn't tell me anything else. I want to know what happened. Now."

Jackass. As if him ordering her to do something would ever work. She'd take a page out of Mirren's handbook and divert attention. "Why in the hell were you two discussing me?" Coll's cheeks flushed. They honest to God turned the palest pink of a trailing azalea.

Three guilty throat clearings later, he answered. "When you got mad at me the other night at dinner, she said it was my fault from that night, and that's why you're so ... prickly with me."

She'd prefer to never think of that night, let alone tell the man she used to fantasize about the embarrassing things some of those girls said to her. "It's in the past. You had nothing to do with any of that old business. I'm not saying another word about it, so forget it. I'll be having a few choice words with Grandma. I can assure you. If that's all you needed." She turned around, ready to ignore his unignorable presence, and picked her pestle back up.

Two hands gripped her shoulders, and an embarrassing yelp slipped past her lips. She spun around to find Coll's six-foot-two-inch frame looming over her. "What the hell?" she spluttered.

"You're lying, Cat," he growled. "Tell me the truth."

She felt her whole body flush with heat. He'd never stood this close before. She was suddenly very conscious of her attire, or lack thereof. She couldn't let her younger, infatuated self take the wheel, though. "I will not discuss anything to do with that night. Not with you. Not tonight. Not ever. It wasn't even that big of a deal. Please leave."

Coll shocked her speechless when he raised his hands and skimmed his fingers lightly over her apron-covered hips before stepping back several paces. "Keep your secrets for now. I will find them out."

Wanting to extinguish the tension that was building between them, she asked, "You're off to the States next week, then?"

Several tense seconds of him staring and her staring back passed before he answered. "My new running blade prosthesis is ready for fitting."

He hated discussing his leg. For him to do it now, with her, meant a lot. "You'll be happy to be running the moors again."

He dipped his head in acknowledgment.

"Will you be going home soon?"

"Tomorrow."

Cat held her sigh of disappointment in. Barely. "I'm working on a liniment that I think would benefit your leg greatly. I should have it finished by the end of next week. Will you try it?"

More staring and fist clenching. "Yes. If you'll let me build you a new website."

She could feel her eyes widen in surprise. Had Mir spoken about it? "Umm—"

He cut her off. "It would take me a few weeks. I would need pictures and media."

Her head snapped up at that. "Not of me?"

"Of course, of you. You're the heart of MacGregor Farm."

"Not of me," she said more firmly. "The flowers and plants speak for themselves. Mirren said she would help me this summer. There's no need to trouble yourself."

"It's no trouble. Do you think your ... ointment could help me?"

"Oh!" She started excitedly, grabbing one of his hands with both of hers. "I really do. I've thought a lot about what would help you the most. I'm almost there with the formula. I'm sure of it. Your input would really help. I also joined an online amputee forum so—"

Coll interrupted her. "Why in the bloody hell would you do that?"

"Overreact much? Jeez, Coll. I joined, obviously, to learn." She could see he was about to ask another question and spoke before he could. "I wanted to know more about your particular amputation and how prosthetics work. According to the forum, you are very fortunate to have the use of your knee, but Janice's husband had an amputation similar to yours," she explained, "and said that in the beginning, Stanley's knee would give him all sorts of fits.

"Even with the best fitting prosthesis, your gait will always be altered, putting extra stress on the knee joint. I'm glad to know you're going back to get everything fitted properly again." She stopped talking for a second to make sure Coll's statue impersonation wasn't actually a medical crisis.

He blinked, so she continued. "Anyway, massage is extremely beneficial, and I began to wonder if I could create some lotions that might help. I got my massage therapy license last year and have been practicing some weekends at Raigmore Hospital. They have quite a few veterans with amputations."

Coll held up a hand. "Stop. You got your license, and you ... you massage men's ... bodies." He finally choked out.

"Christ, way to make it sound X-rated. I don't give happy ending massages, weirdo. I've been able to practice on men *and* women. It's all volunteer work, but I've been told I do an excellent job.

"I would have brought it up sooner, but you ... we ... never really talk. It never came up," she added lamely. "So, will you try some of my products? And massage?"

She thought for sure she'd offended him completely by talking about "the leg," but he surprised her. "I'll try it but only if you let me help you build a new website."

"You're stubborn."

"I am. So are you, lass."

"I am. Fine. I agree to the terms." She'd no sooner finished speaking than her reminder alarm went off. "Damn. I have to get ready to meet everyone." She was about to turn back to her work and begin tidying the space when Coll gripped her hips, stilling any movement.

"You will eventually tell me what happened that night."

"No. I won't." His only response was an irritating smirk.

"Behave tonight, Kitty Cat." With that absurd announcement, he left as silently as he'd arrived.

5

Coll cursed as he left through Cat's office. He had not done himself any favors by coming here, being alone with her. Talking. She'd been wearing practically nothing under her apron. Her round, firm ass on display had hypnotized all sense out of him. From what he could make out, and he'd done his best to see around the edges of her heavy apron, her body was lean and muscular. Powerful like her personality.

He'd watched her work, watched her hips sway to the music, and listened to the off-key lilt of her humming. He'd creeped on her privacy like the worst type of stalker. She was different, surrounded by her plants, in her element. He hadn't seen her with her guard so fully down for years.

Four years to be exact. Perhaps he should pay a visit to her old school friend and prom date, Duncan. Coll was sure he could intimidate some answers out of him.

Not since she'd been a child had they had such an easy time conversing as they had this evening. She was passionate and animated, clearly knowledgeable in her field. He hadn't lied. He was interested in trying one of her oils or liniments, as she called them. There were days his knee ached fiercely, and it limited his activities. He hated limping. He especially hated it in front of his family.

He knew very well that they did not look at him differently. It would be like if he looked at his sister's bald head as if it were an offending sight. Ridiculous. He knew Aileen hated her wigs. He could tell by the way she touched her forehead or fiddled with the strands around her face. She probably understood how he despised being different better than anyone.

His sister wasn't the woman she used to be either. She was braver, stronger but still loyal and loving ... a survivor. Perhaps he should try to look at himself the same way he looked at her. Thomas had never treated him differently. He'd made it clear he didn't care if Coll went back in the field or ran teams behind the scenes. He just wanted him all the way back with their family. Thomas wanted him to move home, and maybe he should. What would Cat think about seeing him every day?

He was still reeling over the fact that she'd joined a damn amputee forum. It sounded like she still regularly chatted with the group. Then, she mentioned that she got a massage therapy license. People don't normally go to such lengths for others. "Christ, but that woman does nothing by halves." He grumbled as he crunched over the gravel to his old farm truck.

He was staying at Grandma MacGregor's for the night. He'd wanted to go home after the cookout, but he had made a promise to spend more time with the older woman. When he asked if he could take her spare room for the night, she'd been thrilled. It made his heart squeeze comfortably knowing she loved him no less than her own grandchildren.

Thomas and Jo had gone round her house after the cookout to give her the news but he figured they were already back to Thomas' house so Josephine could meet the other women.

Had he really agreed to allow Cat to massage his stump? What in the ever-loving hell had he been thinking? He felt his face burn in embarrassment. Obviously, saying no to her was as difficult as it had been when she was a feisty five-year-old, begging him to let her have extra biscuits when her mother's head was turned.

Picturing her massaging another man left him uncomfortably jealous. Picturing her massaging his body ... had a very different effect. Then, when the crazy girl casually mentioned a happy ending massage ... Christ.

"She shouldn't even know what those are," he groused to himself. If he were honest, certain parts of his anatomy didn't mind her knowing. He was still adjusting his severely underused appendage from just hearing the words leave her lips. He instantly pictured things he shouldn't. He'd left Catriona five minutes ago, and his dick was still giving him hell.

He didn't blame the damn thing. Coll hadn't had sex since the accident. Two years. Sex was the last thing on his mind for the first several months after surgery and rehabilitation, and then it was on his mind, but he'd gotten so far in his head about the logistics of it all that his sex drive plummeted before it ever had a chance.

Did you take the prosthesis off or leave it on? Would the stump be a turnoff to his partner? Lights on? Lights off?

He wasn't an indecisive person. He hated that he had allowed himself to become a Nervous Nancy. His little sister was braver than he was, but he was determined to change all that. Starting with his new running blade and ending with ... a massage?

As he slid onto the worn, cracked seats of his truck, he paused, cursing himself for his lack of attention to his surroundings. One thing South America had taught him was that distraction killed. The moment he shut himself inside the cab, he felt like something was off.

He would have sworn that one of his dirty T-shirts had been laid across the passenger seat. There was nothing there now. However, as wound up as Catriona had him lately, his truck could have had graffiti spraypainted up and down its sides, and he might have missed that too. The most likely explanation was that he'd stuffed the shirt in his overnight bag in preparation for leaving in the morning.

Coll started the engine, shifted to drive, and began the short trek toward Grandma MacGregor's. The more distance he put between him and Cat, the more guilt began leaking from his pores. He was covered in guilt by the time he got there.

He was circling Thomas' sister like a shark. He might have tried to lie to himself like he was only seeking her out because he was curious about prom night. The truth was ... the truth was he wasn't willing to admit to the truth, but in his heart, he knew he was on a path that had the potential to drive a wedge between him and Thomas.

He needed to pull back. Reassess. He needed to get out of Bunchrew before he did something he'd regret.

Dinner was waiting, fried cod and crispy chips. One of his favorites. Why had he ever teased Thomas about being Grandma's favorite little boy who got all his favorite little treats? He closed his eyes, hoping he hadn't seen the meal prep.

"I asked Thomas to dinner since Jo is going out, but he said he'd hate for you not to get your fill since it's your favorite. As if I'm not capable of fixing enough food for my boys," she grumbled.

Fucking Thomas. To think, not a moment ago, he was considering not wanting to hurt the bastard's feelings. He settled at the worn kitchen table and prepared to be pampered. His phone dinged a text notification.

Is Colly's cod yummy?

Fuck you.

"I heard you went by Cat's office," Grandma said as she placed a heaping platter of fish in front of him. When he went to grab a piece, she swatted his hand. "Grace."

Chagrined for his lack of manners, he quickly said, "Bless us, O Lord, and these Thy gifts, which we are about to receive from Thy bounty, through Christ our Lord. Amen."

"Good boy. Now you can eat. So, how was Catriona?"

Coll didn't bother asking how she knew. The old woman sniffed out gossip with more efficiency than a Cairn Terrier rooted out vermin. "Working." Coll took a huge bite to he wouldn't be required so say more, but the fish was blistering hot, and it took all his willpower not to howl in agony. Grandma only raised her brows in admonishment and dumped hot, salty chips on his plate before taking her seat.

Once he breathed through the pain and was able to swallow, he was more careful with the next few bites, tucking into the feast and suddenly not caring about Thomas' jibes.

"What's she working on now? I hope a new rose-scented lotion. She was supposed to try using some of those beautiful peach-colored roses. They're called The Lark Ascending or something lovely like that."

Was the whole meal to be about Cat? Coll wondered darkly. "No. A liniment of some sort." Coll kept his head down and hovered over his plate so the busybody wouldn't catch the color gracing his cheeks. He could feel the heat blooming, just waiting to tattle on him.

"Oh. I see."

She sounded smug. *Don't ask, Coll.* "See what?" *Idiot.*

"She finally worked up the nerve to tell you she's been working for months on just the right formula for your leg."

Coll looked up sharply at that and quickly denied the claim. "It isn't just for me." Her only response was to lift her brows. Clearly, she didn't agree. "It isn't. Did you know she massages all sorts of men. I bet she uses her creams on them!" God save him. Could he sound more ridiculous?

Grandma kept eating as if his outburst hadn't been a bother at all. "Testing."

Don't ask another question. Do not dare. "What do you mean testing? How different men's bodies feel?" Screw dinner. He needed whisky.

"I suppose she might be experimenting with that as well, but no young man. I was referring to testing out her different pain liniments on veterans and asking for feedback," she tsked, making him feel like an ass. "She hasn't been completely satisfied yet. She told me the other day that she was close."

"Oh." Thank God and all His mercies that his mouthy niece wasn't hearing this. Mirren would tease him until he was dead and buried.

"Hmm," was her response.

Admitting defeat, he sighed. "What do you mean by hmm?"

"Did you agree to try it?"

He agreed to a whole lot more than that. Specifically, letting her see his naked leg ... and to touch it. "Yes, but only so she would agree to let me build her a better website. Thomas told me her current one is shit, and I looked. It is. She's too stubborn."

"Most say the same of you and watch your language. She cares for you. I'm glad you're letting her. Now," Grandma started, tapping the tines of her fork against her plate, "finish your dinner. I made those pecan brownies you love. Thomas did take one of those."

Coll didn't even care that Thomas knew about the special dessert. *She cares for you.* What did Grandma mean by that? What kind of caring? The family kind? The friend kind? The happy ending kind?

Coll was a thirty-seven-year-old man. It would be beneficial if he could remember that. Still ... *She cares for you.*

6

Why did Catriona think walking the half mile to Grandma's would cure her hangover? She hadn't intended to walk, but the flatbed truck that she used around the farm wouldn't start, so she convinced herself that walking was a better idea anyway. In reality, walking was the literal opposite of better.

It was a lovely morning, and yet she had sweat running down her back in a most disgustingly uncomfortable manner. "Grandma better have a hangover cure waiting for me." She whined to the cow that stared blankly at the huffing and puffing woman walking by its fence.

She would have never pulled herself out of bed quite this early, but Coll was an early riser, and she didn't want to miss telling him goodbye, which was silly. She didn't plan on admitting she was there specifically to send him off, but after they'd talked yesterday and managed not to piss each other off, she thought he might want to say goodbye too.

At the pub last night, Jo had told her about all the food Grandma had made Coll and how Thomas was crowing about teasing him the next time they saw each other. She couldn't resist texting Coll to rib him.

> Was dinner special?

She immediately saw bubbles appear. A full minute of bubbles.

> More like your brother every day.

She grinned at the memory, momentarily forgetting her misery. It's not like it was some grand reply, but he had replied, and that was something. Last evening, Coll reminded her of the man he used to be before the accident. He wasn't as closed off, or at least, there was a hint that he might try being a part of the whole again instead of always stepping outside the circle.

She understood that sometimes not all the pieces seemed to fit together. Not because she'd had a traumatic event like Coll but simply because her own circle was small, and she'd always felt a bit like the odd man out. She was fifteen years younger than her brother and his friends. Growing up, she envied their close relationships.

Cat hadn't done well at finding her person. That one friend who was always there to laugh with and cry. Aileen was a good and loving friend, but even her ex-sister-in-law treated her more like a younger sister. Now she had Josephine who was amazing and only four years her senior, but Jo was ... a world traveler, posh, and put together. Everything Cat was not. It was hard not to feel like a frumpy little farmer next to Jo's svelte form and blonde goddess looks.

She knew unequivocally that Jo's beauty was inside and out, and the insecurities she felt came solely from herself. In fact, Jo would probably kick her ass if she knew.

The Byrne sisters did do a banging job of dressing her last night. The oldest sister, Raven, chose Cat's dress, and it was perfect. It was such a dark green that the silk appeared black unless the light hit it just right, and then a shimmer of emerald was revealed.

It was made to look like a man's long-sleeved button-up. It had come with a belt, but the consensus was no on the accessory. River and Rowan unbuttoned a few more buttons than she would have dared to on her own. When she complained that she didn't have any assets to reveal, all four women busted up laughing.

Cat had felt her face start to heat when Raven explained. "Men like women's bodies pretty much every which way they come—short, tall, curvy, slim."

Rowan took over. "Round ass, no ass, big boobs, small boobs."

"And seriously, Cat," River added. "Your breasts are perfectly sized for your body, and the way the silk drapes your chest, giving just a hint of nip ... I'd be shocked if you left the bar alone tonight."

"Haha. You guys are crazy," Cat rejoined, but secretly, she was pleased with their comments. The dress did look lovely, and it made her feel all woman, which was quite a change from the norm. She drew the line at wearing high heels. She had a lot of work to do at the farm, and a broken ankle would really slow her down. Strappy sandals were more her thing.

She was going to braid her hair, but again, she was overruled. So, the red mixture of curls and loops and waves was left to fall down her back. Before they left the hotel, she tried to pay for the dress and sandals, but Rowan said that Hugh was picking up the tab.

"He said he wanted me and my friends to have the best night," she said dreamily with a wide smile. "He is so romantic."

"Is his dick romantic because you smile just like that at his crotch all the time?" River snarked.

"Christ, you guys," Jo interrupted. "Let's get pictures taken to send to our men so they'll be jealous they aren't taking us out, and then we're off!"

Rowan set up the camera because she had a remote for her phone and they all lined up and did several poses. They were all laughing so hard by the end, Cat had to touch up her makeup. Maneuvering around two baby bumps was work.

They settled on their favorite one, and Rowan sent a group text to the guys. Right before she hit send, Catriona saw Coll's name had been added. "Did you mean to add Coll?"

Row looked up and raised her brows as if she were surprised by the question. "Sure. Colly's one of the guys, isn't he?"

"Sure," she answered with only a slight crack in her voice. Rowan looked at her again and winked. Had she somehow figured out she had a crush on Coll? *God ... How embarrassing.*

Would he think she looked nice? Would he even notice her surrounded by a bevy of beautiful women?

Regardless of her obsessive Coll thoughts—after ten years of them she was used to tuning them out—she'd decided to enjoy the evening. She could have done with about two less mugs of Guinness and at least three less shots of Glenmorangie.

River's speculation earlier that she'd snag a guy happened to be accurate, much to her shock. A gorgeous Russian man, Feodor, approached after only an hour of partying with her friends. Aileen, who'd met them there, was trying to give her two thumbs up, which the man totally saw. Mortifying.

He approached their table and introduced himself to the group before turning his stunning blue eyes her way. In heavily accented Russian, he explained that his family had recently immigrated to Scotland and were working on building their delivery business in Inverness. Mainly heavy freight, but Cat had perked up when he mentioned they had an established relationship with freighters going to the States.

She explained her business and admitted that she had been considering expanding her trade to the United States. He was as passionate about his family's business as she was about her own. It was nice. Really nice.

It was just a shame that Coll had looked her way not three hours ago. *Pathetic, Cat.*

Feodor joined their group seamlessly, and all the women at the table thought he was amazing. She relented when he asked to exchange numbers.

"Even if you won't let me take you on a date, Catriona, please consider our delivery service if you do expand. But … please consider the date."

Lord, but his light blond hair and dimpled smile were a stunning combination. She finally relented. "I'll consider it. I promise."

Remembering her words, she felt her face flush even more, and it had nothing whatsoever to do with her hangover. She felt funny entertaining the idea of another man taking her out when her every feeling was wrapped up in Coll Barr.

"Reel it in, Cat," she reminded herself as she finally, finally, thank you Jesus, came up to Grandma's front porch. Coll's truck was gone. She'd missed him, then.

Letting herself into the front door, her grandma was bent over the stove frying bacon. Thank you, Lord, for small mercies. "Hey, Gram."

"You just missed Coll," was her response.

Ignoring the blush that wanted to take root, she said instead, "It's you and your hangover-curing breakfast ways that I'm interested in." *Lies.*

"If you say so, lassie," her grandma sassily replied.

Save me from any truth bombs this morning. Please, God.

"Colly seemed a bit out of sorts this morning before he left. I happened to walk behind him while he was working on his computer. He mumbled something about a Russian. Mean anything to you, sweetheart?"

Someone sent a picture. *Kill those bitches ...* "He must be working on a new job. Tommy didn't mention it, but I'm sure we'll hear something about it soon." Redirect. Redirect. Redirect. "Bacon. Yum."

"My hairdresser's niece's cousin said a stranger to town was chatting you up last night. Bess said he was foreign."

This was turning out to be a real shit morning, sun bedamned. "The girls and I did speak to a stranger. I'm surprised I was singled out as being the man's focus. There were five other women at our table."

"Yes, but you were the only one seen exchanging numbers."

Kill me.

7

> I just landed in Maryland.

Why was he sharing his itinerary with Catriona? He decided before he left Scotland to keep his distance from her, but he'd been fiddling with his phone for hours, and the moment his phone was off airplane mode, he sent her a message.

> I came to see you at Grandma's before you left. You were already gone.

That made him feel dangerously satisfied that she would try to seek him out. It was probably for the best he'd left early. He would have been tempted to ... he wasn't sure, touch her in some way.

> Oh.

He shook his head at his lack of game, but then he remembered he shouldn't be trying to have game with Thomas' little sister. *What in the hell was he doing?*

> When will you be coming back to Bunchrew?

He knew she would ask. She'd put so much work and effort into her oils and massage skills, and he was going to disappoint her.

> It will be a while. Your brother sent me a new job. Work takes priority over visiting.

> I see. Okay.

He could almost feel her disappointment through the phone and tried to lighten things up.

> I get the blade today.

> Send me pictures.

Speaking of pictures, he was still fuming about the group text Rowan thought it was a good idea to add him to. The first picture sent was of the Byrnes, Josephine, and Cat all dressed up for a night out. Cat was always beautiful. In that picture, she blew his mind. Her dress was simple, like a man's shirt, but the material touched and caressed her body in a way that left his mouth dry.

He must have looked at her smiling into the camera a hundred times. The more he blew the image up, the more it looked like she was smiling just for him—until the next few pictures were sent.

Her smiles definitely weren't for him in those.

The last one was of a big blond man with his arm draped over Cat's shoulders. He was smiling down at her while she grinned at her friends. Her green eyes sparkled. She was having the time of her life.

Catriona

The caption for the photo was simple and infuriating. *Cat's Russian.*

He wanted to call Thomas and make sure he knew a man was hitting on his baby sister. He talked himself out of it, thank God. Thomas was in the same text group for one, and secondly, if she ever found out, she'd kill him. His best friend might also begin to wonder why Coll was so bent out of shape. She was, after all, not in high school anymore.

In fact, she was a grown woman, a college graduate, and running a growing business. She deserved an evening of fun—the fun better have ended at the pub. If she took that man home to her cottage, he'd be ... what would he be? Furious? Hurt? He had no right to either emotion where she was concerned.

> I'll try to remember.

You never forget anything.

> I don't remember what hurt you the night of your senior prom.

Enough, Coll. You'll have to come home eventually. You promised to try my liniment and let me massage you.

He really wished she would stop putting those two words together, "massage you." He quickly envisioned stepping in a fresh pile of cow shit at his folk's place to divert the direction of his dick's thoughts.

The truth was, he wasn't going to get out of seeing her. They had made a deal the last time they spoke, and he wouldn't go back on it.

> Two weeks.

> Fine. I have a special massage table at my house. See you in fourteen days.

～

COLL CALLED Thomas once he was settled in an Uber. It would take at least thirty minutes to get to Johns Hopkins, and he figured he would use the time to get information on the new case. To say he was shocked when he read the email brief was grossly underplaying his emotions.

Thomas was asking him to revisit the South American case. The one where he lost part of his right leg in a Peruvian jungle. Thankfully, his accident hadn't compromised the case, and the Drug Enforcement Agency, the DEA, was able to use a lot of Coll's research to close one of the largest and most brutal manufacturing cartels in the area.

The wealthy businessman that had hired MacGregor Security originally wanted them to locate his young son, who had been stolen during a vacation and forced to work in the facility making cocaine. He had tried two firms before MacGregor. Neither had made any headway in the case.

It had taken several months and hours of surveillance to locate the boy and extract him. By then, he'd been missing for two years. Jean had turned twelve the month before his rescue. His health would probably never be the same, having been forced to work with the harsh chemicals used to process coca leaves into paste.

The DEA had been aware that Coll was working for a French citizen, but because their goals were similar, they were more than happy to share intel with each other. He'd stayed on an extra month to finish scouting a possible new manufacturing location. Hindsight would have had his ass out of the jungle and home as soon as the boy was rescued. Hindsight rarely does a person any good.

The new case had nothing to do with the original contract, but it did have to do with the facility where the boy had been held. The DEA raided it and burned it to the ground. The leader, Inti Alvarez, was a sadistic bastard who was cruel to his workers and downright vicious to the camp women and children. The abuse he had witnessed kept him sleepless for months after.

He was scrolling through the file when Thomas answered. It was late afternoon in Scotland.

"Did you get the file?" was how he answered the phone.

"Looking at it now. I see Alvarez was murdered six months ago in prison. If anyone deserved that end, it was him."

"Agreed."

Thomas was unusually short for a newly engaged man. Coll could feel the hair on the backs of his arms raise. Something was off. "What's the case? Did DEA contact you again?"

"They did, but this isn't a case. Not in the traditional sense."

"For fuck's sake, Tommy. Spit it the fuck out already." Coll's angry outburst got him a disgruntled look from the Uber driver. He stared back until the man turned forward once more.

"Fine," Thomas replied tersely. He was clearly reluctant to say whatever it was he had to. "Did you ever have sex with a woman named Amaru Alvarez while you were living in Peru?"

That jolted him like he'd touched his tongue to a live wire. "What the hell, Tom?" Coll wasn't embarrassed that he'd had sex with a local. He'd been stationed there for months and on the rare occasions he and his team had a night off, they would go to local taverns for drinks and chatting up willing women.

He remembered Amaru. She'd been gorgeous in a sultry yet dangerous femme fatale kind of way. After a few shots of some rotgut liquor, Coll had thrown caution to the wind and let her lead him back to her lodgings one night.

"I would never invade your privacy, brother, if it weren't important."

That settled Coll's ruffled feathers. He had instantly been indignant, which probably had more to do with his recent impure thoughts about Thomas' sister and less to do with the invasion of privacy. "I know. I know. Yes, I did sleep with Amaru. I didn't know her last name was Alvarez. She hit on me at a local tavern one night, and I went home with her. What's this about?"

"Did she say or do anything strange?"

"Besides fuck me within an inch of my life? For hours?"

"Yes."

Coll thought back to that night so long ago. It was actually the last time he'd had sex since he lost his leg, so he did remember it well despite his alcohol consumption. There was ... something.

"When I woke up, she was gone. We'd gotten there after one in the morning, and the owner of the hostel woke me up the next morning around seven and told me my time was up, so it hadn't been her place after all. The last time we had sex had been around five, and I went to sleep after that."

"Impressive," Thomas said dryly. "Anything else?"

"She spoke Aymara. She spoke Spanish too, because I knew enough Spanish phrases to communicate. It was Frank from our team who told me earlier in the night that she was speaking the less common language of Aymara."

"Nothing else?"

Coll was disgusted to feel his cheeks heat. Glancing at the driver, he lowered his voice. "I used condoms. Four. I flushed everyone. Jesus, are you saying I got her pregnant or something? There's no way," he hotly denied.

And then it was like a light finally clicked on a memory that had been slumbering just under the surface of his skin. It was probably nothing, but still.

"I had a deep cut on the inside of my left forearm, which I hadn't gone to bed with. It took forever to heal. There was blood on the sheets. And," he hesitated, trying to remember everything about that morning, "there was an old rickety wooden table in the room. I remember wondering if I had somehow missed the ... the hell, I don't know. It looked like a small fire had been lit on the top.

"The whole room smelled like sex and burnt hair. It was weird, but I never thought about it again. I was hurt two days later and hoped to never see Peru again." This whole conversation freaked him out, though. Thomas' silence wasn't helping to improve his mood either.

The car he was in came to a stop outside the hospital. "We've arrived at your destination," the driver announced.

Coll grabbed his overnight bag and slid out of the car's backseat. "Thank you," he said absently, still focused on Thomas' silence. Once he was out on the sidewalk, he found a bench off to the side where he could privately finish the conversation.

"My appointment's in forty minutes. Tell me what in the hell this is all about."

"I can't believe this shit myself, but apparently, Amaru is the head of the Alvarez cartel. It was never Inti, who was the oldest, or even the other two brothers. Amaru ran it all, and the DEA discovered that the other processing facility you were looking into was hers as well—still operational because security was quadrupled after the first takedown. Landmines, cameras, guerilla armies. You name it, the nasty bitch has employed it."

"Still, what does this have to do with me?"

"There is probably not a more dangerous criminal in South America. The DEA has been trying to take her out for a year now, and no luck. It was recently discovered that her family has been longtime followers of Brujería, a form of witchcraft. Amaru, herself, is a leader among the Brujas, or women practitioners of her family.

"Brujería isn't always bad. In fact, it has roots in Catholicism. However, her family practices the darker arts of the religion. It's not a surprise, considering her line of work. The little fire she must have made in that hostel room points toward her practicing ... Jesus, it sounds ridiculous, but magic shit, I guess. And you were cut. You smelled burnt hair."

"Surely, I would have woken up if someone was doing some weird voodoo crap on me, and no matter how drunk I'd been, I would have woken up to the smell of smoke."

"My guess is she drugged you."

"This is all disturbing as fuck, Tommy, but why is the DEA contacting you about my involvement with the woman. Obviously, had I known who she was, I would have stuck a knife between her ribs before ever sleeping with her, but still, I don't get what's going on."

"The DEA has a spy working as a soldier, or enforcer, at one of her larger production plants. He said that the local gossip has it that she and her brother Inti weren't just in business together. They were lovers. Openly. Sick as fuck, I know," Thomas gritted out.

"The spy also reported that she hadn't been seen in over a week. She checks on the product almost daily, so her absence has been noticed. They tracked one of her private planes. She left Peru six days ago. DEA lost track of her plane the moment it was in the air. Where she went and why is anyone's guess. They believe she is trying to set up her own trade routes. Cut out the middle supplier, and she'd be a queen among drug peasants."

"Why can't they track her?" Coll asked, dread knotting his stomach.

"Even though the South American authorities work well with the DEA, it would be foolish to believe she doesn't have many officials in her pay. She can ghost whenever she feels like it."

Coll felt like he'd been thrown into the ocean and left to tread water or drown. None of this, absolutely none of this, was connecting for him.

"Let me try to understand. I had sex with an incestual, brother-loving woman who happens to be the head of one of the most violent drug-producing cartels. The facility that was destroyed when Inti was taken was just one of many.

"For reasons unbeknownst to us or the DEA, she sought me out specifically after the raid, which probably means she or her people figured out the Scotsman in their Peruvian midst was to blame for the loss of business.

"She took my blood because she's some sort of witch, and she thinks to enact some spell or curse over me." Looking down at his legs, he tapped his prosthesis. "Maybe she did manage to curse me after all."

"It actually gets worse."

Good God in Heaven. Worse? "How's that?"

"One of the lead DEA officers that had been stationed in South America for the past five years was seen going home with her two days before she made contact with you."

"Jesus. Should I have my dick scanned for unusual and disgusting diseases while I'm here in Baltimore?" Coll was only half joking. He was getting more disgusted with his past life choices by the second.

"I wish it were only about venereal diseases. The DEA officer went missing. His body was discovered ten days later after you were injured and left the country. He was tortured. They would like to believe he didn't give up any information, but since that time, the woman has been not just one step but ten steps ahead of them.

"A few DEA officers that specifically worked with you began to question if there was a link between their guy and our team."

"Why would they suspect that?"

"The spy reported several weeks after Inti's death that Amaru had met with three of her top security. When the group walked by his position where he was posted as a guard, he heard Amaru say Scotland.

"He wasn't able to hear anything else, but he reported it because it was odd. Scotland would be one of the last places a drug lord would try to set up camp. Of course, there are the ports, but it would take one good Catholic dock worker to see or hear something nefarious before running home to his mum to tattle. Every God-fearing neighbor would join forces to oust the sinners."

Coll cracked a smile at Thomas' depiction.

"Anyway, your teammate, Frank, had been dating one of the DEA at the time, and he mentioned to his girlfriend that you'd gone home with a local. It was only after the spy mentioned Scotland that their suspicions were aroused.

"They started going over old surveillance footage from the cameras that they'd set up years ago in and around the city where the Alvarez cartel was known to venture.

"They knew the date of their officer's disappearance, so it was easy then to go back and find him entering a hostel with Amaru. The same hostel she took you to. They now believe their officer gave more than DEA confidentials, but MacGregor Security's as well."

"My God, Thomas. I've compromised our business and possibly our family for a mindless fuck. I ... I ... Christ, I'm sick."

"She found you because the other man gave you up. You

didn't do a damn thing wrong, but we do have to meet this threat head-on. I assembled a team of our best computer brains, and they are going to work night and day until they find a way to hack into Alvarez.

"In the meantime, I have a contact, Maddy, a young college student who is an electronics genius who I've been trying to recruit, who is going to meet you after your appointment to scan your phone and laptop. She's working on her Computer Science PhD at Johns Hopkins Uni."

"Oh shit. You think the bitch has been tracking me."

"Possibly. It could be that after her brother was offed in prison, she remembered that you played a key role in her brother's capture. She clearly had some motive for taking you home that night. You weren't a random hookup. The witchcraft bullshit ... who knows.

"Our security software would have corrupted any breach to our system and not allowed access. However, it could be something as simple as a location chip. She's not the type of person to let the destruction of one of her huge facilities and the death of her brother go. She'd want revenge, and that's why I've already taken measures to secure our family."

"I'll head to the airport immediately."

"No. No, Coll. You're already there. Keep your appointment." He cut him off when he was about to protest. "No. As your best friend, I'm asking you to keep the appointment. You need it," he repeated. "I'm sending your parents on holiday and my parents to the States. They are going to Hugh O'Faolain's Oklahoma compound under the guise of planting flower beds for the Byrne sisters."

"Aileen? Mir?"

"They had already discussed with me about going with Charles to Cambridge, Massachusetts, to help him pack up his belongings. He put in his notice at Harvard and will be teaching again at a Uni here in Scotland next year. They agreed to stay while Charles finished the year out. Mir's all-important fucking prom isn't until June. They'll be back by then."

"You've been busy since I left town." Coll was trying to sound anything but devastated. He didn't manage it.

"This isn't your fault."

"Who's fucking fault is it then? Josephine is pregnant, Tommy. I screwed a nutcase, and she might turn her bloodlust toward everyone we love. In what world is any of this not my fault?"

"We will handle it like we always do. I'm moving with Jo to Dublin, and we'll stay at Hugh's mother's apartment. I think it's best to live anywhere but our hometown for now. I hired a few ex-military buddies to guard Grandma since the stubborn woman refuses to budge."

"Catriona?" Coll's heart was in his throat.

"She has a business that requires her presence. She'll be guarded. When you get home, you'll be the one guarding her yourself, though I hope this all blows over, on our end at least. DEA will know when her plane is back in South American air space. They will contact us immediately. Hopefully, this is just a short-lived inconvenience."

"Does—" he cut himself off before he said Cat's name and outed his panic. "Does anyone in the family know the specifics for the caution and upheaval?"

"Josephine. She took it in stride, though. I think pregnancy is making her a tad bloodthirsty."

Coll couldn't help the smile that twitched his lips at the thought of Thomas' fiancée. "Why is that?"

"She said she would do anything I needed her to do, but that the crazy bitch better not keep her from decorating the baby's room. Her words."

Thomas sounded awfully pleased for a man having to

uproot his life and move to Ireland. "The moment I'm back, I'll go home and pack up my things and let the lease go on my cottage there. I'll take care of Gram and Cat until this blows over."

"I know."

Coll sat on the bench a moment longer after they hung up, letting Thomas' confidence in him be a balm. He understood that it was another man who had given up information, but it didn't negate the fact that he'd fallen into her trap too. It could have just as easily been him who'd been captured and tortured.

Opening his phone back up, he texted Catriona.

> You didn't tell me you knew about the threat to the family.

She answered within seconds.

> I'm not concerned. You and my brother will handle it.

Coll tried not to puff with pride at her confidence.

> We will. Clean out your spare room.

Why?

> I'm moving in.

No. You aren't.

> We both move in with Grandma, or I move in with you.

I'm calling Tommy.

> Good luck.

8

Catriona was in a foul mood. She had just got a lift from one of the part-time gardeners to the auto repair shop in Inverness. Brant was the owner and a good friend of her dad's. He, Dad, and Mom all went to school together. When Brant got married, the two couples always made sure to stay close.

When her truck broke down last week, Thomas had it towed to Brant's, and he'd finally called that morning to say that it was ready to go.

She'd been furious to find out that some asshole had put water in her fuel tank. The prank had cost her five hundred pounds, all told. It had to have happened during one of her stops, but Brant said if that's when it happened, it was a miracle that the truck started, let alone made it back to the farm.

"I have too much to do today to deal with this shit," she groused to the empty truck cab as she pulled out of Brant's crumbling parking lot to head home. It wasn't just the truck pissing her off. It had been four days since Coll texted her that he was moving in, and she was still fuming.

She couldn't just have a guard patrolling the farm like her grandma was getting. Oh no. "Wee Cat needs an actual babysitter living with her." She thumped the steering wheel with the flat of her hand, releasing some of her pent-up anger.

And she knew, she *knew*, that her rising temper was not that her brother and Coll were swooping in to protect the women of the family. She was afraid that Coll would revert to seeing her as a little sister to shield instead of ... well, she had thought he might have finally started to see her as a woman.

Thomas could coddle her all day long if he chose. It was his right as her big brother, and she was well used to his overprotectiveness. She just wanted Coll to do it for different reasons.

Thomas explained the seriousness of the situation. Cat understood completely. She didn't have peas rattling around in her brain, for heaven's sake. It was a slim chance, but if that drug lord from South America targeted MacGregor Security or Coll specifically, only a foolish person would disregard the danger.

She had lost her temper at Thomas—not an unusual occurrence—when he didn't take her side about not letting Coll move in with her.

"If Coll wasn't glued to your side, then you would be glued to mine, and I'm going to Dublin these next few weeks."

"Tom!" she screeched. "Just give me a guard like Gram."

"Gram is almost eighty years old and would never bake me another special treat if I pushed her. You, Catriona Elizabeth, are my baby sister, my Wee Cat. I need to know you're safe, and there is no better man to see to you than Colly. You know this. You're just being argumentative because it's your nature to be so."

"Can he stay with Grandma? She has more room and would love to have him." The year before, Cat had talked her grandma into swapping houses. She'd been living in her childhood home since her parents had moved, but it was too big for her and further from the greenhouses than she liked.

Gram's old two-bedroom cottage was warm and cozy and

practically in the middle of fields and greenhouses. As Cat had expanded the business with more crops, the cottage looked like a fairy getaway surrounded as it was by rows of plants. Plus, any big family get-together was always at Grandma's. She needed the space more than Cat. Thankfully, she agreed.

"Please. For me, Wee Cat."

Damn her brother. He wasn't playing fair. She might lose her temper more often than not, but she could never tell him no. She would never add to his stress. He had a family to protect, and she wouldn't burden him further.

"Fine, but if he leaves the toilet lid up one time, one time, Thomas, I will kick his ass to the curb and good riddance."

"I accept your terms."

Just remembering the amusement in her brother's voice had her shaking her head in exasperation. However, if she were being honest, there were a few benefits to Coll's proximity. He could be her full-time test subject for her creams and oils. A bit of giddy anticipation tweaked her nerves at the thought.

She parked the flatbed in the lot closest to her office and main greenhouse, catching a glimpse of her new hire, Réka. Her beat up old 1999 Vauxhall Corsa was the only other vehicle in the lot. Her other employees lived near enough to bike in, but Réka lived a few miles away in Inverness.

She was a bit of a mystery, but a hard worker. She'd come to Catriona's office the same day Coll had gone back to his hermit home. That's what she called his house because it was situated in the farthest reaches of the Highlands. Réka was Hungarian. Her first language clearly wasn't English, but even with her thick accent, they were able to communicate just fine.

She was reserved and kept to herself, intentionally opting to take on jobs that kept her isolated from the other gardeners. There was a story to Réka that Cat hoped the woman would eventually feel comfortable to share, but for now, they both spoke plants. Her family had been big into gardening, she'd said, but that was the extent of her past revelations.

Cat got out of the truck and waved to her newest employee. Réka smiled shyly and waved back, the ends of her colorful head scarf lifting in the breeze. She should ask the woman how she wrapped all her hair so carefully that none escaped the confines. It might be worth trying on her own riotous mess.

It was nice to have another woman on the farm. If she stayed as diligent with her work as she was now, Cat decided she would hire her full-time. She did have a Hungarian driver's license, which meant that as soon as Cat could teach her how to drive the delivery truck, she could start helping with that chore.

Truth be told, Catriona loved the direction MacGregor Farm was taking. She might grumble about the work, but her careful planning and management were panning out. Now that Coll was going to be an uninvited guest in her home, she knew he would immediately start on the new website. He said he would build her one, and he'd never go back on his word.

Now that her initial irritation over her brother and Coll railroading her into the arrangement, she could see many, many extra benefits to having a man move in. She'd often wondered if she could cohabitate with the opposite sex or if she'd feel like she had to act differently, especially since it was a man she dreamed about in a nonplatonic way.

She had a vivid imagination. In her dreams, waking and asleep, she and Coll had done some pretty spicy things together. The ideas mainly came from books. *Thank you, Romance authors.*

She'd find out soon enough. Coll would be here tomorrow night. After work, she planned on clearing out the spare bedroom. It didn't have much besides a tiny bed with a chest at the foot to sit on and for storage and a rickety dresser.

She had considered letting him take her room. Her bed was

slightly longer and wider. His feet might not hang off. She wasn't sure she wanted Coll in her personal space.

Shaking away thoughts for tomorrow, she went back to ticking off her mental to-do list. The spare room wouldn't take but a moment. It was all the massage therapy equipment and a table that needed to be moved to the living room. It would be cramped, but no matter. If she could live in a dorm room with the sloppiest girl in the UK, then she could handle tight spaces as long as they were tidy—and Coll Barr had always been precise with his things, just like her brother. Royal Marines for life.

She needed to give the bathroom a thorough scrubbing and make sure there were enough towels for two people. She wasn't about to do laundry every day. She already stocked the kitchen with Coll's favorite snacks and drinks. He was a steak lover. She preferred fish. They both loved vegetables. Her small garden behind the cottage was bursting with variety, so she was good there. Crips and Guinness were a must for both of them.

It wasn't hard to know a person's likes and dislikes if someone grew up watching them like a preteen predator.

She managed to get hours of uninterrupted work done with her tinctures while Réka, bless her, tended the largest of the greenhouses. She was ready to call it a day. Her back ached pleasantly as she stretched, flexing her shoulders back and forth to relieve the tension. She'd finally finished Coll's warming ginger oil and couldn't wait to try it on his leg.

She was about to hang her apron on one of twenty hooks in her greenhouse when her phone notifications announced a text. It was a group text from Thomas to Coll and her.

> DEA update. Amaru Alvarez was spotted in South A an hour ago surrounded by armed guards. There was no sign of her plane. She might have flown in with someone else.

> So, no need for sleepovers?

Cat tried to tamp down her disappointment. She made a fuss about the roommate situation for two reasons. The most important thing was that she didn't like to be told what to do, and the other was because her brother would have instantly homed in on any odd behavior. She and Coll had been poking at each other for years, so if she'd suddenly opened her home willingly to her nemesis, Thomas would have taken note.

> I'm on my way to Bunchrew now. What do you think?

> What do you mean you're on your way now? What happened to tomorrow night?

Unsurprisingly, they acted like she wasn't a part of the conversation.

> My gut says wait for the DEA spy to confirm it's really her.

> I agree. We continue with the original plan.

> Yes. Cat. Talk to Coll about the plan. I'm taking Jo to dinner.

Talk to Coll ... *Brothers sucked.*

> Try to stay out of the supply room this time.

She quite enjoyed the two minutes of silence, knowing her big, tough brother was blushing, his ears bright red. The Byrne sisters had regaled her with the story of Jo and Thomas hooking up in a storage room of a pub in Dublin. She and Aileen almost fell out of their chairs. No one could tell a story like Raven, River, and Rowan Byrne.

Finally.

> Paybacks, Cat.

Knowing the text thread was finished, she wasted no time in calling Coll, who answered the first ring. She didn't waste time getting to it. "So, I assume from the conversation you two assholes had with each other that you're still going to live with me until the woman's identity is confirmed. Is that correct?"

"Yes."

Keep your temper in check, Cat. He knew that short answers were extremely annoying to her. That's why he's doing it. "Why are you a day early?" She was pleased to hear her voice sound unruffled. *Cool. Calm.*

"I decided to."

Powder keg fuse ... lit. "Do you think you should have fucking asked me first? I haven't even cleared the damn room out yet." *Shit.*

"You still have an hour. I'll pick you up for dinner at Grandma's then."

Never in the history of man could there have been one more annoying than him. She hung up before she gave him any more satisfaction. She had to learn to not give him the responses he expected.

When she considered that night after the cookout that he'd visited her workshop, she'd talked to him with nary a snarky comment—and it had thrown him. He hadn't known how to handle the dynamic. She needed to learn how to give him the unexpected more often. Throw him off his gruff high horse.

Maybe it was time to put herself out there. She was tired of mooning over the asshole, and she was really tired of being too scared of getting hurt or rejected to try. There were a few times where he'd looked at her like maybe ... he wanted her too. There was no better time than during forced proximity and her brother being out of town.

Smiling to herself, she closed up her office and began meandering around the paths between greenhouses, looking for Réka. She was always the last one to leave. She found her by one of the many water hydrants washing out fertilizer buckets.

Cat made sure to get in the woman's line of sight so she wouldn't startle her. Cat had noticed on more than one occasion that the new hire scared easily. They both smiled when the other woman noticed her. She turned the faucet off and tipped the last of the buckets over to dry overnight.

"I'm glad I caught you. You've been doing excellently this past week. I'm losing another part-time high school kid who's moving away for college in a month, and I wondered if you might consider working full-time."

"Oh." Her eyes lit up, and she clasped her hands together at her waist. In her thick accent, she answered, "I would be honored."

"Well, I don't know if it's much of an honor," Cat laughed, "but I think you are a perfect fit for MacGregor Farm. I thought you could make deliveries in the mornings as we have them and continue to help with the greenhouses in the afternoon. I'll make sure you're comfortable driving the truck, of course.

"I was also thinking that if you started at seven in the morning, you could finish your day by four. You'd have an hour for lunch and a couple of breaks as you see fit.

"You mentioned you live with an elderly cousin. Feel free to stop by during your errands to visit or eat lunch."

She nodded her head. Today's soft peaches and cream-striped scarf brushed against the woman's strong shoulders. It was hard to tell her age with her hair covered, but she was tall, slender, and fit. Her features were symmetrical and lovely.

"I would be pleased to accept this offer," she replied in her thick Hungarian accent.

"Oh, I'm glad to hear it. If there is ever a need for you to work a Saturday, I'll ask that you take off Monday. Well," Cat started as she and Réka walked side by side to the parking lot, "I'm ready to head home. I have to get my place ready for an unwanted house guest who'll be staying with me for a few days."

"Oh?"

"Coll. He's a friend of my brothers. No big deal." It was a huge deal.

"Is he … your boyfriend?" Réka asked shyly.

"Oh no. Nothing like that." She wished it was like that. "I only told you in case you saw him around. He's tall with dark hair. Grumpy but harmless," she smiled at the other woman. "Are you dating anyone?" She couldn't help but be curious. When Réka's mouth tensed right before she looked away, Cat knew she shouldn't have pried.

"You don't need to tell me, Réka. I'm sorry I asked. Scottish folks can be a bit nosy."

She hummed in amusement but visibly relaxed and even bumped Catriona's shoulder. "I left him. He left me." She shrugged. "I'm still not over it. I couldn't keep living in the home we were once so happy in. I'm starting over." She studied Cat for a moment, appearing startled that she'd been so open. Finally, she added, "He may eventually look for me. I pray he never does, but … well … I hope he doesn't." She shrugged and moved to her car.

Cat was thrilled she'd opened up as much as she had. Her ex must have been a real bastard to leave a kind woman like Réka. "Enjoy your evening. I'm eating dinner at Grandma's.

Maybe you could bring your cousin to Gram's house one evening. She lives to cook for people."

"I would love that. Ceila has good days and bad. Perhaps on one of her good days, we could join you. Thank you again for the full-time position. Your trust in me means a lot."

With that, she climbed into her ratty car and slowly left the farm. Cat now only had forty minutes to clean Coll's room, shower, and put on her sweetest face. It was time to enact her 'Make Coll Want Me' plan.

9

Coll put his truck in park outside Catriona's cottage. The gazillion plants and flowers covering every nook and cranny of the residence advertised its owner more efficiently than a four-foot placard would have.

He'd been anticipating their verbal sparring since she'd hung up on him an hour ago. His truck bed was full of his belongings, but they could stay there until tomorrow. He only needed the worn duffle sitting beside him. Grasping the leather handles of his bag, he shoved open the stiff door of his truck and slid out of the cab. Dodging five planters and hanging ivy, he finally made it to the front door.

His hand was raised to knock, but Catriona beat him to it. She yanked the door wide, and her beautiful smile was the first thing to greet him. Her glorious red hair was unhindered by bands or braids and tickled all the way to her lower back—her naked back.

What the hell was she wearing? It looked like similar undergarments from that night they spoke in her workshop. The tiniest, tight shorts and a sports bra sans apron this time. He felt the last bit of his saliva dissipate when he was confronted with the most mouthwatering breasts, small, firm, and high. Sure, the bra was full coverage and totally modest, but there was nothing modest about the perfect tiny pricks that her little nipples made in the fabric.

"Come on in. I've got your room all ready. I want you to lay down on the bed, and we'll see if it's going to be too small for you."

She grabbed the hand still numbly holding his bag, and dragged him over the threshold. He barely took note of the small living space before he was in a tiny bedroom. She pried the bag from his numb fingers and dropped his belongings to the floor, tugging and shoving him toward what had to be the world's smallest bed.

"Here now, lay down. Let's see if your feet stick over too bad. I know you'll probably only be staying here for a few days, but you may have to sleep in my bed." She chuckled as she manhandled him into sitting on the mattress. Was it his imagination, or was she acting odd?

He sat, and the squeaking was earsplitting. The level of mattress sag was alarming. "Cat—" he tried to interrupt, but she wasn't having it.

She placed her hands against his chest and shoved none too gently. For such a wee creature, she was strong. He found himself flat on his back with a scantily clad woman staring down at him, hands on hips.

"Christ, Coll. If you could see how ridiculous you look. No question. You'll sleep in my bed."

He sat up so fast, and she was so close that he almost knocked her over. He couldn't stay on his back and chance her noticing his dick, though, which was slightly thicker than it had been a moment ago. Hearing "You'll sleep in my bed" come out of her mouth was giving him way too many fantasies.

"With you?" He did not just say that. He. Did. Not.

She gripped his hand and pulled, bringing his much bigger body flush with the front of her petite one—and in that moment, he wanted to grab her and pull her tight against him. Grinning up at him, she only said, "Of course not. Unless you'd like me to." Cat dropped that bomb as she spun on her heel and headed out of the room. The firm globes of her ass flexing in those ridiculous shorts. Moving in here may have been one of the biggest mistakes of his life.

∾

Thankfully, Cat pulled on a pair of light joggers and a loose t-shirt before they made their way to Grandma's for dinner. The older woman insisted on a plate of food being taken out to Lyle, the burly guard that Thomas had hired to surveil the house and surrounding property.

"Take this out to Lyle for me, Cat, before we sit down. Oh, I meant to tell you. I've been chatting the boy up. His family's from Wales, but he travels all over as a freelance bodyguard. He looks very strong and capable, if you know what I mean."

She winked at Catriona. What the hell was she winking about?

"He's twenty-six and single," Grandma helpfully provided.

"I've always wanted to visit Wales. Their National Botanic Garden is supposed to be extraordinary. I'll have to ask this Lyle if he's ever been."

Cat was reaching for the plate of food, but Coll snatched it before she could. "I need to speak to the guard. I'll take it." Before either woman could protest, he was out the door. Finding the 'perfectly single' Lyle was easy enough. He was rounding the corner of the house, presumably finishing a circuit of the perimeter.

Coll met the man at the bottom of the porch steps and stuck

his free hand out to shake. "I'm Coll Barr. I work with Thomas MacGregor. All quiet?"

"Lyle Evans." He shook his hand with a firm grip. "Nothing to report. I only came on duty an hour ago. My partner will relieve me at six in the morning."

Did the boy have to be quite so handsome? He handed the dinner plate over. "This is for you." Coll enjoyed seeing the slight tinge of pink grace the other man's cheeks.

"I told Mrs. MacGregor she doesn't need to feed me, but damn, she's a better cook than my mum."

He couldn't help the chuckle that escaped his throat at the boy's honesty. "Telling Grandma MacGregor no never works out well for anyone. I'm with Thomas MacGregor's sister, Catriona. The woman who runs the farm. We live together in the small cottage behind the greenhouses." Coll was aware that he made it sound like they were a couple—he'd done it on purpose.

"I'll keep her and the farm secure."

"Understood."

Coll actually believed he did understand. Satisfied, the men parted ways and he joined the women who had placed at least eight different platters of food on the table in his absence. He noticed the table settings immediately.

One plate was placed where Grandma always sat, and two were placed side by side on the opposite side of the table, even though there was plenty of room to spread out. Coll was beginning to think that Cat was trying something. She'd done a complete one-eighty since their phone conversation.

She now seemed ecstatic that they were to be roommates, almost exuberant. Cat was not a giggler or a gusher. She laughed and enjoyed herself, but her personality ran more toward no-nonsense.

And here she was now, smiling and bringing him a glass of

water. She would rather cut off her own hand than serve him unless her grandma browbeat her into it.

As surely as he'd known the mouthy brat for twenty-two years, he was positive she was

up to something. Maybe she was trying to lull him into a false sense of security, and when he least expected, she'd strike. She could be killing him with kindness because she knew it would put him on alert, keeping him on edge so he wasn't able to relax.

Or she may have decided to try her hand at flirting. He thought he'd crushed any old flames she used to carry for him, but ... what if he hadn't?

She'd dated in college. He knew because Thomas had periodically done background checks. Coll tried not to ask too many questions about her boyfriends because the truth of it was it pissed him off.

He eyed her as she pulled the chair out next to him and sat. And then ... nothing. She didn't mention their sleeping arrangements again—not that she was likely to do that in front of her grandma—or bat her eyelashes up at him. She didn't accidentally touch her thigh to his, and there was no sleeve brushed against his arm.

He'd know if any of those things had happened because he was doing nothing but watching her. Whatever the hell her plan was, she managed to capture his complete attention. Not that she didn't always capture his attention.

Cat was telling Grandma about how well one of her new hires was doing and that she couldn't wait to have the woman and her elderly cousin over for dinner.

"She's going to start making some of my deliveries. That will free me up considerably. Already, with her help, I've had more time to spend on my oils."

"I'm glad you finally hired another full-time person. You

work too hard," Grandma admonished. "She's Hungarian, you say?"

"Yes. Her English is great, though her accent can make a few words tricky. She said her family back home are big gardeners. She knows her way around plants. Maybe she could teach us some traditional Hungarian recipes."

"That would be lovely," Grandma agreed. "Have you finished Colly's liniment since you've had all this extra time?"

Coll's eyes snapped to the older woman. He couldn't detect any meddling on her part. She was a canny woman, though.

"Oh, yes, I did. I can't wait to use it." Cat turned to face him. Finally. "As soon as we get home, I'll set everything up for a massage. Your feedback will be really helpful."

"We're doing that tonight?" He thought he'd have a few more days to work up to the idea of her seeing his leg.

"Of course. Why wait?"

Why indeed. Why? Why? Why? *Think, Coll.* This was too much, too fast. "I have work. I'm aiding a team with research, and I need to start laying out your new website."

"Oh."

Christ. She was disappointed. He'd disappointed her. She was fiddling with her fork and knife, the silence an uncomfortable bit of condemnation.

Grandma shot him a sharp look, but thankfully, she took mercy on him and asked him a question.

"Any news on that drug woman from South America?"

He internally sighed, not wishing to discuss Amaru Alvarez. Still, it was better than listening to Cat's silence. "DEA will let us know the moment their spy has eyes on her. So far, she hasn't shown her face at their processing plants. Thomas and I believe that until she's found, vigilance is the best option."

"Thomas mentioned she might be specifically targeting you. Why you, when so many others were in South America too?"

A headache was building at his temples. Catriona had set down her utensils, still and focused on his answer. "She killed a DEA agent. It's believed he might have given up DEA mission objectives and those of MacGregor Security."

Grandma tsked and shook her head. "Bless that man. He was tortured?"

"Yes." He looked at Cat sitting next to him. Her eyes were wide. He hated that she would carry that knowledge now.

"But why you? Why does the DEA suspect it's you and not someone else on your team that she might be targeting?"

Catriona was always clever. "She made contact with me once. I didn't know who she was at the time. Not until a few days ago."

"What do you mean she made contact?"

Ignoring her question, Coll stood abruptly and started picking up the dishes. "Thank you for dinner, Grandma. Let me help clear the table." He heard the women finally begin to move. He kept his back to them and started rinsing dishes so he wouldn't have to see their questioning glances.

Ten minutes later, he and Catriona were loaded up in his truck and headed home. She hadn't spoken a word since he'd ignored her question. He'd hurt her twice that night. That was a record even for him.

Coll let them in the house, asking Cat to stay by the door while he checked the interior. There was no good in him living here if he didn't take the job of Cat's safety seriously. "Clear." He announced as he walked back into the living room. "If you'd like the shower first, I need to walk the perimeter and mark where to install security cameras." At her silent nod, he let himself out.

As he shut the door behind him, he felt defeated. His chest felt tight. There were so many emotions clanging around his body, he wanted to roar with frustration.

10

When Coll walked through the front door after securing the outside of the house, Catriona was waiting for him.

Her hair was up in a clip, escaped tendrils trailing her neck, chest, and back. She wore wholesome, white cotton panties with a white cotton tee. Her exterior screamed innocence, but her interior was a bubbling cauldron of fury.

His eyes found her immediately, darkening to burnt umber. She crossed her arms across her chest, ready for battle.

"You don't trust me." In her mind, tonight's whole debacle began and ended with that truth. He didn't trust her with his leg, and he didn't trust her with his work. She was pleased to see his fists curl and flex at his sides.

"I do."

"Your actions spoke differently tonight. Have I ever betrayed you? Purposely sought to hurt you? Would I ever be so foolish as to speak of your and Thomas' work? Would I ever make you feel less over an injury? Is that the type of woman you believe me to be?"

"No."

"Then why?" She'd considered letting tonight's disappointments go. Forgive and forget. But she was done not speaking her mind when it came to this man.

"Cat—"

She interrupted. "If you aren't going to give me answers, then tomorrow I will move in with Grandma for Thomas' sake, and your presence here in Bunchrew will no longer be necessary."

She could see his jaw flexing and his chest heaving in agitation. He didn't want to tell her anything. He didn't want her to know ... him.

His eyes closed, opened, closed, opened. In prayer, perhaps. "I'm not ready for you to look ... for you to see what my body looks like now. I'm not ... fuck." He cursed, running both hands over his head and face. "I'm not ready to know whether you'll see—I'm not ready," he finally ground out.

Now, that was honesty, and it was the type of honesty that required the same level of truth back. "I'll give you however much time you need, Coll. I'm not going anywhere. Though looking like you do," she shook her head in wonder, "I'm gutted that you don't see what I see. What everyone else sees."

They stood looking at one another for several moments, each digesting the recent revelations. She couldn't let it go at that, though. "And how does the drug cartel woman know you?"

He took a moment to remove his boots, gathering his thoughts or shoring up the bits of the story he planned on imparting. He couldn't lie to her. She'd know.

He was so handsome, standing there in a worn tee and work pants, stockinged feet pressed against the worn, wood floors of her cabin. It mattered less than a grain of sand's space that he didn't have two matching legs. He finally spoke, and it wasn't what she wanted to hear.

"I'll tell you about Amaru if you tell me what happened four years ago at prom."

Bastard. What an unscrupulous asshole. Her psyche went from tender to wanting to strangle him in under a second.

"Trust goes both ways, Kitty Cat."

She hated it when anyone got the best of her in an argument. Coll just doubled down on her truth throwdown, and it pissed her off something fierce. "Jesus, Coll. My high school woes are so minor. I'm shocked we're even discussing them." She felt the telltale heat creep up her chest and cursed her complexion for the millionth time in her life.

"If it's so inconsequential, tell me ... and I'll tell you."

And to think, she'd been flirting and acting ridiculous all evening to make him notice her. As soon as she admitted ... *Damn. Damn. Damn.* The truth was, she was insecure about her body, but so was he. If she wanted him to trust her, he was completely right in saying she needed to trust him too.

Taking a deep breath and concentrating her attention on the darkening window behind his body, she started. "I knew you or my brother would find a way to watch over me at prom. I didn't like it, but I had resigned myself to it months before. Duncan and I were only and always friends, and it seemed silly, yet I still knew not to fight it.

"I only had a few not very close friends in school. Most of the popular girls made it their life's mission to make my life hell."

"What the fuck does that mean? You never told us your classmates were assholes."

Coll's indignation almost made her smile. Not quite, though. "Just let me get it out," she said in exasperation. "For years, I was the butt of every joke. My crazy hair, my ... my ... my," she stuttered before finally getting out, "body. All jokes. I looked like an ugly duckling amongst puberty-enhanced swans.

"I was only ever invited to birthday parties as a joke. I stopped going to those when I was eight. I would think a boy might fancy me, but then the pretty girls would tease him until he ignored me too. I didn't want to go to prom, but Mum really, really wanted me to. She was ... popular in school. She didn't ... I didn't want her to know how bad it was.

"I did feel pretty that night. I stuffed my bra," she admitted with an embarrassed shrug. "At dinner, I wondered if you knew my chest was a wad of cotton stuffing."

"You were beautiful, lass."

She brushed the comment aside with a swipe of her hand. "Of course, you would say that. You and Thomas are gentlemen, I'll give you that. So, that night, as soon as I saw you at dinner, I knew I was in for it, but ... I didn't care. I only cared what you thought. I was silly," she admitted, her cheeks turning redder at the confession.

"The whispers started during the appetizers and grew deafening by the main course. I'm honestly shocked you didn't hear any of it. I'm glad you didn't."

"Tell me. What were they saying? You were as lovely then as you are now. What did they say, Cat?"

"Oh, the same old things. Nothing to go on and on about."

"Tell me. Trust," he reminded.

Trust. "Umm, things like *'The runt still needs a babysitter. Poor Coll Barr, so handsome but relegated to babysitting a dud. He must have a strong stomach. Her tits look like two flea bites in that ugly dress. Pedophile's wet dream,'* and my favorite, *'Why wasn't she homeschooled? It would have saved us from having to look at her.'* And then, later at the dance, you were dancing and practically making out with one of my teachers, and the same lovely girls from dinner made an executive decision to drop by and deliver more insults throughout the night until it was finally, blessedly, time to go home.

"So, prom wasn't necessarily out of the ordinary. I just felt like, had you not made yourself so visible, I maybe wouldn't have been given such a hard time." She could see him start to speak, but she didn't want to endure any platitudes. "I was angry at you for it, I admit. I also admit it was unfair of me and immature. I don't hold any grudges about that night. It was always their opinions, and though I hated it, I don't think of them anymore." Much, she didn't add.

There. She puked her most embarrassing moments up for Coll's perusal. Trust. "How does the drug cartel woman know you? You specifically."

"I want to talk about those piece of shit girls from your high school, not—"

She cut him off. "I trusted you with my truth. I never said I would discuss it. I asked about—"

"She approached me at a bar one night in Peru. One of the rare nights the team and I went out. She wanted me. I wanted her."

"You mean ... what? You slept with a woman like that?" Catriona was sick at the thought.

"I didn't know who she was." He gritted his teeth in obvious discomfort.

"What did you do?" It was a childish question. She knew it the moment it left her lips.

"What do you think, Cat? We fucked for hours."

She had to swallow several times before she felt like she would be able to stop all the comments trying to escape. *We fucked for hours.* He said it so casually. Did he have no clue what a statement like that ... what a blow it was ... to her?

"Oh." Oh. That was all she had. As she turned to walk to the guest room where she planned on sleeping so Coll could have her bed, the man of the hour grabbed her arm and swung her back around.

"Cat." There was a desperation in his voice that she couldn't interrupt.

"Please. I'm to bed, Coll. Let me go. We told each other our truths. Perhaps we shouldn't have." She whispered as she pulled her arm free of his grasp.

11

Dear Brother,

Your loss grieves me. I walk our beloved jungle paths and feel nothing. I am alone in my grief. Our brothers do not mourn you. Soon, they will pay for that slight.

I feel as though my flesh has been stripped from my body, and each step without you by my side feels like acid raining down upon my raw, skinless form.

I am nothing without you, Inti. Nothing. I know you are on your own perilous journey. Mountains. Rivers. Dark forests. The Underworld awaits you, but I beg you, do not take that final step.

I can't follow you there. I am working on a way to bring you home, bring you back to me. My arms feel like banded weights at my sides because they don't have you to hold.

I lay in bed at night, summoning my memories. Sometimes, I feel breath warm against my skin, and I know that you have found me even though your trials must be brutal.

I want to feel the weight of your body, your tongue sliding against my own. I want to feel you between my legs

... when our bodies come together, the Seven-Headed Palm shivers its branches in joy.

I will go mad without you.

You need me as I need you.

Our bodies were never meant to be apart.

Believe in me, my love. I have not forsaken you. I will never let you go.

There is a way. It is dangerous, but my life is nothing if you aren't here to share it. I will make a million sacrifices until the Old Ones hear my plea.

Your beloved,

A

12

Mortification, thy name is Catriona MacGregor. She didn't sleep last night. She *couldn't* sleep and not from the damned uncomfortable bed. She weighed next to nothing, but she could have sworn her ass bottomed out and touched the floor with every twist of her body—and the squeaking ... like a screaming rat in a trap.

Oh, how she wished the bed were to blame. Her sleeplessness began and ended with each replay of her confessions. One after the other after the other. It was like once she started remembering the slights she couldn't help uttering them.

And did she have to tell him she stuffed her bra? *Christ, have mercy.* She scrubbed her hands over her face, terrified she might burst into embarrassed tears the moment she saw Coll's face.

Confessing one's most embarrassing moments was supposed to make them feel light and free. That hadn't happened yet.

And then there was his confession. Did she think Coll didn't have sex? No, but she also did her level best to never, ever think about it either. To hear him say ... how he said it ... for hours. She felt beyond foolish.

She also instantly envisioned him and some voluptuous, exotic woman, all curves and red lips and smooth, flowing dark hair. As opposite of her own image as possible. She hadn't cried, but it'd been close.

Clearly, it was meant to be a one-night stand. The woman must have had ulterior motives to have chosen Coll ... but none of that mattered. He'd thrown the intimacy in her face after she'd barfed all her insecurities. She knew she'd been kidding herself about Coll one day falling madly in love with her.

He certainly didn't see her as a one-night stand kind of woman.

She'd tried to date in the past in the hopes of ridding herself of her feelings, her unrequited feelings, for him. It never worked. Maybe it was time to try dating. Really try. No more halfhearted attempts.

In the meantime, there was nothing for it but to avoid, avoid, avoid.

She had a packed day and had never been more thankful that she had an unusual number of clients coming in. She wouldn't even have time for lunch. Perfect.

Cat was up well before dawn and snuck into the bathroom that separated the two bedrooms. All she wanted, no needed, was to get out of this house before Coll was up. "Please, God," she whisper-prayed, "do me this one solid, and I promise to go to Mass more than once a month."

She already regretted the promise. "That's not true, God," she was quick to amend lest He hear her thoughts, "I don't regret the promise. Not at all." She added while pulling a lovely, thin gray jumper over her head. Her mother had gotten it for her for Christmas two years ago, and it was still one of her favorites.

Since she had clients coming, she couldn't wear her normal shorts or exercise pants, so she opted for light-wash jeans and gray trainers. A bit of mascara and powder. She kept nude gloss in her desk to apply right before a meeting.

She cringed when she finally looked at her hair. The level of crazy vibes it was putting off was a code red. She should have braided her hair before bed. "Brush, brush, brush." She mumbled while opening and closing every drawer and cabinet. "What the heck did I do with the damn thing?"

Growling in frustration at the wasted time, she attempted a light finger comb with minimal results, as her fingers weren't up for the challenge. She finally opted to pull the mass back in a low ponytail. Restrained, the ends of her hair hit her jean's back pockets. It would do. It would have to do.

As she exited the bathroom in the still, silent, dark living area, she raised her eyes up toward the heavens. "Thanks for that."

On light feet, she left the house and locked things up behind her. On her way to the office, she mentally ticked off her to-do list. Check her emails for new orders. Print out delivery invoices for Réka. Beg Réka to stop by Boots and grab her a new brush—she'd probably accidentally thrown the damn thing away when she was tidying like a mad woman for Coll. Time wasted ...

"Don't think about Coll," she chided herself. Back to the list. It was early enough to get a good few hours in at her workshop—reminder: lock all exterior doors while working so no one can interrupt. Specifically, tall, dark, and handsome men.

"Don't think of him," she warned herself. The first client appointment was at nine. The owner of a new Italian restaurant in Inverness would be stopping by around eleven-thirty, and that appointment shouldn't last more than an hour to an hour and a half to discuss the regular delivery of fresh flowers. He wanted the elegance of real, but as it was a new business, cost was very important to him. When they spoke over the phone, his tastes seemed classic and simple. She felt they could work out a deal he'd be very satisfied with.

The moment that meeting was finished, she would change into her gardening clothes and spend at least two hours walking through each greenhouse, ensuring that her plants were well cared for and healthy, and making note of any low stock.

That would give her less than thirty to change her clothes again in time for her second client appointment. A daughter wanted to pick out flowers for her parents' seventy-fifth anniversary. "What would that be like?" she wondered aloud. "Seventy-five years." She shook her head in speculation.

Her last appointment was a blushing bride picking out her wedding flowers and the flowers for the reception. Unfortunately, the blushing bride's overbearing mother, who was also attending the appointment, was the one who would make the appointment difficult and twice as long. She'd had the displeasure of speaking to the woman over the phone.

Cat smiled at the terrible schedule. No time for roommate troubles today.

The last of her day would be spent in her workroom. Soft music, stale trail mix, a can of Diet Pepsi, and no Coll.

Satisfied with her planning, she came around the side of her glass office and froze. Cat craned her neck back to get a look at the few lingering stars in the sky. "God ... you have some explaining to do," she said under her breath. Coll Barr was leaning his back against her front door as if he had nothing better to do at five-thirty in the morning.

~

THE STILL OF the early morning allowed sound to carry. Coll heard Catriona long before she stood there facing him. His casual pose hid a conscience overflowing with guilt and remorse.

He couldn't have handled last night worse if he'd paid someone to write the conversation as a Shakespearean Tragedy.

In his defense, he'd been reeling from Cat's school revelations and been hit with fury

and guilt in equal measures. That his presence had made that night so hard for her. That he'd

been flirting with one of her damn teachers while she was being verbally assaulted. He'd never

forgive himself.

He didn't deserve her blasé forgiveness, as if what she endured wasn't worth mentioning.

I was angry at you for it, I admit. I also admit it was unfair of me and immature. I don't hold any grudges about that night. Well, she sure as hell should hold grudges.

Had he been able to calm himself, he would have never said what he said about his night with that Alvarez drug lord. He was angry at himself, but he took it out on Cat because she made him talk about it. What she didn't understand was how ashamed he was of that night. He *needed* her to understand. He wanted a chance to explain.

Her wide eyes and rounded mouth were proof that she thought she'd escaped the confrontation that was about to happen. He had listened to her toss and turn for hours, knowing that she was as upset about the way things had been left between them as he was.

He also knew her well enough to know that she would try to sneak out and avoid him. He wasn't going to allow that.

"Good morning." He watched, fascinated by her transformation. She went from shock and surprise at seeing him to embarrassment. Her reddened cheeks colored a path to anger. He didn't care if she was mad. They were going to talk.

"I'm not sure why you're here so early, but I have a very tight schedule today, and you aren't on it."

Ouch. "I won't take up much of your time."

"No, you won't because you aren't getting any of it. Listen, Coll. Do I wish I hadn't confided in you about school? Yes. Am I embarrassed this morning? Definitely. Coulda, woulda, and shouldas won't change any of it. So, we move forward. You and I are family. Our little tit-for-tat information share, though unfortunate, doesn't change who we are.

"But you don't get to insist upon anything when it comes to me unless it is a matter of keeping me safe from the woman you've fucked, and only will I allow your inconvenient presence because my brother insists.

"Now, I hope this clears up any misconception you have that I need more, or anything, from you."

She forcibly shoved him away from her door's keypad, which he allowed because he was reeling from the massive put-down she'd just delivered. "Cat. Pleas—"

She held up her hand to stop his plea. "I would appreciate you giving enough of a shit about my feelings to at least switch places with the men Thomas hired. You watch over Grandma instead of them."

Well, that hadn't gone as planned, but then why did he ever think she would behave in an expected manner? Cat was fire and left scorch marks in her wake. He barely grabbed the heavy wood and glass door before it slid shut, locking him out.

When she whirled around to confront him, he grabbed her shoulders and held her still. He was going to get out what he wanted to say one way or another.

"I'm sorry, Cat. I'm desperately sorry for making your prom one of your worst memories instead of one of the best. I'm sorry I want to track down the girls who hurt you in school and ruin their lives the way they tried to ruin yours.

"I say tried because the joke's on them, you're stronger, smarter, and a hundred times more beautiful than they ever hoped to be. I wish you could see that they hurt you out of jealousy. Nothing more, nothing less. You are extraordinary, and my guess is that they realized early on they'd never measure up.

"I'm sorry I got into my feelings about it and got angry instead of pulling you into my arms. I should have comforted you, and instead, I was selfish, which tends to be a theme where you're concerned.

"I'm sorry you have to be guarded and worry about your safety because of my work ... and because I slept with a woman who meant absolutely nothing to me.

"I'm sick that I spoke to you like I did—as if sleeping with a stranger was normal for me and that your feelings meant nothing. I don't know if you remember, but I hurt your feelings before I left to go back to South America that one night at a family dinner. Well, to be fair, I hurt your feelings *and* my sister's. You were ... seeing someone, and it was the first time I realized you were dating." He winced at the omission. He was going to give himself away if he wasn't careful.

"I felt out of the family loop and behaved badly. I'm sorry for that night too. South America was a disaster personally for me on so many levels. First, I slept with a woman whose name I didn't even know, and then I got part of my leg blown off, and now I look like a ... a ... a science project. I wish to God I'd never told you about her or at least not told you the way I did.

"I'm angry and sensitive about it for two reasons, and I took those reasons out on you. It was childish and beneath me. I never want to hurt you, Cat. I hope you believe that, though after last night, it seems I'm a repeat offender."

She never interrupted him, and for that, he was grateful. Her silence was unnerving. Forcing himself to get it all out, he confessed, "I haven't had sex since that night two years ago. Meaningless sex no longer holds any appeal, and I ... I'm not the same."

WELL. Well, then. His apology sure made it difficult to shove him out of the doorway and lock him out. It also made Cat's simmering anger and embarrassment feel churlish and childish. Sighing, her conscience riding her, she decided Coll's friendship was worth getting everything out and moving on.

"I appreciate that you care enough to want to set things right. The truth ... well, the truth is you have nothing to apologize for. As for prom, it really isn't that big of a deal now that I'm older and have more perspective. I only agreed to tell you because, for some reason, Grandma decided to bring it up.

"I've thought about why quite a lot. Clearly, she knows you well enough that she wanted this exact thing to happen. She knew you wouldn't be able to let it go, and you didn't. Her reasons are her own, and you know as well as I do that she'll never fess up.

"As for your admission, you obviously didn't know who the woman was. You're certainly free to have sex with whomever you please. You just drew the short straw on partners this time." She tried a small smile to put him at ease before she dropped the uncomfortable secret that really wasn't a secret.

"I reacted badly to you talking about fucking someone for hours," he flinched at either the coarse phrase coming out of her mouth or the reminder he'd said it first or both, "because we both know I've harbored an embarrassing crush on you since I was little, and I guess you describing what you did with another woman stung my pride."

Her face was blazing red now. She could feel the heat traveling from her cheeks to her neck and below the neckline of her sweater. "I'm glad we finally got everything out. It's actually a relief. I embarrassed myself for years, and you were a trooper to tolerate it so well. Plus, you never ratted me out to Thomas, which I really, really appreciate." She laughed and patted her cheeks—the attempt to cool them was unsuccessful.

"I decided it was time I moved on from little girl crushes anyway, and your truth bomb gave me the needed kick in the ass." Coll hadn't moved or blinked since she started. He was probably mortified that she brought up her crush, but none of what she said was news to him, and he knew it.

She did feel better for talking it out. It was a long time coming and maybe now they really could become closer without all the tension. She wouldn't lie and say there hadn't been a small part of her that hoped that he might surprise her and admit he had feelings for her too. She sighed inside, shaking off the disappointment.

Since he wasn't moving, she moved before him and slowly put her arms around his waist. At first, he didn't respond, but then his arms went over her shoulders to hold her to his chest. It was the most intimate moment the two of them had ever shared, and God, he smelled amazing. A mix of her favorite things, outdoors and pine. She could have stayed standing there for hours, cocooned in strength.

Knowing if she didn't let go soon her announcement to move on wouldn't hold much water, she forced herself to let go. She unlocked her hands from his lower back, unable to resist sliding them against his sides as she unglued her body from his. Coll was slower to release her, but she was finally able to slip free.

As she turned to walk toward the workshop's entrance, she paused. "You need to give yourself a break about the woman, Coll. You also need to stop seeing yourself as different. Missing limb or not, you will always be one of the best men I know. Now, I've got to get busy." She slid the barn door open; the comfort of the space's scents a balm. "I probably won't see you until tonight."

13

"The DEA's plant reported that Amaru Alvarez still had not visited her growing sites or processing facilities. Even if it was an area he didn't guard personally, he would have heard about it. Any news about the Alvarez family travels quickly." Coll could tell Thomas was frustrated.

"What about her other two brothers?" The two Amaru wasn't sleeping with, Coll wanted to add, but the sickening reality of that family didn't bear speaking out loud.

"Those two didn't get the entrepreneurial gene that Amaru and Inti possessed. The sister was always the head of the Alvarez family. The two brothers have been holed up partying in one of their luxury estates in Brazil. They take helicopters to Peru no more than once a month, if that, and probably just to ask their sister for money. Neither of those boys work in the business.

"They are still being monitored, but the DEA believes they are not the keys to taking down the operation. Their sister didn't interact with them before the DEA arrested Inti and put fire to a large portion of their production."

"It's unfortunate that neither our team nor DEA's people

hadn't connected the dots before they moved on Inti. Inti's portion of the Alvarez drug kingdom only made up about thirty-five percent. That bust cost them, but in the scheme of things, it was a minor irritant."

Coll wiped a few beads of perspiration from his brow, briefly leaning his hip against the ladder. He'd been hardwiring in security cameras all over the property and had finally worked his way back around to Cat's office and personal greenhouse. He knew he'd pay for the ladder climbing with a throbbing knee later. The discomfort was well worth it since he'd gotten to watch Cat walking through the greenhouses and amongst her plants. Some water here, a bloom caress there.

She'd acknowledged his presence but didn't seek him out for conversation. It was for the best. If he didn't want her to know that she wasn't the only one in their friendship who was trying to set aside a crush, distance was necessary.

Coll was getting more concerned by the hour that distance wasn't going to work for him. He tracked her every move, each step, smile, laugh ... this was the first time he'd ever spent so much time with her, just the two of them. Living together. He had to forcibly shake his head to rid his imagination of him and Cat in such a domestic partnership.

"How is Dublin?" he asked Thomas quickly before he got off the ladder and searched his obsession out. It surprised him how much he missed having his friend around. Once Coll had decided to stop hiding from his family, the thought of living apart from them again held little appeal.

"Fine. We are coming back to Scotland tomorrow."

Coll felt his eyebrows lift in surprise. It was unlike Thomas to deviate from a plan that he himself had put into motion. "Your reasoning?"

"Josephine and I are getting married tomorrow in a civil service. We need you and Cat to witness."

He knew they were going to get married soon considering, Jo was already four months along, but ... "Tomorrow?"

"Yes." Thomas huffed a laugh. "The more ideas Jo's family and friends, especially the Byrnes, have had about wedding plans, the more we wished we could just do it ourselves. No fuss. We decided to do exactly what we wanted. We aren't telling anyone besides you and Wee Cat. If Mir were here, she would be there too, of course.

"Married tomorrow, a two-week honeymoon directly after. Jo is looking into locations, but I already have the honeymoon booked. She just doesn't know it yet. Once this Alvarez business is taken care of, we'll let our family and friends plan a reception to celebrate."

Listening to Thomas' even voice list the most important events of his life like a grocery store list, it would be easy to believe his friend wasn't that invested in the big event. Coll knew Thomas better than he knew himself, though, and could hear the barest crack of nerves in the deep voice. Coll was also a good enough friend to not mention it.

"You've got a strong plan, then. Cat and I will stand up with you, of course. Do I need to tell your sister, or have you already?" *Christ, Coll.* Any excuse to seek her out.

"Tell her now so she can free up her morning. Jo will call her tonight with the details. I have a planning meeting with the team headed to Kentucky this afternoon for the security detail gig. Remember the wealthy client is a rising politician with a wife and three young children?"

"I do. It took two weeks to assemble a team willing to relocate. The job could be months or even years depending on if he gets elected."

"I'm glad not to have to take jobs like that anymore," Thomas admitted.

"Especially with a second child on the way," he teased.

Thomas' only reaction was a grunt, but it definitely held satisfaction. The overbearing bastard was thrilled to have knocked his girlfriend up, Coll realized in amusement.

"I'm off," Thomas stated.

"Tomorrow." Thomas' only response was another grunt before the call ended. Coll tried to ignore the thrill of having an excuse to interrupt the end of Cat's day. Surely, her last client was gone.

He let himself into the back of her personal workspace, where he could enter her office if she wasn't already hard at work over her plants in the back. Damn, the lights were off. She was still in her office then, but he didn't hear any voices, so he slid open the barn door that divided the spaces and let himself in.

Big mistake. Cat was leaning against her desk facing the seating area and three very unhappy-looking women. Well, one was crying, one looked mortified, and the older one looked like she'd just eaten a shit sandwich.

Cat heard him enter and immediately stood at attention. "Sorry for the interruption, lass. I thought you were done for the day. I had some news from Thomas, but it can wait. I'll let myself back—"

Before he could finish extricating himself from the obvious meeting gone wrong, one of the younger women, the one not crying, interrupted. "Coll Barr. Oh my God, I can't believe it. It's been years."

Obviously, it had been enough years not to recognize the highly doctored and polished brunette currently getting to her feet.

Unfortunately, his lack of response didn't put her off. "It's Winnie Platt. We went to high school together. Don't you remember me? We went out a few times, if you'll recall," she chuckled, starting to fidget in embarrassment.

He recalled the name, but ... her face looked like plastic, and her chest ... her giant breasts and tiny waist weren't quite how he remembered her, but there was just enough of teenage Winnie's smile left that he did recall them being friends or friendly anyway.

"Winnie. Of course." There was nothing for but to walk forward with his hand out. He meant for it to be a quick handshake and a quicker exit, but the brunette Barbie had other ideas. She practically skipped into his arms, smashing her breasts to his chest while her long arms squeezed him like a boa constrictor.

He patted her back twice and, in a panic at the continued compression, looked over her head toward Cat. Annnnd ... that was a bad idea. She did not look happy. He really should have checked the front parking lot to see if the clients were still there before barging in.

Coll felt his balls start to shrink, pulling inside his body where they'd be more protected. Cat did not take kindly to anyone interrupting her work. But Jesus, she was even more glorious when her temper was fired up.

∾

Fury and no little amount of misery flooded her system at the sight of Coll hugging that woman. Well, she was hugging him, but he hadn't pushed the limpet off yet, either.

She took three deep breaths while she watched Coll gently push Winnie away, trying to regain her composure and a modicum of professionalism for a client meeting that had already gone well past south before Coll's arrival. The interruption had probably given the bride a well-needed reprieve. The nicest thing she could say about Winnie and Ginnie's mother was that she was a bitch.

Not ten hours ago, Cat had made a promise to herself and Coll that she was hanging up her crush for him and moving on. She hadn't moved on. Clearly. She could, however, fake it. Even if it killed her.

"Well, this is a fun surprise." She fake-smiled to the room at large, clasping her hands at her waist as if she could barely contain her excitement. *And the Oscar Award for Best Actress goes to ...*

"Coll, you know Winnie, but let me introduce her mother, Mrs. Platt, and the gorgeous bride-to-be, Winnie's younger sister, Ginnie." Ginnie made a halfhearted attempt at a smile, but the wobble of her lips wrecked it. Coll kindly shook hands with the two women, giving each compliments that even had that nasty Mrs. Platt blushing. That gave Cat a great idea.

"Coll, maybe you can be our tiebreaker." She pointed to the table of four arrangements that she had created especially for this appointment. "Winnie's favorite is veronica, and I agree, their slender spires have beautiful movement. Mrs. Platt picked the pale pink roses, which are lovely and timeless. My favorite is the lisianthus arrangement. The delicate ruffles are so elegant. Ginnie adores," and here she briefly looks at Coll with a slightly pleading look, "the hydrangeas in white and pale green."

Without missing a beat, Coll said, "Roses are always a classic choice. Winnie and Catriona have chosen flowers that I've never even heard of, but surely you ladies will forgive my ignorance."

He grinned and winked. Cat puked in her mouth, but she was woman enough to admit the Platts were eating it up.

"Cat's brother is good friends with some oil billionaires from Oklahoma, the O'Faolains. They recently bought a distillery in Ireland that they've been remodeling as not only a working distillery but also a venue for retreats and weddings."

"Oh, aye," Cat agreed, not sure where he was going with the story.

"The O'Faolain wives own a high-end interior design business in Dublin, Triskelion. They travel the world for special clients," he said as an aside to the Platts. Who knew Coll was a closet thespian? "I only know what type of flowers they have planted all over the property because the Byrne sisters, the decorators," he explained, "told me that they used hydrangeas because they were the current in ... dang it, what was the word? In vogue? That's right." Cat was surprised he didn't add an "Ah shucks."

"Hydrangeas are the most sought-after flower for wedding photography, I guess. I admit I don't know anything about flowers. They all look pretty to me. I don't think you could go wrong with any of them, and just because one is trending more than others doesn't mean you have to choose it."

Holy crap ... And Cat thought she was a good actress. Mrs. Pratt was frantically googling on her phone, presumably searching the Byrne's business that Coll had just name-dropped. To Cat's immense satisfaction, the old biddy had a smug look on her face.

"I think you might just be right, Mr. Barr. Hydrangeas do seem to be making a comeback."

Ginnie's face instantly lightened, and her back straightened. Her mother clearly mentally beat her daughter to a pulp on the regular. Cat had been at her wit's end watching the rotten family dynamic play out. She was about to wrap things up and move the ladies toward the exit when Winnie decided it was her time to shine.

"Now that flowers are settled, Coll," she giggled, "how about you take me to dinner and catch me up on all the local gossip. I swear, since I moved to London, my family doesn't tell me anything."

The batting fake lashes were hypnotizing and nauseating all at the same time. When Coll didn't immediately shoot the idea down, Cat felt her ire rise once again. Damn him for making her an emotional example of what not to do when jealousy finds you in a weak moment.

Should she have taken a deep breath or ten before answering? Yes, one hundred percent, yes. Did she? No.

"Oh, my goodness, Winnie. What a great idea! I'm meeting up with a guy at Gellions. They still have live music every night. The four of us could meet." *What in the absolute hell are you doing, Cat? Stop. Now.*

Too late. "That sounds amazing. What do you think, Coll?" Winnie clapped with joy, bouncing until her tits were probably mesmerizing the cobra lily on Cat's desk that she'd been nursing back to health.

The thought of Coll taking that woman, any woman really, on a date chafed. Sitting there watching it unfold in real time ... a horror movie. Why, oh why, had she let her temper get the best of her. He might not have even accepted Winnie's invitation if Cat hadn't forced it and then doubled down with her own date.

She could always meet Coll and Winnie and explain that her "date" had to cancel, and she'd just grab some takeaway food for home. Coll was too smart. He'd see her blush—and she would blush—and know she was lying.

There was nothing for it. She had to nail down a date for the night. She was avoiding Coll's eyes, knowing he probably wanted to kill her for encouraging Winnie, but if he wanted to discourage her, he'd had the chance.

It was unfortunate that Winnie was both stunning and seemed genuinely nice, if a bit dense. Her mother mentioned Winnie's divorce more than once, causing Winnie to cringe and look at her hands more often than the flowers. It seemed like the hag enjoyed hurting her children with verbal barbs.

Time to move this show on the road. "Well, Ginnie. I think we made some great progress today. By next week, I will email you with ideas for the wedding and the reception tables. You can pick and choose any or all of the combinations, and from there, I'll send you an itemized price list. I think from some of the pictures you brought in, I have a pretty good idea what your wedding vision is." There were rare times like these when Cat was able to give the florist a blueprint of what the client wanted, and that was extremely satisfying.

With thank yous and a hug from the bride, the Platts finally walked out the door, but not before Winnie grabbed Coll's hand and asked for his number so she could text him her address.

"Catriona and I will meet you and her date there. My truck is having issues, so she'll be giving me a lift. I hope that isn't a problem."

It sounded like he hoped it was a problem.

"Oh, of course, I'll see you there. Seven?"

"Fine."

And then there were two. When she tried to nonchalantly sidle past Coll to escape to her workroom, he took a large step to the side, effectively blocking her escape.

"Why?"

Cat decided to take a few steps back and casually lean against the edge of her desk. Her body felt awkward, so she definitely wasn't pulling casual off. It did allow her a moment to ponder his question. Why what? *Why?* What did that mean?

"What's your problem?" Always best to go on the defensive with Coll.

He raised his irritating brow, visibly expressing his thoughts on her maneuver. "You knew I didn't want to go out with her."

"Could have fooled me. She was practically dry humping you, and you let her." Cat winced as she heard the hiss of a spitting mad cat in her tone. Would he notice that this wasn't the behavior of someone no longer crushing on him? *Pitiful, Catriona.*

"Dry humping," he repeated softly, not impressed with her description.

"She's gorgeous. I don't see why you're mad about it." *So gorgeous. FML.*

"I'll text Winnie my apologies. We both know you don't have a date. Let's put an end to this evening before it becomes awkward, lass."

There were no breaths deep enough to quench the flames of outrage that flared to life at his words. The arrogant nerve. That it was true meant less than zero. She was swimming in a loch too deep in anger and embarrassment to back pedal now.

She wouldn't lose her temper. No. not this time. She would make him swallow every last arrogant syllable he'd just uttered.

Straightening from the desk, she met him toe to toe and smiled sweetly up at the scowling giant. She even grasped one of his muscular forearms to make sure she had his undivided attention. She barely controlled the gasp that wanted to escape her parted lips at the feel of all that masculinity under her fingertips.

"I'm sorry I pushed you into doing something you didn't want. It was childish, and I can see why you're peeved." His look of confusion was delicious.

"Okay ..." he drew out the word.

"Let Winnie know you can't make it after all." Was it her imagination, or was his body beginning to lean ever so much closer to hers?

"I'll do that."

She forced her body to twist away, the exact opposite thing she wanted to do. With the same gentle smile, she spoke her last words over her shoulder before entering the workroom. "I'll be keeping my date, of course."

14

Coll had to rewire one of the outdoor office cameras three times because his concentration was shot. "Goddammit." He cursed after dropping his pliers again, forcing himself to climb down the ladder once more. He kicked a rock, sending the projectile pelting into the side of the long tool shed fifteen feet away.

At a startled gasp, he spun on his prosthesis, causing the tender appendage a jolt of pain. He shook his head in chagrin as he watched a woman wearing loose overalls and a yellow headscarf scurry quickly into the greenhouse located behind the shed.

"Damn, me." That was Ms. Farkas. He only knew that because Cat told him she always wore her hair wound in a scarf. Cat said she was skittish of men and to attempt to either keep his distance or try not to startle her. "Get it together, dickhead," he scolded himself.

He'd have to let Cat know so she could make his apologies. He certainly wasn't going to chase after the woman to do it himself. Cat said she'd been an amazing addition to the farm, and she'd have his balls for breakfast if he caused the woman to quit.

He was tempted to call it quits for the day, but this was the last camera on this side of the office, and he wanted to get it done. He could finish the rest the day after tomorrow, since he'd be busy witnessing Thomas and Jo getting married in the morning.

He just remembered he never told Cat her brother's news, and that was the whole reason he'd gone to her office in the first place. What a debacle that had turned out to be. Jo would have called Cat by now, either way.

He envied Thomas his new life. He and Aileen and Mirren were still a strong unit, but now his best friend was gaining a new wife and his second child all in one go—and Coll and Cat were standing up for them. He had never been a dreamer, but he would be lying if he didn't admit to picturing himself in Thomas' shoes, speaking words of forever to Cat.

Sighing, he climbed the ladder, hopefully for the last time today, and finished the job. Before dinner tonight, he would make sure the cameras he'd gotten installed today were named for their location and working as they should. He'd need to download the app on Cat's phone and walk her through how to use the program.

He was doing his best to think of any and everything besides their "double date" tonight. She'd been jealous of Winnie and no amount of her attempts at sidetracking would convince him otherwise. He was so turned around that his first response to her anger was satisfaction. She wasn't over her feelings for him yet.

He would swear on his life that Cat had been lying about having a date. She'd never mentioned it, first, and second, she'd only hours ago admitted to her crush on him. He didn't like remembering how she said she was going to move past it ... him. He selfishly didn't want her moving past shit, which was totally unfair, considering he was doing his damnedest to ignore his lust for the woman and keep his hands firmly away from her body.

But a date? Tonight? With whom? She'd refused to answer any of his questions and ordered him out of her workshop. He'd been stewing over the possibility that he'd misconstrued her wide-eyed look of dread when she'd brought it up to Winnie. He supposed there was always a chance he was wrong, and she did have a date.

As he was putting his tools back in their bag and folding up the ladder, his phone dinged. "Please, Christ, let it be Winnie canceling."

> Can't wait to see you. Winnie xx

"Fucking kill me."

"I'd like to most days." Catriona laughed as she walked out of her shop to join him.

"Haha." It seemed like they were back to being in a good place. Maybe she'd decided to cancel after all.

"We better head home. We only have an hour to shower and change before we need to head to the pub. Thank God I don't have to wash my hair." She joked as she grabbed his bag of tools and placed them in her workshop while he did the same with the ladder.

Still going to dinner then. It was better to think of her on a date than in the shower. One reaction he could hide, the other not so much. "Fine," he gritted out.

As they walked back to her cottage, she told him that Jo had called. "I'm so excited for tomorrow. I'm going to get up early and make the perfect bouquet for Jo. She's wearing a simple cream-colored wrap dress, and I know the perfect flower to complement the dress and her lovely hair," she said excitedly. "I have several pots of perfectly bloomed ranunculus in a golden shade of yellow."

Coll was transfixed by Cat's animated cheer. When she tended to plants, harvested plants, or created arrangements, she was at her happiest. "I'm sure Jo will love whatever you choose."

"That's what she said." She huffed and shook her head. In her excitement as they walked, she grabbed two of his fingers and squeezed, her hand wasn't nearly big enough to engulf his. "It matters though." She must have realized she was holding his hand because she quickly dropped it, much to his disappointment.

"They sound pretty." He didn't know a flower from a weed. His attention was snared by the woman exiting the greenhouse to their left. It was the scarved woman he'd seen earlier. Cat waved goodbye. The woman briefly looked his way and ducked her head, giving the barest wave before hurrying toward the car park.

"Please tell your new hire that I didn't mean to startle her earlier. I didn't know she was anywhere around and," he hesitated, "she may have heard me curse or see me kick a rock. Tell her I meant no harm."

"Oh, dang. Poor Réka. She doesn't like anyone getting too close. Though she's doing better with me, she really struggles around men. I think her ex hurt her."

"Do you want me to look into her past?"

"I would, but I wouldn't feel right unless I discussed it with her. It might set her mind at ease to know exactly where her ex is now. She would surely be relieved to know that he isn't hiding around the corner waiting to pounce, but she's private, and I understand. I'll let you know. Thanks for thinking about that."

"Of course." They were home by then, and she offered to let him go first since she would take longer in the bathroom.

He went to his, or her room rather, to grab a change of clothes. Before he took a shower, he tried one more time. "Cat."

She glanced up from looking at a magazine full of flowers. "Yeah?"

"If we stayed home tonight, I would cook us dinner."

∼

He looked so hopeful that Cat almost caved in. There were two reasons why she wouldn't and couldn't cancel their plans. Coll wasn't interested in anything but friendship with her, and she'd used up every ounce of her nerve asking Feodor, the super cute Russian with the shipping company, if he would like to go out on a double date with her tonight.

He accepted immediately, much to her relief and chagrin, because she was, in essence, using him to teach Coll a lesson. If the man of her dreams—years and years of dreams—could just make himself less appealing, Cat would totally be into Feodor. Regardless of how pissed she was every time she thought of Coll and Winnie on a date, she was attacking this evening like a therapy session. Exposure therapy. To other men.

"As amazing as that sounds, knowing that you can barely manage a grill, we've both accepted an invitation to dinner. We can hardly back out this late." Invited would have been a more accurate description of her date, but she wasn't going to quibble about the details.

"Right. Your date."

She could tell he wanted to say more, but thankfully, he restrained himself, choosing to close the bathroom door instead. While he showered, she went into her bedroom which Coll was currently occupying and chose her clothes for the night.

They were meeting at a well-known pub, so she pulled on a sheer white linen button-up with a bronze silk tank for modesty beneath and boyfriend-cut jeans. The shirt was sheer enough to be considered reasonably sexy, while the delicate tank molded her breasts just enough to give the illusion that, well, she had breasts. White Sperrys with brown leather laces would finish off the outfit. Cat usually preferred a shabby chic look.

She rummaged through her jewelry box next and couldn't resist choosing a simple gold necklace with a tiny flower pendant. Coll had gotten it for her thirteenth birthday. She should have chosen any other necklace besides that one. She had time to change her mind, but wearing a necklace he had given her, even when she was a child—yeah, probably a sign that exposure therapy wasn't going to work.

She couldn't help the immature need to one-up Winnie, either. She might be on a date with Coll, but Cat was wearing his necklace. *Could you be any more immature, Cat?* Probably.

Coll exited the bathroom in a cloud of steam, and without a word, she took his place.

15

The drive into Inverness was tense. Coll tried to rouse her temper before they left, and the belligerent bear was still trying her patience. He hadn't liked her outfit. One would think she was wearing an ass-cheek revealing club dress instead of baggy jeans for crying out loud.

"You sure as hell aren't wearing that out in public." He threw that gauntlet down the moment she'd exited the bathroom. She simply walked by him, adjusting the butterfly hair clip that held back the sides of her hair and rested at the nape of her neck. The delicate gold wings were lifted in flight from her curls. She loved the clip. Mirren had gotten it for her last birthday.

"I'm wearing jeans, Coll. Christ. Don't start with me."

"Jeans and a bloody see-through shirt."

He was huffing like Puff, the Magic Dragon—too bad he wasn't big, green, and precious. She was in no way dressed provocatively. However, she did feel like she looked attractive, and he wasn't going to ruin it.

"I refuse to entertain your mantrum. I don't want to be late." He mumbled under his breath all the way to the truck, slamming the passenger door. He could have driven himself, of course, but he'd lied to Winnie about his truck, so she was stuck with him since she didn't want the whole evening to blow up before it began.

She found a parking spot decently close. Before they could exit the truck, her phone dinged. *Oh no.* It was a message from Feodor.

> Got off work a little late. I am home and changing now. I will be fifteen to twenty minutes late. Forgive me. I am hurrying.

Thank you, little, tiny baby Jesus, she prayed in her head—in Ricky Bobby's voice, of course. For a second, she thought he might have to cancel and then Coll would never believe that she'd had a date.

> I just parked. No worries. My friend is with me. We will get a table. See you soon.

"Did your date cancel?"

The slight sneer to his voice was a light to her fuse. Thankfully, she had just enough control left to not fall for his tactics. "I appreciate your concern." Neither admit nor deny. Let him stew and wonder. He and her brother were so used to bossing her around that he could barely stand not being in charge.

Coll's limp was more pronounced tonight. He must have overdone it today, damn him. She had to bite her tongue to keep from asking after his leg. If he'd just consent to trying her new warming ginger massage oil ...

Before they stepped into Gellions' brightly lit interior, she threw caution to the wind and tugged on his arm. "Let me massage you tonight." The scowl that instantly dressed his face wasn't encouraging. Good thing Cat grew up with scowling men. They didn't faze her.

"Please, Coll. Just think about it. I desperately want to know if my new oil is any good. I would have already gone to the hospital and tried it on a veteran, but this batch is bound to get warmer on the skin than my other attempts, and I want to make sure it isn't too hot."

"I don't know. Maybe. We could have done it tonight, but here we are." He waved an angry arm to the pub's façade. "At least at home, you wouldn't be showing your ... your breasts," he practically choked on the word, "in public."

She felt her eyes bulge in surprise. Was he serious? What sort of caveman bullshit was he trying to pull? "You need to make an appointment with an optometrist, you lunatic. My breasts are ... nothing special," she spat. "It's a wonder you've made it this long with such shitty eyesight." Frustrated that yet another argument had broken out between them, she said, "Let's just go inside. Forget I asked about the massage. I'll try it on someone else." She pushed by him, but he grabbed her arm.

She waited for him to say something else that would make her want to kick him in the nuts, so when he did finally speak, his words surprised her.

"Your breasts are perfect." Then he ruined the compliment by adding, "Next time, cover them up. Oh, and you will stop massaging other men."

He opened the door with an arm above her head, ushering her in before him. The moment they hit the warm lights and laughter, she vowed to try and enjoy the evening and not let Coll's mood bring her down.

As they moved through the front of the house crowd, she jolted when she felt his thick-fingered hand clasp her waist. She knew it was just to guide her, but her body didn't care. Warm awareness tingled under his palm and spread between her thighs. She might have let out a tiny moan, but the pub chatter was the perfect cover.

Her second moan, which was more of a groan, unfortunately, had nothing to do with the pleasure of his touch. Winnie was already there and had secured a four-top table. She jumped up when she saw them, an athletic feet considering she was wearing gravity-defying stilettos and a dress—a generous description—which consisted of no more than two napkins worth of material.

As Winnie bounced her way toward them, squealing and clapping, her nipples threatened to make an appearance, as well as her private below bits. She certainly knew how to draw a man's attention. About every male's head swiveled as she created a spectacle across the room.

Cat pretended that Coll snatching his hand from her waist didn't hurt her feelings. Before Winnie was close enough to throw herself at him, she looked over her shoulder to see his face. "I see what you mean now. That's exactly how I look in this shirt." He tried to grab her arm before she moved away. She heard a growled "Cat," but that was muffled as Hurricane Winnie pounced.

She actually threw her arms around his shoulders, which she could reach because she was a good nine inches taller than Cat, and she wore heels. As she rubbed her front all over Coll's chest, Cat could feel her vision going red. *No, no, no, no.* She was an adult, and she had set the whole damn night up. There was nothing for it but to endure the next few hours.

It might have been nice had Coll pushed her off, but he seemed to have trouble managing that. When Winnie kicked her leg up, Cat felt vomit begin to creep up her throat. *Someone* must have watched *Princess Diaries* recently.

Deciding it was best to leave the exhibition, she walked to the table where Winnie had left her purse. Shocker, it was tinier than her dress. Cat hung her clunky tote off the back of her chair and straightened her shirt. She had liked how she looked in this outfit. Correction, she liked how she looked. Just because she wasn't a supermodel like Winnie, she still managed to be passably attractive when she tried.

Coll and Winnie finally joined her. For his part, he looked desperate to escape. Cat had taken a seat that gave her a view of the front so she would see when Feodor got there. Cat sat across the table diagonally. She assumed Coll would sit across from Cat and next to Winnie. Winnie probably assumed that as well, but no, Coll sat next to her.

She casually leaned toward him and spoke low enough that Winnie wouldn't be able to hear over the music. "Why don't you move next to your date so *my* date can sit next to me."

"No."

Count to ten, Cat. Do not let him rile you into an argument. Knowing good and well, he wouldn't change his mind. She placed her phone on the table in case Feodor called or texted. She forced herself to look at Winnie's face and not be distracted by her chest, which was currently taking a nap on the top of the table.

"I can't wait to send your sister some of the flower arrangement designs. I want her to love everything about the day, and flowers are so important." It was hard for the woman to pull her eyes from Coll, but she finally managed.

"I'm sure she'll love them. Ginnie and her fiancé are simple. Their simple tastes should be perfect for the simple, boring life they plan on leading."

Cat felt her hackles rise at the dismissive way Winnie spoke of her sister. Where was the woman's loyalty and love? She felt her hands clench into tiny fists in her lap, and she was gearing up for a lecture on how Winnie might consider being a supportive sister instead of an asshole when Coll's hand slid over her thigh and tightened in warning.

It wasn't his warning that had her backing down but the

proximity of his fingers between her legs. She pictured his fingers sliding up the seam of her jeans, which made her squirm and flex her thighs. As Winnie kept up a stream of mindless chatter—which sister was simple?—

Coll moved the finger closest to her center ... closer. What the hell was he doing? What was *she* allowing?

Cat placed her hand over his, not sure if she planned to push him away or pull him closer. She'd never know because in that moment Feodor walked in.

Standing from her chair like it was on fire, she excused herself. "Excuse me, I see my date." Before Coll or Winnie could say a word, she was trucking it across the pub. Feodor saw her coming and smiled.

She'd forgotten how handsome he was. His light blond hair was tousled as if he'd quickly showered and used his fingers for a comb. His blue eyes twinkled as they met. His dimples were one hundred percent sigh worthy. He was dressed in jeans and a black T-shirt that was just fitted enough to show off his muscles.

Cat shook off the thrall Coll's fingers had temporarily put her under to greet her date. Knowing Coll, he hadn't even realized where his hand was. "Feodor! I'm so glad you could make it."

"Catriona. I apologize again for being late."

"Seriously, no worries. We haven't even ordered drinks yet." As they walked back to their table, Feodor placed his hand on her back. Men sure liked to pull out that possessive move whenever possible. She kept her smile firmly in place even in the face of Coll's scowl. Leave it to Winnie to break the tension. She popped up and vigorously shook Feodor's hand.

"Winnie Platt, this is Feodor Kuznetsov." Thank God she practiced pronouncing his surname. Feodor kept his eyes above the tit parade. He deserved points for that. Out of the corner of her eye, she saw Coll rise. The two men were of a height, but

Coll was definitely broader in the shoulders. *Don't you dare compare them, Cat.*

Once Winnie sat back down, she introduced the men. "Feodor, this is Coll Barr. You'll remember his sister, Aileen. Coll, this is Feodor."

Feodor shook his hand firmly. "You have a very kind sister."

"I do."

Cat would kill Coll later for his taciturn reply. "Why don't we run to the bar and get everyone a drink and grab some menus." At his agreement, she took the drink orders. They were almost away when Feodor asked Coll to switch places.

"Would you mind? I haven't seen Catriona in a while, and it would be easier to catch up if we could hear each other. I imagine you'll want to sit closer to Winnie."

The hell? If she wasn't mistaken, Feodor was purposely baiting Coll.

Coll didn't respond, but he did move seats. Winnie, of course, batted her lashes in Coll's direction and used her arms to push her breasts to record heights. Any higher, and she would risk injury to her eyes.

At the bar, Feodor placed the drink orders and then leaned his side against the bar so they could face each other.

"Tell me. Am I here because you don't want to date Coll, and this is an in-your-face message? Or am I here to make him jealous?"

Catriona spent at least sixty seconds opening and closing her mouth in a most unbecoming fish out of water performance. "Umm...," she dropped her shoulders in defeat and shook her head, "how did you guess? No, before you answer, I'm sorry. I really do like you and the night we met, I felt a connection with you."

"A friend connection or something more?"

Feodor wasn't beating about the bush. "I wished for more.

No, I wished I was emotionally available to want more." She cringed. This was not the part of the evening that she had foreseen being difficult.

"How long have you loved him?"

She didn't bother to deny it. "Years and years and years. Even now that I'm quite old enough to date, he isn't interested. I'm just his best friend's little sister."

"Hmm." Was his only response.

"What does that mean?"

"Don't make it obvious, but glance over at our table. Act like you're laughing at something I said."

She did as he instructed. Coll was turned in his chair, completely ignoring his date and staring at her and Feodor. "Oh, well, it may seem like he's interested in me, as a woman that is, but really it's that he takes his job of protective 'brother' to the next level."

"I respectfully disagree." He laughed to let her know there were no hard feelings either way. He really was a great guy. "I actually have a confession of my own, and it should make you feel less guilty about using me tonight."

She looked up at her date, and they both burst into laughter at their predicament. "Please tell me you're a closet gay, and you were thinking of bridging the gap with a woman who has no feminine curves." She laughed at her joke, but he didn't. In fact, he became serious. A sober look replaced his previous grin.

"Don't do that."

She was taken aback. "Do what?"

"Talk down about yourself. You aren't seeing what everyone else sees. I approached you because your laugh was infectious but also because you stood out over every other woman in the bar that night, and you're sexy as hell. Women like Winnie sell themselves short. She thinks all she has to offer is her body. It comes off as desperate.

"If the woman I've loved for twelve years hadn't called me two hours ago and told me she'd made a mistake letting me go and that she was willing to move from St. Petersburg and make a real go of it, I would do everything in my power to make you forget Coll Barr ever existed, but if there's even a chance with Daria ..."

Cat wasn't sure where to begin sorting out Feodor's words. Blushing was a given. Denial about Coll's feelings was hot on its heels. Finally, she latched onto the news that had nothing to do with her. A much safer option.

"Oh, Feodor! I'm thrilled for you. When will she be here? I would love to meet her and show her around. You've met my friends. They would love to meet Daria too. Wait," she paused, a spark of anger smoldering in her chest, "why are you here? With me?"

"Don't get all bent out of shape. I told Daria about you and that I wanted to come and explain things in per—"

Cat cut him off. "Unlike what I was willing to do." She grimaced in chagrin.

Feodor laughed. "You meant no harm. I know that, rest assured. Daria knows that we've not so much as breathed on each other. She trusts me, and she'll get a kick out of you and Coll ... and Winnie."

"God, don't remind me. Text me Daria's number. I have a feeling we'll become fast friends."

He took one of her hands in his own and brought it to his chest. "I would be beyond grateful. I want her to love Scotland. I really want her to love me enough to live anywhere in the world," he admitted.

"I'll do my best. A word of advice."

"Yes?"

"Don't make her live with your parents. I'll help you find the perfect house, but don't expect an independent woman to make her home in another woman's home." His surprised look said it all. "Jesus. How are men so dense? Also, I know very well you are holding my hand to piss off a certain someone." Cat could feel the wrath of Coll hitting her peripheral in terrible waves.

Feodor's smirk and shrug said it all. "The drinks are here. Shall we have a good time at the expense of the man who isn't interested in you?"

This night just got exponentially better. "Absolutely."

16

Coll had held out hope that Cat had made up her date and that he would magically not be able to make it at the last minute. He'd been positive he was right, arrogantly so. Feodor was the man in the picture from the night she'd gone out with the girls. Had she been talking to the prick since then?

He kept telling himself that he had no right to be angry. Sure, he and her brother needed to vet anyone she dated, and he planned on finding every little, hopefully incriminating thing he could on the Russian once he was home, but he didn't have the right to forbid her from seeing other men.

Not many hours ago, she'd admitted to her feelings for him. Were they magically gone when the first blond-haired, blue-eyed asshole looked her way?

Currently, his eyes were locked on Cat who was chatting up her date at the bar. They were having quite an animated conversation. Watching Cat laugh and smile so easily with another man made him crazy. She was more likely to bite Coll's head off than chat.

The interloper just took her hand and placed it against his chest. She let him do it.

He felt a tug on his shirt and had to grit his teeth as he turned back around to his 'date.'

"Tell me everything you've been up to since high school. I already know you're still as handsome as you ever were." She leaned into his side, batting her fake lashes.

If he could survive the South American jungles, he could survive this date. Though it was feeling less likely with every word Winnie barfed. He never thought he'd be thankful to see Cat's date, but he showed up with drinks at the perfect time.

Cat set a beer in front of him and some godawful neon orange drink in front of Winnie. "A Guinness for you, Coll, and a Sex on the Beach for you, Winnie." *Of course, she would order that.* Feodor sat down next to Cat and handed her a pint of Guinness as well and some clear drink on ice for himself. Vodka, most like.

Not one for silence, Winnie jumped right back into it. "Thank you, Cat. Don't you just love sex on the beach?"

Coll could feel his cheeks heat at Winnie's less-than-subtle double entendre. Cat didn't even bat an eye.

"I've never tried it. Sounds like a good way to get sand in some pretty sensitive places." That took some wind out of Winnie's sails. Turning to her date, she asked, "How is business? I haven't had a chance to come by and check out your store, but I plan on it next week."

"Good, good. Any day but Tuesday. My parents are taking the day off for their anniversary, and I want you to meet them."

Why would Cat need to meet this guy's parents after one date? What was this asshole playing at? And why was she avoiding his gaze like the plague?

In a gratingly overloud voice, Winnie tried to gain everyone's attention. "Coll was just getting ready to tell me what he's been up to since high school."

Not that Coll wasn't relieved that Winnie interrupted the

'meet the parents' talk, but he had no desire to discuss his life. "There isn't much to tell." Hoping to sidetrack Winnie by talking about her favorite person, herself, he asked, "How long have you lived in London?"

"Close to twelve years. I would consider moving back to Inverness with the right motivation." This was followed by a sigh that magically managed to raise her breasts by two inches. "After I caught my piece of shit husband cheating on me, I divorced his ass and took as much money of his as I could, so I have more than enough to relocate."

"I'm sorry your husband did that, Winnie." Cat might be a stick of dynamite on the regular, but she couldn't stand to see anyone hurt.

"Oh, don't worry about me. I couldn't stand him. I figured out real quick that college wasn't for me, so I had to make a living somehow."

She shrugged as if she hadn't just made herself look like a gold-digging bitch. Cat did look at him then with round eyes. She wasn't used to associating with people like Winnie.

"Tag, Coll, you're it." She booped his arm. He was beginning to recognize the signs of a person who never matured past ... well, never. "It's your turn to tell me about you."

Her childish giggle was grating, and then, to top off this garbage dump of an evening, Feodor took that moment to put his arm around Cat's shoulders. She turned her body toward what was practically a stranger pawing at her and ... smiled. If she thought he wouldn't tell Thomas about her behavior tomorrow, wedding or no wedding, she was sorely mistaken.

Before he could stop himself, he gave Winnie what she so desperately wanted. "After high school, my best friend and I joined the Royal Marines. Thomas is Cat's brother. After we served several years, I helped Thomas begin a security business." That was a very loose label for the services that MacGregor Security performed.

"I took a job in South America." At this announcement, Cat's attention became riveted on him. Did she think he might bring up Amaru? That only pissed him off more. "I got part of one of my legs blown off. Did rehab. I wear a prosthesis. Now that I've moved full-time back to the area, Cat and I are living together."

"You have a missing ... leg? That sounds ... umm ... yikes."

He announced that he was living with another woman, and Winnie's only concern is his missing limb. He tried and probably failed to hide his flinch about what she thought of amputees. It was his greatest fear that a woman might find his body less desirable.

The flat of Catriona's hand slapping their tabletop startled him from his pity party. She had the look of an avenging angel, and her wrath was squarely focused on his date.

If he hadn't lost his temper and spouted off his personal business, Cat wouldn't be losing her temper now in his defense. His Cat loved fiercely. She was as honorable as her brother and no mistake.

That didn't mean he wanted her to lose a big client on his behalf. And Winnie and Ginnie's mother was a nasty piece. She'd love to switch venues if for no other reason than to not let her youngest daughter get the flowers she wanted.

"Cat," he warned.

"Don't you Cat me, Coll Barr. No one, and I mean no one, will speak to you in such a way. I don't give a rat's arse if I lose a client." She'd stood up by this point, all furious fairy, ready to drop the wrath of the gods on Winnie's head.

She pointed her finger at Winnie, who resembled a deer in headlights. She was about to speak but took several deep, hopefully calming, breaths instead. Cat must have thought better of what she was going to say and let both hands drop by her sides.

"You and I could volley insults between us, but that isn't the kind of woman I am. However, I would warn you against further derogatory remarks at this table."

She finally sat down and casually smoothed her shirt, her see-through shirt, as if she hadn't just handed Winnie her ass. Coll would normally be embarrassed to have someone speaking for him, but he was too busy looking at his wee Kitty Cat in wonder.

Cat took a careful sip of her Guinness and seemed to be coming to a decision. "I apologize for the outburst, everyone. I usually don't lose my temper like that."

Coll's snort of disbelief earned him a glare, but in Feodor's favor, her date simply grinned and shrugged his shoulders in humor. Winnie was still frozen. Cat had that effect on people.

Coll felt like he should try to get the evening back on track since the whole debacle happened because Cat had felt the need to defend him. "Does anyone want to order food?"

"You might look like a little boy, but you're a real bitch, aren't you?" Winnie found her forked tongue.

He looked toward Cat. She was bravely trying to hide how badly Winnie's barb had hurt. Cat was foolishly sensitive about her figure even though she was stunning. Feodor looked disapprovingly at Winnie before whispering something to Cat.

Coll stood, ignoring Winnie completely. He stuck his hand out toward Feodor because despite how much Coll wanted to despise him, he appeared to be an honorable man. "Feodor. It was good to meet you." He looked toward Cat with concern before standing and shaking his hand. "If you don't mind, I think Cat and I will head for home."

"Of course. I am ready for home as well," was Feodor's reply.

"Cat." He held his hand out, and she took it, allowing him to pull her to her feet. Turning to Winnie, he said, "Will you be able to find your way home? Or do you need me to call a car for you?"

Winnie looked shocked at the abrupt change of plans. Did she think her comments and venom were a precursor to a night of fun and frolicking?

"Coll?" Winnie whined.

He didn't bother with a response. He just took Cat's hand in his own and led her to the parking lot. He slipped the truck keys from her front pocket and lifted her onto the passenger seat. She hadn't said a word so far. Her silence wasn't going to work much longer.

They drove for several minutes still not speaking. "I think we can both agree that you are shit at matchmaking." In the dim light of the truck's cab, he saw her lips twitch. It was a hundred million times better than tears.

He didn't park at the office lot but drove the last little bit to her cottage. She slipped out as soon as the truck was in park, but he was faster and caught her on the front porch, caging her body between his chest and the front door.

"I'm sorry I lost my temper. Again," Cat apologized.

He gently grasped her shoulders and turned her around until she was forced to face him. He tipped her chin slowly until their eyes could meet. "Do you think if you see my leg, it'll make you see me differently?"

Her little fist instantly struck his chest. "What the hell, Coll? You know better."

He did know better. With her, he knew better. "When I look at your body, what do you think I see?" he growled softly. His mouth dangerously close to her own. He really needed to pull back, but he would be damned if he didn't make her see the truth.

"How ... how ... how would I know?" she stuttered.

"Do I need to tell you?"

"I guess you do," she answered with a little more spirit.

He pinched her chin and used his thumb to slowly swipe over her lower lip, barely containing a groan of pleasure. Being this close and not touching her the way he'd dreamed of doing was killing him.

"Fine then. I've dreamed of fisting your glorious hair and pulling your head back until your throat is bare for the taking. I've wondered hundreds, maybe thousands of times what your sweet, round ass would feel like fisted in my hands."

Her breath was starting to get ragged against his fingers. "I have traced every inch of your body, every dip, every muscle, every smooth, ivory inch of you—my hands have memorized you, head to toe. In my dreams." He shifted his hips the barest inch closer.

"Do you want to know what I think of your breasts?" She barely jerked a nod. Yes. "Ask me then."

She tried to move her head to the side, but he wouldn't let her. "What do you," she paused, clearly struggling, before, "think of my breasts?"

"I think of your perfect tits more than my job, more than my damn leg, and more than any man who is best friends with your brother and too old for you should do. I can tell they are perfectly round and high.

"When you don't wear a bra, and I see the tiny prick of your nipples against the material, like tonight, all I can think about is stripping you bare and sucking them deep into my mouth. I want those hardened nubs stroking my tongue and between my teeth.

"If you felt between my legs right now, you would never doubt your feminine appeal again."

"Coll, God."

His breath caught in his throat as he watched her raise her hands and place them on his chest, light as a feather and then firm enough to make him arch his chest to encourage her exploration. When her hands found their way behind his neck and tugged, he was helpless to stop himself from bending.

She licked her lips as he closed in until he could feel their breaths joining. "Jesus, God, Cat." He was out of his mind for this woman. He was doing this. He was finally going to find out what her mouth tasted like—until his phone began ringing just as their lips barely touched. He jerked back, stumbling a few steps back, startled out of a lust-induced fog. He pulled his phone from his pocket.

"It's Thomas."

17

Dear Brother,

Do not forsake me. Your return has become my life's work. The witch elder from our mother's village has given me direction.

I must have a pure heart and pure intentions to fulfill my tasks to bring you back.

Seven consecutive days of ritual and fasting. Seven sacrifices.

Know that my resolve is unwavering.

What is pain?

What is suffering?

What is sickness?

Depravity?

Five sacrifices have been made already. I started with our brothers. They begged for mercy, for which I gave them none.

They were the easiest to string up like the pigs that they are and bleed them dry.

They did not mourn you, and I have made sure that no

one will mourn them. I hope it amuses you to know that I replaced them with lookalikes who are satisfied to drink and whore their days away.

Meanwhile, their corpses rot in unmarked graves.

The next three sacrifices were more of a two-birds-with-one-stone convenience. I needed a house to plan your return, and three people happened to reside in the one I chose.

The sixth—undecided.

The seventh and final—your new body's true love. She cannot exist if our souls are to be reunited.

Your beloved,

A

18

Cat let herself into the house, leaving Coll outside still talking on the phone with her brother. "Damn you, Thomas," she mumbled. It was unfair to blame him, but fairness wasn't playing a part in her emotions at the moment.

She cringed remembering the look on Coll's face as he'd backed away from her. Shock then guilt, and maybe this was hopeful thinking on her part, disappointment and frustration. She was certainly frustrated.

She dropped her purse on the narrow credenza just inside the door, flicking on the living room table lamp next. Her eyes snagged on the massage table, an idea beginning to take shape.

Cat knew, as sure as she knew her own face, that Coll would come inside and pretend that he hadn't been about to kiss her or that they hadn't been seconds away from tearing each other's clothes off.

She tapped the table, making up her mind. The decision was made, and Cat practically sprinted to her bedroom and grabbed some night clothes before hurrying to the bathroom. For her plan to work, she needed to be in the shower when he came in. Clipping her hair up, she made quick work of washing her face and jumping in the tub to wash her body.

Timing was important. Coll was smart, give him too much time and he'd come up with a surefire way to avoid her. Too little and he'd run.

Coll was leaning against the kitchen counter when she stepped from the steamy bathroom, wearing a soft white cotton sleep camisole and tiny matching shorts. She'd left her hair back in a ponytail.

"How was Thomas? The wedding is still on, I hope. I'm so excited, I probably won't be able to sleep tonight." His expression barely changed, but she could tell she'd surprised him by acting as though not thirty minutes ago, he'd described in detail what he wanted to do to her breasts ... admitted he was hard for her.

"Fine."

Ahh, pouting. He didn't like her nonchalance. Good. It was fake anyway. That's why she was clasping her hands at her waist to hide their shaking. She knew that the best way to get what she needed from the stubborn men in the family was to throw them off balance.

"Great! Well, go shower while I set up the massage table. Don't put any lotions on."

"I didn't agree to that."

His clenched jaw and crossed arms screamed at her to back off. *Coll, Coll, Coll. That crap doesn't work on me.* "You said had we not gone out tonight, I could have massaged you. Well, our date lasted a hot second. We're home." She used her hands to take in the living room.

"No."

Don't lose your temper, Cat. "You also told me I couldn't massage 'other' men. Meaning I could massage you. Listen, Coll. I know you overdid it today. Let me show you a simple thing like a massage can make such a huge difference in your everyday life."

All of that was true, but she also wanted to force him not to run from her. She'd given up hope that he would ever want her in a sexual way, and then tonight happened. He *had* been jealous at the bar, and he admitted to dreaming about her body. He would try to pull away now over some bro code with her brother. She wasn't going to let him do it.

She saw him flick his eyes around the living room behind her and the massage table leaning against the wall before quickly looking at the lamp. It was bright in here. Not necessarily soothing. Then it dawned on her. He had admitted that he hadn't been with a woman since the accident.

He didn't want her to see his leg. *Crap.* He deserved to have his feelings about it, but it was also time that he faced them. Maybe she could make it less awkward.

"Since I don't have any soft lights for relaxation set up in here yet, why don't we do this on my bed? The closet light would be plenty for me to work by but not blinding for you." She could see some of the tension leave his shoulders and knew she'd made the right call.

"I know you just showered before we went out, but the warm water will begin the process of relaxing your muscles. Remember, no lotions."

He didn't move from the kitchen counter, probably wondering why she wasn't discussing the near kiss and also if he might be able to weasel his way out of her services.

"I'd prefer not to do this tonight." Bingo.

"Well, I do, so tough shit."

"Jesus, she's a menace." He mumbled quietly as he walked by her, clearly wanting her to hear the comment.

It only made her grin. Before he shut the door to the bathroom, she threw over her shoulder, "No clothes. Just the towel."

She quickly gathered her ginger oil and grabbed an old sheet to cover her bed with. She had to be prepared to start immediately. He was in that shower right now, attempting to come up with a last-ditch Hail Mary to get out of her seeing or touching his leg. Even if her brother was knocking at the door, it wouldn't matter.

She was getting her hands on his body. Tonight. Sixty minutes and he would be a massage convert ... hopefully a Cat convert as well.

∼

COLL WAS out of the shower and staring at his reflection in the clouded mirror. He had a towel wrapped around his waist.

"What in the fuck are you doing, man?" he asked himself. He'd been a second away from devouring Cat on the front porch, and that was only after he'd talked about her tits and practically mauled her with his hard-on.

Thomas calling had been the wake-up call he needed, but here he was, naked and about to submit to Cat touching his body. Her hands would ... "Christ. Stop."

She acted as though the porch scene never happened. As if she hadn't practically been panting his name. Like having a man's hands on her body was just another day in her life. Never had a woman tied him in so many damn knots.

He still hadn't asked her if she was serious about Feodor. He didn't know what he would do if her answer was yes.

If he walked into her bedroom, she would see his leg. She would watch him take off his prosthesis like a Mr. Potato Head. He gripped the sink hard enough he was surprised it didn't crack. He knew she didn't care about his leg ... "Damn it. I know!" he growled to his image. Cat would no sooner think less of him than Thomas would.

Look at the way she'd defended him to Winnie tonight. She'd been downright vicious, or at least she was prepared to be.

Cat was his family. Her childhood crush aside, she cared for him, and he ... he cared for her too. His lunacy from earlier aside, they could still keep this thing between them platonic. If he were honest with himself, and up until a few days ago, he usually was, the massage would be their biggest test.

Sighing, he yanked open the bathroom door and killed the lights. The house was dark except for a faint glow coming from her bedroom. He exhaled a small breath of relief and reminded himself that there were a million amputees out there, and he needed to stop being such a little crybaby about it.

"Come on, Barr." As pep talks went, it could handle some improvement. He tucked in the towel's end at his waist for the fiftieth time and forced his feet to move.

Cat was waiting for him—wearing the tiniest scraps of white cotton surely in existence. When she'd come out of the bathroom earlier, he'd been sure she was trying to seduce him. "I'm ready." If he sounded like he was about to give his deathbed confession, well, it felt like it.

She whirled around at his voice, giving him a perfect view of her tiny, pebbled nipples. Off to a great start, he thought ruefully.

"Great. I'm ready. Sit on the edge of the bed first. I want you to show me how to take off your prosthesis. If I'm going to be your live-in, unpaid," she coughed, "masseuse, then I need to understand the mechanics of it all."

Her slightly teasing, matter-of-fact attitude helped him not snap an instant no. Before he had time to say yay or nay, Cat was kneeling on the floor at his feet and speech became ... difficult.

His dick twitched under the thin weave of the towel. She was not on her knees for that ... *Don't think about her between your legs. Think about how hungry you are. You never got dinner.* But she was on her knees.

She had become a masseuse for him. She had been working on a special massage oil for him. The least he could do was not wave his dick around in her face.

All thoughts concerning his dangly bits flew out of his head when he felt her hands on his knee and sliding down over the cold metal. He couldn't help but flinch.

She kept her hands on him but met his eyes. "Coll," she spoke softly as she reached for his right hand to bring it down to his leg, "trust me with this. Just walk me through the steps. My hands are about to be touching a whole lot more than this leg in a few minutes."

As distractions went, she nailed it. Prolonging this was only going to make it awkward. More awkward. He took a deep breath and then launched into the lesson. "I'm fortunate that my knee was unharmed. It still functions the same. It just gets sore much easier. I'm going to start taking it off and explain what each piece is called. My new running blade is similar to this but has a few different parts."

"Have you gotten to try it out yet?"

"No. I haven't had a chance to. The doctor said I would need to work up to my old distances and not to push too hard too fast, but I admit, I can't wait for the freedom of it."

"I'll want to learn how all of them work. I know there are different feet and special nylon socks and a ton of different shoe inserts depending on what you're wearing."

He couldn't help the small smile tugging his lips at her look of concentration. Everything this woman did was to the best of her ability. "I'll show you all of it." He went through the names of everything, their placement, and care. From the liner-liner, to the liner, socket, and sleeve. He remembered being overwhelmed when he saw all the gear. Now, it was nothing to put on and remove.

"How do you shower?"

"Good question. I have a shower leg, but I haven't needed it here. The shower is tiny, and when Grandma lived here, she put a stability bar on the wall. I keep my core strong, so my balance is excellent. Still, it takes me a lot longer than it used to. If I use the shower leg, I put it on before I walk into the shower. If I don't, I have to get in and then remove it after I'm in and then replace it before I get out.

"Tonight, since I'd already washed my leg thoroughly before we went out, I used a waterproof sleeve so I didn't have to take it off and on. I have crutches, too, for when I'm home and want a break from wearing anything."

"I would think you'd always want to use the shower leg. Much more convenient."

Thank God the lighting was dim. He could feel his cheeks heat. "The ... ahh ... the bathroom is tiny, and I didn't want to leave a wet leg lying around while it dried." It was like leaving pieces of his body all over the floor. Weird.

"For fuck's sake. You'll use it from now on. I'll remove that big clothes hamper and set it in the hall. That will give you plenty of room for a whole area for your gear. And you can lean a pair of crutches anywhere."

"Fine."

"I know it's fine," she snapped. "I expect you to tell me when you need something."

Christ, but Cat could turn anything into an argument. He secretly loved it but only grunted in response, knowing she hated nonverbal answers. "Will you tell me when you need something?" His question sounded suggestive. *Damn him.* She didn't miss a beat.

"Sure. I'll even use lots of adjectives."

He didn't touch that statement. Instead, he gave her a demonstration of how to remove everything, going over the names and uses again as he went. He was down to the last layer, the liner-liner.

He was about to pull it from his residual limb. Determined, he hooked his thumbs in the cotton sock. She laid her hands over his, stopping him.

"Let me."

At his nod of assent, she gently peeled the last layer away to reveal the ... stump.

"Coll. How much you must have suffered." Her delicate fingers slid over the ugly scars. It looked a lot better now, at least. "I wanted to come to you. In the States. Thomas said you didn't want me."

He placed his hand over both of her small ones, stilling her movements. "I didn't want anyone. Your brother included. I was grieving and angry and a total ass. I didn't want my family, Aileen, Tom, or you to see me like that."

"Then you spent months and months having a pity party, huh?"

He snorted in amusement. "Pretty much."

"Okay. Class is over for now. Lay face-down on the bed. We'll start with your back first. I have a lighter oil for that and will save the good stuff for your legs."

"Both legs? Why?"

"From what I've read and been told, your other knee takes its own share of stress because you're compensating for the other side. Hopefully, if we get your residual limb in better shape, you won't have trouble with the other side. Enough chitchat," she clapped her hands, "it's showtime."

It's showtime. As he made his way to the head of the bed, hoping his crawling didn't look as silly as it felt. He glanced sideways at Cat, who was fiddling with her jars and not paying him a whit of attention. He was about to settle on his stomach when she piped up.

"Undo your towel first."

He did as she bid, knowing full well that resistance would most definitely be a wasted effort.

"The plan is to make your body so relaxed that by the time I get to your right leg, you'll be putty in my hands."

He almost said, "I already am," but instead managed, "I'm ready."

19

It's not like Cat hadn't seen Coll with his shirt off dozens of times before, whether he was swimming in a pond with Thomas and friends or working out in the summer heat. This time was very different. As unprofessional as this made her, she was practically dancing with giddiness at the thought of touching all that skin.

Ropey muscle wrapped his arms and broad shoulders, and his sculpted chest was dusted with dark curls, with small dark nipples that looked absolutely lickable. And don't get her started on his abs—cuts and divots and a V-line that disappeared under his towel. She wanted to disappear under that towel.

His thighs were thick and powerful ... his ass ... she'd dreamed of that ass. She took a moment more to drool over the man laid out on her bed before rubbing her hands together to warm them up. She might appreciate the view, but she was determined to make this a truly healing session for him.

"All right, Coll. Working on the bed won't be as easy as the table, but we'll make it work. My goal is that tonight, you'll sleep better than you have in months. I need you to tell me if I do anything that causes discomfort or if you just don't like it. Ready?"

"Yes."

He wasn't ready at all. She could tell by the tension in his back and neck. She closed the closet door, taking even more light from the room. The tray of oils was within reach. She climbed on the bed and knelt beside his waist, making sure to adjust his towel for modesty. She poured some juniper berry oil into her hands and began working it until she felt it begin to warm. It wasn't as strong as ginger, but juniper berries were amazing muscle relaxers.

"I'm going to touch you now." And then she did, starting with his thick upper back. He groaned but quickly cut it off. She huffed a laugh. "Everyone makes noises when they get a massage. Let it out. Focus on how it feels."

She worked his full back, neck, shoulders, and arms. He was so pliant under her fingers that she might have thought him asleep except for the occasional grunt or moan. He was right where she wanted him before starting on his legs.

Reaching for the ginger-warming oil, she scooted down the bed until she was kneeling between his spread legs. He felt her move and started to twist his upper body up and off the bed.

"No." She placed a hand on his left leg, the springy dark hair soft against her palm. "Settle, Coll. Let me make you feel good. I've got the new oil right here." He'd twisted enough to look at her. He looked so vulnerable just then that she almost relented and stopped for the night, but that wouldn't do him any good on more than one front.

He needed to let another person touch his stump, and he needed the pain relief it would bring. "Lay back down. You're going to like this part," she promised.

After another moment of locked eyes, he finally settled.

Shaking her head at his stubbornness, she picked up the ginger oil again and got to it.

She spent twenty minutes on his left until he was once again melting into the mattress. From his calf to below his buttocks, she worked on every sore muscle. While she was still on the first leg, she'd preplanned and poured a large dollop of oil on the back of his right leg but kept working on the other.

It was time to switch, and she didn't have to stop for more oil, she just seamlessly switched to his right. He stiffened. She expected it and ignored it. Without warning she placed both her hands on his residual limb. She started light. She needed to gage his tenderness to pressure.

The ginger was doing its work, his skin was getting hotter. "You'll need to guide me this first time. I'm going to try different strokes, direction, pressure, all of it—I need your words. Tell me what feels good."

He was silent for several more minutes as she kept things light. Then finally, "Harder. Try ... try as hard as you did on the left side."

She instantly changed direction and pressure. Kneading deeper and deeper, creating runnels with her fingers from the tip of his stump to below his butt cheek before returning to where his limb ended. Her thumbs dug deeper and deeper. His moans grew in frequency.

After another fifteen minutes, she switched to working both legs together. The oil slick beneath her hands created no resistance to stroke after stroke. Cat realized her breath was coming in heavy pants. Coll's groans had turned to moaning her name. She made a pass up the back of his thighs, her thumbs tunneling between his legs until ...

"Oh, Christ! Cat ..."

Her thumbs had touched his balls. She'd gone too high,

apparently. "I'm ..." Sorry? Not sorry? Want to do it again? "Accident," she finally squeaked out.

From one slow, mortified blink to the next, Coll was on his back, her waist gripped in between his powerful hands. He pulled her sex even with the base of his, only a modest cotton towel and the sheerest cotton pajama bottoms separating them.

"What are you doing to me?" He growled, his hips barely pumping beneath her spread legs.

She was a hairsbreadth away from apologizing ... but why? "Do you want a happy ending, Colly?" From that moment until she was an old woman, she'd never know where she got the nerve.

"What do you think?" He pulled the towel from his groin, revealing ... "Jesus, Coll. Is your dick compensating for your lack of personality?" A slap on the rear was his answer.

"So?" she taunted.

"This is a very bad idea, lass." He gritted his teeth when she rolled her hips.

"Come on, asshole. You admitted to wanting me not two hours ago." No man was that hard if they were waffling with their feelings. He wanted her.

"No one has ever ... your hands ... Christ, Cat, it's been two years."

She wiped off the ginger oil and poured a small dollop of sandalwood into her palms while he debated with his conscience. Sandalwood smelled divine, and Cat also knew it increased some people's sexual desire. Unneeded in this instance, for them both, but it was a fun fact to know.

It was clear Coll was going to spend the rest of the evening deep in denial and excuses. She wasn't patient as a rule, so she took his considerable girth in her oiled hands and gave his length a slow, firm pump.

He closed his eyes, and she missed his dark gaze immediately. She wanted him to see exactly who had him in hand. "Open your eyes and watch me."

He obeyed, and his dark eyes latched onto her face first before landing on her hands. His back arched, her small frame lifting with every undulation of his hips. She pumped him slowly, enjoying his firm flesh sliding through her fingers.

This moment was surreal. Just like the unoriginal movie stars said during their red carpet interviews, only she wasn't an actress and could forgive herself for the uninspired, unoriginal thought.

Catriona MacGregor was jacking off Coll Barr.

Her slick hands increased the pace, barely squeezing the crown of his sex before she descended.

"I won't last," Coll rasped. "I want you ... need to feel you ... slow dow—"

"I can't," she interrupted with her own panting need. "Come for me. Me, Coll. Your Kitty Cat. Come for me," she repeated.

20

Coll woke to sunlight flickering around the edges of Cat's fabric blinds. He reached for his phone on the nightstand. "Holy shit. Eight-fifteen." He couldn't remember the last time he'd ever slept so late.

He lay there slightly befuddled as he took stock of his body, which usually fretted him the most in the mornings. His leg felt loose and limber. He went through a series of stretches that he did each morning before putting on his prosthesis. There was no discomfort. No wonder he'd slept like the dead.

It could have also been that he'd come harder than he ever had in his life. Memories from the night before started to flicker through his mind. Cat between his legs. Him pulling off his towel. Slick, oily skin. Cat's hands wrapped around his—
"Fuck," he dragged the curse out.

What had he been thinking? He'd already been half mad with wanting her. Once her magical hands touched his skin, it was game over. He'd been able to keep his lustful thoughts at bay while her hands had gone to work on him, but once she got to his legs ... once her fingertips started to graze his ass cheeks ... once her thumbs glided over his sac ... his control snapped, and the already tearing need to have her became a roaring want in his ears.

He'd never felt anything so good as her stroking him off. Her hands looked tiny and delicate, but there was strength and power there. She'd worked his flesh like a master. He hadn't wanted to come so soon. Cat and his body had other plans.

He erupted all over himself and her hands. His dick was hard and throbbing from remembering what she did next. The wee hellion brought one of her fingers to her mouth and licked, closing her eyes briefly. Her look was one of delight—as if his seed were delicious.

He reached for her then, wanting desperately to give her pleasure like she'd given him.

"No. Tonight was about you, Coll. While your body is loose from the massage, and your ... release," she smiled at that, "you need to rest."

"So, you gave me a good chugging, and I can't return the favor?" he'd asked.

"Exactly. I imagine we'll find plenty of time to explore. Just not tonight. You need this rest. Don't argue."

Then the bossy woman had taken up a damp rag and cleaned her hands and his cock as if she handled men's appendages all the live long day, removed her tray, and covered him with a sheet and blanket. She gathered her things, flicked the closet light off, and left him alone.

He would have sworn on his life that he would never sleep after what they'd just done together, but he had.

Now he was being a layabout, daydreaming about what he wanted to do to his best friend's sister. That was the cold shower thought his body needed to get moving. Throwing off the covers and ignoring his hard dick, he began the task of putting his gear on.

It was easier to think of his fake leg like military gear. It was a task to be completed like any other. He got dressed in the clothes Cat had laid out for him before they'd gone on their date. Dark blue slacks paired with a light blue button-up and brown leather dress shoes. They were more like half-boots and more secure feeling with his shoe insert than loafers.

He grabbed his laptop, intending to go over all the camera feeds from last night and make sure they were working properly. He also needed to finish mapping out where he wanted the rest of the cameras before they left for the wedding.

Cat was in the kitchen fiddling with some yellow flowers. Presumably, Jo's wedding bouquet. She looked up when he walked in, her eyes widening enough to make him believe she liked what she was seeing.

"You look very handsome, Mr. Barr."

If she felt awkward about what happened between them last night, he couldn't detect it. "Thank you. You picked it out."

"Of course I did. My dress is blue striped. I wanted us to match, and then there's the fact that you and Tommy would wear jeans and T-shirts if you could get away with it. Our blues will be a lovely compliment to Jo and Tom's creams. The yellow flowers will tie it all together. I was glad to hear Jo hired a photographer."

She stopped speaking and looked at him in question. He realized he was just staring at her. He loved watching her talk. He didn't bother to tell her that the prettiest color at the wedding would be red. Cat always looked like one of the beautiful flowers she grew.

Christ, Coll. Get ahold of yourself. What's next? Poetry?

"Oh!" She jumped like an alarm was going off. "I need to get ready myself. I didn't realize how late it was." She was about to run by him but turned before running to the bathroom. "I almost forgot. I had some leftover scones from Gram, and I made you a couple of bacon, egg, and cheese sandwiches. They should tide you until the wedding luncheon."

She shut the door before he had a chance to thank her. Not only for breakfast but for last night. Not for jerking him off but for the massage and sleeping good and ... "Christ, you're a damn idiot." He found his breakfast warming atop the AGA, and careful of his attire, he dug in.

His best friend was getting married today, and not thinking about his sister's hands wrapped around his dick was the least he could do to celebrate the day.

Shaking his head, he sat and opened up the security camera app, flicking through each camera and noting any holes that he might improve on. He left the camera running on Storage Shed from last evening's feeds while he worked on a separate screen of notes.

Movement on the screen had his head whipping around. "What the hell?" He backed it up and paused. A person was leaving the shed at four-forty-two this morning. Leaving ... He backed the camera feeds up. He saw the video of him and Cat leaving for the pub, and then ... "There you are." Not forty-five minutes after they'd left the property, the same person was caught entering the shed dressed in loose, dark clothes. A large hood hid their face. There was no telling whether it was a man or a woman.

Did Cat have a squatter? He went to the bathroom and knocked—maybe pounded since she pulled the door wide like the bathroom was on fire. She stood there in a sheer nude bra and panties. He could see ... Christ, he could see everything. Saliva filled his mouth at the site of her hard nipples, and ... oh God ... her pretty little slit was covered by the barest trace of red curls.

"Jesus, Catriona. What the hell are you wearing?"

"My underwear, for the love of God. What the hell are you about, Coll?"

What was he doing? Thinking was so hard when all of his brain power was being redirected to his hardening cock. "I ... I ... there was—"

"You've never kissed me. Will you?"

He wanted nothing more. He didn't waste time on words but grasped her waist and lifted her to his body. Her legs locked around his waist. A growl of satisfaction rumbled past his lips as one hand secured her ass and the other tunneled into her curls.

"Give me your mouth, Kitty Cat," he whispered against her lips. There was no hesitation and then finally, finally he tasted her. "Oh, Christ, baby."

It was like time stopped but also like he was dropped in the middle of a hurricane where he knew he was in danger and the consequences would be severe. He didn't give two shits. Nothing mattered but that Cat was in his arms.

The first time his tongue slid against hers, he knew he was addicted. She was his drug. There was no living without her taste. The moment their mouths fused, Cat went wild in his arms. She ground her center against his erection.

There was still a grain of working brain left to recognize the trouble he was in. He needed to keep his distance from this woman, but he would kill to be close. There were no warnings strict enough for him to heed.

"I want inside you, baby."

She touched his mouth with her fingertips. "We don't have time. If we don't leave here in five minutes, we'll be late for the wedding."

He was satisfied to hear the whine in her voice. She wanted him to take her and was pissed that it wouldn't be happening.

"I'll make you come, then."

"Yes."

Agreement. Surrender. *Mine.*

Coll leaned her back against the open door, using his free hand to first pinch her delicious nipples before he brushed his fingers against her silk-covered sex. Watch me, Cat." He moved her panties aside. "Watch as your body swallows my fingers."

"I'm already so close, Colly. God, yes," she hissed.

He worked her body, fingers plunging, thumb pressing her nub until she stiffened and then screamed her release. He plunged his tongue deep into her mouth, matching his fingers, swallowing every sound that passed her lips.

As her quivering body shuddered and draped against his, he understood that he'd just done something that he couldn't undo.

21

Dear Brother,

I grow weary of fasting. My body suffers, but my mind is strong.

You would not recognize me, Inti. I live in the shadows, laboring each day for you. The city I must reside in is shadowy, dank, and dreary.

Nothing like our beloved Peru.

Here, I am covered, keeping my identity secret is paramount.

I finally found a distant cousin of ours that could be my twin. Her presence amongst our soldiers and workers will allow me more freedom here. The cops will soon believe that I am again untouchable behind our fortress.

Only a few trusted men from our vast army are with me —more would have drawn attention. They keep this house secure and the curious at bay. My job lies only in fulfilling the witch's commandments.

Your new body is no longer perfect, but I think you will

be pleased nonetheless. The body you'll inherit pleased me greatly. Many times.

Do not be jealous, my love. Each time he took my body over the edge of pleasure, it was your name I whispered into the night. I sought his company to learn more about our enemy's plans, but even drugged, he gave up nothing. He is powerful in body and mind. I remembered him long after our one night together.

It was fated that he would become you.

Soon, you two will be as one, and what came before will no longer matter. You know you are the only man I have ever loved. Since I was a child, you taught me what it meant to truly be loved—it's only ever been you.

I do not want to burden you, but your body is living with a woman. She flaunts her body in front of you, or what will be you. He does not truly want her, but he is a man with a man's needs. I performed a spell on him that night, binding him to me. If he could only lay eyes on me again, he would forget all else. Still ... I fear she will wear down his resolve.

I do not want her touching what is mine. She is the seventh, and I dare not take her before the Guardian's Gede spirits tell me it's time, but ...

I hate her Inti.

I hate the way you look at her.

You watch her like you used to watch me.

I beg you to turn your head away.

The red devil will suffer for trying to take what is mine. If I was not so fearful of making a misstep, I would kill her now.

I will do nothing to jeopardize your precarious hold. Your soul cannot slip any closer to the Underworld.

Do not let the afterlife beguile you.

Thank you for last night, Inti. You cannot fathom what seeing your face did for my morale. I was near the end of my penance, kneeling for hours and hours on a cold concrete floor. I closed my eyes, and you were there.

You smiled, and my heart sang. You brushed your fingers against my cheek and took all my pain away. You spoke to me, though I couldn't hear your words.

Until finally, my ears were opened, and I heard you whisper ... I love you. I love you too. Thank the blessed Bawon Samedi, guardian between the world of the dead and the living.

Endure everything. Sacrifice anything.
For you, Inti. I will not fail us.

Your beloved,
A

22

Cat was still flushed from the epic orgasm Coll had given before they left. They were meeting Thomas and Jo at Inverness Town House, a lovely old municipal building on High Street. She was excited about the wedding, but the smile that kept creeping out had more to do with the scowling man driving.

She wouldn't let his silence and frowns ruin her post-coital bliss. She knew the moment his fingers left her body that he'd have a mantrum of guilt and regrets. He hadn't come to terms with the fact that she was his best friend's little sister, but he was desperate to get in her pants.

He was afraid Thomas would be angry if or when he found out, but really, Cat didn't see what the big deal was. They were all adults. Thomas was about to be happily married. He was expecting his second child, for heaven's sake. Minding her business should be the furthest thing from her brother's mind.

Coll's eyes had heated when she walked out in her wrap dress. It was modest but lovely. She felt pretty in it, at any rate. He'd done a brilliant job of ignoring her since.

"I need you to look at a video from one of the farm's cameras when we get home. A person appears to have stayed the night in the storage shed. There were two videos of them entering last evening and another of them leaving early this morning."

That shocked some of her bliss off. "What? Did you recognize them?"

"No," he sighed. "The video was dark, and the person was wearing a hoodie. I plan on adding motion lights so that won't happen again. While you got dressed," his cheeks turned a precious shade of pink, probably thinking about what they were doing before that, "I ran over to the shed. Everything is neat and tidy. Nothing appeared out of place. The half bath was clean." He shook his head in irritation.

"Do you think it was," she hesitated, "the woman from Peru?" The one you had sex with all night, she didn't add.

"No, and I would have thought that too, but Thomas texted me right before we left that he had good news on that front. I assume that means she has been sighted at her compound and is no longer a threat to us. He said we'd talk at lunch."

She was relieved by the news but also deflated. If the woman wasn't coming after Coll or his family, then that meant he'd be moving out. Just thinking that made her cringe at how selfish she was being.

"Are you going to tell Thomas about the person sleeping in my shed?" Now that the shock had worn off, she was beginning to wonder if it was her new hire, Réka. She was opening up more, but Cat got definite vibes that the woman wasn't being completely honest about her past. Cat would watch Coll's video and if there was any chance it was Réka, she would speak to her.

His hands gripped the steering wheel tighter than necessary. Interesting.

"I would prefer to not bother Tom right before his honeymoon. He'd only worry about you the entire time, and I'm perfectly capable of taking care of you myself."

Cat didn't miss the slight hesitation in his declaration, and she wouldn't stand for him to second-guess himself. As if her brother was better suited to the task. *What shit!* "Of course, you can handle it. I'm not worried." He only nodded, but it was clear to her that he was pleased.

She didn't want to bring up her concern concerning Réka, but it would be foolish not to. "The squatter might be my new hire. If it is, she wouldn't mean any harm by it. From the few things she's admitted, her past wasn't ideal. I will talk to her if you think I should."

"Don't worry about it now. Let's enjoy your brother's wedding. I'll pick up extra lights on our way home and get them installed. I'm also going to add a lock to the shed."

"Sounds like you'll have a busy afternoon. Should I schedule you in for a massage tonight?" She kept her face blank. Barely.

"No."

Liar, liar, pants on fire.

~

THE WEDDING WAS BEAUTIFUL. There were no two happier people in the world at that moment than Thomas and Josephine. There had been some trial and many errors—on her brother's part—but they'd made it to the other side.

The party of four had just settled at a cozy table at Lauders, a lovely pub that had great views of Inverness Castle and the River Ness.

"I know I've told you a thousand times already, Jo, but you were a beautiful bride."

Jo grinned, her happiness sparking Cat's own.

"She's still the most beautiful bride," Thomas groused. Always game to bring a mood down.

"She isn't a bride anymore, numbnuts. She's your wife."

His only response was a well-timed grunt. Typical.

"I'm going to have my bouquet preserved so that I can somehow use it in our wedding album."

"Oh, Lord! Don't pay anyone for that. I preserve flowers all the time. I make sachets for my clothes drawers. Just leave it with me, and I'll turn the ranunculus into keepsakes. No worries."

Coll was sitting at her side but one would think they were strangers. It was time to end his 'trip into regrets' feelings tour. She quickly tapped out a message.

> Did you taste me on your fingers like I tasted you on mine?

His phone dinged. She looked out of the corner of her eye as she ordered a Guinness. She would have laughed out loud, watching his eyes peel wide as he read. When he set the phone down without responding, she was disappointed but far from defeated.

While Jo spoke of their honeymoon and what a romantic her brother was—Cat did her best not to chuckle—Cat tried again to get a response from Coll.

> Did you like the bit of hair between my legs? Would you prefer me bald?

Again, he picked his phone up, and again he set it down but not before adjusting his privates. Progress.

> Two questions. First. When I give you another massage, what is the one thing you were dying for me to do to you that I didn't? Second question. If I were naked in your bed, what's the first thing you would want to do to me?

She knew she was pushing her luck, but ... He read the text, but instead of setting his phone aside, he typed. She sipped her beer and agreed to an order of grilled shrimp and crab dip for appetizers.

> Behave yourself, Cat.

Her brother, unfortunately, broke her side-ogling. "DEA has had eyes on Alvarez. It appears to be drug business as usual. They are going to keep tabs on her and her brothers because they are still obviously waiting for an opening to take her empire down."

"The family?" Coll asked.

"I didn't want to give everyone the all-clear until I spoke to you."

"I think we're good. You?"

"Yes." Thomas nodded his agreement. "I'll let Aileen and Mir know when we leave here. Will you let Grandma's guards know?"

"Of course. Though she'll probably miss cooking for them." The table laughed. Gram did love to feed people.

"It shouldn't take you long to move from Cat's. I'm sure my hellfire little sister will be happy to have the cottage to herself again."

Thomas didn't mean anything by his comment, but it sent a wave of anxiety zinging through her nerves. She didn't dare look at Thomas.

"I can't wait to move out. Cat's cottage is as wee as she is." He chuckled ... actually chuckled. "My parents have agreed to sell the farm to me. I'll be starting renovations on the house immediately."

I can't wait to move out. Unbeknownst to his sister's heart breaking, Thomas slapped the table in glee. "Christ, Coll, you bastard. When were you going to tell me? We'll be neighbors just like old times." He turned to Jo and excitedly told her where the property lines connected.

For her part, she worked on blinking and swallowing so no tears slipped free.

Blink. Swallow. Blink. Swallow.

When people say something was *a hard pill to swallow*, maybe they had just sexted a man who already had two feet out the door too.

She pathetically kept looking Coll's way throughout dinner. He could have been made from stone. He was probably planning contingency plans in case she made a scene when they got home.

She wouldn't.

23

Coll could feel Cat's pain like his damn phantom limb. The ghosted memory of the jungle explosion and his resulting rendered flesh hurt less to remember than to see Cat's upset and know he was responsible.

He didn't want to leave her. She could live in a shoebox, and he'd happily live there with her.

He'd called her wee and not as an endearment. She was sensitive about her size. Her childhood bullies had made sure of it, and he made light of it.

She was tiny, damn it, but her size made her that much more precious to him. She was a woman with a giant's personality and a femme fatale's libido. He wanted to protect her and fuck her in equal measure.

Panic was beginning to settle in his bones. He could feel her shoring up her defenses and turning from him. She'd trusted him with her truths and her body, and he shit on them both.

Somehow, he made it through the wedding lunch, toasts, and jests. They were on the sidewalk outside Lauger's, giving the newlyweds a proper farewell. He hugged Josephine and thought to shake Thomas' hand but pulled him into a hug as well.

Cat and Jo whispered back and forth, blotting their eyes and promising things that women promised to one another. When it came time for Cat to tell her brother goodbye, he watched in aching wonder as his best friend grasped Cat's delicate shoulders and stared into her eyes.

"You're upset."

"I certainly am not, you oaf," she hotly denied.

Jo gave Coll a strange look. He ignored it. Thomas gently grasped Cat's chin, forcing her to make eye contact.

"I don't want to leave you like this. I won't." His voice was a rumbling growl. A threat and promise.

Coll expected her to lash out with some snarky denial. Instead, she leaned her head against her brother's middle and wrapped her lean arms around him. Thomas' large hand cupped the back of her head and held her close. The moment was so tender, he felt like an unwanted voyeur.

She pulled back and managed a smile. "I love you, Tommy. I'm only sad because I'm going to selfishly miss you and Jo. Now leave already and send me lots of pictures. Presents wouldn't go amiss either," she teased.

The spell was broken, because Cat wanted it broken and the new couple got into their rental and pulled away. He and Cat watched the car until it was out of sight.

Without turning to look at him, Cat spoke loud enough to be heard over the milling passersby. "Go on home without me. A friend is picking me up. Put the bouquet in the fridge, will you?"

Without another word or glance, she began to walk away. Before he thought better of it, he lunged and grabbed her hand, spinning her to face him. "What the fuck do you mean go home without you?" She wouldn't meet his eyes, which crushed him. "Cat?" Her name was a plea for ... what? Forgiveness?

Before he could demand she speak to him, a damnably familiar voice was calling her name. Feodor. That mother ... "You aren't leaving with him." He tugged her hand again, bringing her close enough their sides touched. "No way, Cat."

She looked at him then, fury bleeding across her green eyes. "Have your things moved out before I get home. I know you can't wait. It will go faster without me throwing myself at you. We'll both be saved from further embarrassment." She wrenched her hand from his grasp and took several steps back.

She turned and was walking toward that Russian dickhead when she paused, turning slightly back to him. Had she changed her mind?

She sighed in ... defeat? "There is a full jar of the ginger massage oil in the bathroom cupboard. I fetched it this morning. Use it every night." With that, she walked away. Into another man's arms.

Even though he'd hurt her feelings, she put his needs above her own. He hurt her feelings, and she was worried about his goddamn leg.

He watched as Feodor stooped to hug *his* ... to hug Cat. The man made eye contact and raised his brows in question, like, "What the hell did you do, dumbass?"

He'd been a coward and hurt the one woman he ...

∽

FEODOR DIDN'T ASK her why she needed him to save her. He was turning out to be an amazing friend. Plus, he knew the perfect way to spend the next few hours while Coll vacated her home.

She got to meet his parents, who were wonderful, and was

able to roundtable her ideas of eventually broadening her sales to the States with Feodor's father.

Three hours went by with her only thinking about Coll around forty-two times. She pinched the bridge of her nose to dam the flood of tears that wanted to overflow. Coll had admitted that he couldn't wait to leave her—leave her wee cottage and her wee self.

Damn him but damn her more. Her inexperience with men had never shone brighter than it did today. She was so embarrassingly sure that Coll wanted her as much as she wanted him.

That it was more than sex.

That he might ... be interested in a relationship.

Christ ... It was that last admission that had her cursing her naivety. Would she ever be able to live down texting Coll those explicit messages? No. No way. She'd officially strangled whatever familial relationship they'd previously shared.

"You ready to go home and face the music of your sexting?"

"Not funny, asshole." Oh, how she wished Feodor hadn't called his girlfriend, Daria, and that she hadn't taken their first meet and greet to puke her man woes in the poor woman's face. To Daria's credit, she'd taken Cat's most embarrassing moments and upped her humiliation for humiliation. Daria was amazing.

"I'll call a ride, Fe. Thank you for today."

"Grab your bag. Not only my parents but also Daria would burn me on a pyre if I let you go home alone. Plus, I owe you. Daria is so excited to move here. Just me telling her that you couldn't wait to meet her did wonders, and after today, I know she'll be even more amped. I owe you."

It only took fifteen minutes to reach her cottage. She prayed the whole way that Coll's truck would not be there. Not only was it still proudly parked in her drive, but the man of her most embarrassing hour was sitting on her front steps.

"Oh shit," Feodor cursed.

No truer words ...

"Turn around and drop me off at my office, please. I can't deal with his accusations or apologies."

∽

COLL'S ANGER built to a crescendo as he watched Cat driving toward him with a man who wasn't him. Had he not been here, would she have invited Feodor in?

No. Absolutely not. She wasn't the kind of woman to jump from one man's bed to another.

He finished wiring the last of the cameras, put a few motion lights up, and installed a good lock on the shed. He was waiting there because he needed to show Cat the video of the intruder to see if she recognized them.

Honestly, he was waiting on the front porch like a lovesick puppy because he hurt Cat earlier, and he wanted to apologize. He wanted to see her face and know she forgave him.

He'd only said he was ready to move out because it's what Thomas would expect him to say. He knew that Coll and his sister got along like cats and dogs.

He hadn't been ready for his best friend to know that Cat was texting him dirty texts. Thomas didn't need to know that his sister made his dick harder than it's ever been just from her filthy words. It had taken every bit of his military training to control the powerful need to grasp her thigh and pull her against his side. He desperately wanted to feel her touching him.

He was so far gone for her that he panicked. He was cruel.

He straightened from his lean and stared the two down through the windshield until Feodor did a U-turn and drove back the way they'd come.

She was running from him. He quickly pulled the security

app up on his phone and started flipping through the images. "There you are, Kitty Cat." Feodor had dropped her at her office. He exited the car when she did. He flipped to the next video. They were embracing.

He fumbled his phone in anger, eventually switching from taped to a live feed. Feodor's car was pulling away and Cat must have gone inside her office already. Knowing he was being the worst type of stalker, he flipped to the camera that he had angled to see the interior of her office. It was all windows, and he could see her clearly sitting at her desk.

He didn't bother driving the short distance. He could wind through the greenhouses on foot and be there faster anyway. The farm was deserted. Cat had given everyone the day off to enjoy the football game between Scotland and Germany. It would have been on in every pub and home across Scotland.

He tested the office door's handle. Unlocked. He didn't bother knocking. She looked up, startled from where she'd been reading something on her computer. She didn't look pleased to see him.

"You keep running from me."

"Did you get your things packed?"

"No." He crossed his arms over his chest, ready for a fight.

"Then why are you here pestering me?"

"I lied. At lunch." She gave him no reaction. "I didn't mean what I said to Tom." Still nothing. "I'm not ready, that is, I don't want ... we're new, we haven't discussed. Christ, could I fuck this up anymore?" He dropped his hands and moved a few steps closer. "I lied to your brother, I meant to do *that*, but I swear, Cat, I never meant to hurt your feelings."

She stood, leaning her hip against the desk, still stunningly beautiful in her blue dress. Had he told her that?

"I'm glad you were able to get all that off your chest. Now, please, go pack. I want to relax and read tonight. In peace."

She was still upset. How the hell was he supposed to make her forgive him? "I'm truly sorry, lass. Truly."

"Apology accepted. Goodbye, Coll."

She turned, giving him her back. He decided to go for it. "I licked my fingers until every bit of your taste was on my tongue. I wanted your mouth on my cock. My face between your thighs."

Cat almost gave herself whiplash, spinning around as his words registered.

"Wha ... what?"

"I answered your questions. The ones you asked at lunch."

Her face bloomed red, whether with embarrassment or anger, he didn't know.

"I would prefer to forget how I threw myself at you and how easily you blew me off. I pray I'm intelligent enough to have learned my lesson with you. Finally. Your message was received."

Anger and embarrassment, then. No matter what her conflicting emotions were, he couldn't let her believe that he did something so ridiculous as blowing her off. He moved closer until her body was trapped between him and the desk.

"I admit to being a coward with your brother, Cat, but don't ever accuse me of not wanting you. I want you every minute of every fucking day."

Prying her hand from the lip of her desk's top, he flattened it against the fly of his pants. "Does that feel like I don't want you, Cat?"

Her lips parted, and her eyes were blown wide in surprise. He wondered if she would reject him, but the small twitch of her fingers across his zipper gave him hope. He took her face in his hands and brought their lips together.

The kiss was explosive. It was desperate and dirty—teeth, tongues, swollen lips, groans and moans. Without leaving the haven of her mouth, he untied the side bow on her dress and spread the material wide.

Placing a hand on her sternum, he pushed until she laid back flat against her desk—and made good on what he would do if she was ever naked in front of him.

He pulled her panties down her legs so fast he hoped he didn't leave a silk burn anywhere. It was his last clear thought. The moment the see-through panties dropped from his fingers, his mouth was between her legs and tasting heaven.

"Coll. Coll. Coll." She chanted his name as she thrashed and rotated her hips faster and faster. He could feel her body shaking, her movements becoming erratic. She was close. He would push her closer.

He grabbed her ass and lifted her high off the desk, sinking his tongue as deep as it would go, faster and faster and faster, until she came screaming his name.

With a final long swipe of his tongue and nips to either side of her inner thighs, he commanded, "Take everything off. Now." He leaned down to take her mouth, frantic to have his mouth any and everywhere he could, but her palms pumped his chest back.

"You take everything off too."

He'd never ripped his clothes off so fast in his life. He had to take his shoes off to get his pants off, which would leave him with a bare metal 'foot' on display.

"Coll," she got his attention. "If you keep staring at your damned prosthesis instead of taking care of my needs, I'm going to seriously reconsider who takes my virginity."

"Takes what?"

24

Cat, you idiot. When she felt him come to a grinding halt, she knew her mouth had run away with her.

"You're a ... a ... what?"

"Jesus, Coll. I've done plenty of—"

"Don't fucking finish that sentence," he interrupted.

"God." She huffed, smacking her forehead at his tone. "I think I lost my hymen three years ago with a vibrator. I'm good. We're good. Kiss me."

He capitulated without a fight, his mouth landed on hers, the taste of her sex coating her tongue and making her almost climax again. She reached between her legs and grasped his shaft, pumping in rhythm with his tongue.

"Cat, Jesus, baby, I need you." He took control of his sex and began to rub her seam, making her mad with need.

"Yes, yes, yes," she purred against his lips. She was naked, lying atop her hard-as-hell desk in the middle of her office, and she couldn't find a single thing to complain about. She felt him position his length at her entrance, and nothing had ever felt better.

"Condom." She stuttered out. At least she was still coherent enough to think of the basics.

Coll reared back. His wide-eyed look of panic didn't bode well.

"I'm clean. Two years. Doctors ..."

His rambling would have been cute if she wasn't so flipping horny. "I'm clean. Hello, toys aren't usually STD carriers. I'm not on birth control." His gaping mouth wasn't reassuring in the least.

"Christ, Cat. I don't have any."

His panic was a balm to her virginal soul. He wanted this as badly as she did. If she had any doubts, the fact that the head of his penis kept breaching her vagina, pumping in and out in the barest of increments.

She propped herself up on her elbows to better assess the situation. Cock, loaded and almost locked. Patience, nil.

"Can you pull out? We're good Catholics," she pleaded. "We're taught the pull-out method, right?"

"Right. Yes. The pull-out method." His head jerkily agreed.

"Can you do that?"

"Yes," he pushed an inch further, "yes, yes, yes."

Cat pulled his head down for a kiss. His mouth was a drug she needed. He hesitated to take her mouth.

"We should be in a bed. Your bed. Our bed. Christ! I don't know. Any bed. This is your first time. Our first time. Cat ..."

He said her name with so much angst she couldn't help but feel warm feelings. "Our first time is going to be on this damn desk. Right now." She pumped her hips, taking him deeper. She hissed at the fullness, and she had barely taken any of his length. Sweat started to bead her brow. Bravado could only take a person so far—this might hurt ...

She squealed in surprise as Coll pulled what little of himself he'd managed to get inside of her out. He scooped her into his arms and carried her over to the couches.

He laid her gently against the soft, buttery leather cushions, a relief from the cold, hard wood of her desk. She'd been prepared for a bruised back. He made quick work of taking his prothesis off.

"I don't plan on taking it easy on you, baby. I think the couch is a better option."

So much better. Coll draped his gorgeous body over hers. She thought he would go straight for the main bits, but he never did anything she expected. He spent what felt like hours on her breasts. She would never question her appeal to Coll again. It was an experience in revelations.

He'd told her before that her breasts were perfect. Tonight, she finally believed that they were. At least ... perfect for him.

When he finished worshiping her breasts, he went back to her mouth. The desperation in their joining was fire. Her lips felt swollen and puffy, both of them nipping each other, sucking, desperate moans, and grasping hands. Breathing was no longer life. Only Coll. Only.

He sat up and grasped her knees, slowly widening her legs. He brushed a thumb across her small patch of pubic hair, seemingly fascinated. He glanced at her face, a smile tugging his lips. "I can't believe you're finally naked and underneath me."

"I've wanted it for years," she replied honestly.

His answer was to slowly slide his fingers through her slick folds, causing her to suck in a quick breath. She was so sensitive, her body vibrating with want.

"I want to taste you again."

Her hips bucked at the suggestion, but she had other ideas. "Later. I have things I want to do with you too ... but later. I need you in me now."

He didn't argue but grasped his sex and slowly rubbed the

slick head against her center. "I'll go slow, baby. Tell me if you need to stop."

Her head and shoulders were propped up on the couch's fluffy armrest, allowing her to see everything he was doing to her. He slipped an inch, then another, and another. Her hips were moving up and down of their own accord. The fullness and friction made her crave more.

Coll's clenched jaw and complete focus on where they were partially joined would forever live as a vivid memory for her. Coll looked like a warrior statue, immortalized in the agony of pleasure.

It was lust and wonder for him.

It was love for her.

Ready to complete their union, she pumped her hips higher. He groaned and gritted his teeth and met her tempo. Finally, finally, finally, he was fully seated. She felt not painfully full but uncomfortably so. He was big, and she was not.

"Jesus God, Cat. Your body is gripping me so tight, I could come without moving again."

"Don't get lazy on me now, Colly." She lifted her head off the couch and grinned. He grinned back.

It was lust and wonder and joy.

Having sex for the first time with someone she'd loved and trusted her entire life made this experience better than any dream.

They kissed, their mouths tender and aching. Her fingers gripped his scalp, creating runnels through his thick, black hair. He gripped her hips with increasing strength and began to pump and slide into her wet channel until she had to release his mouth to gasp.

"I'm going to come, baby. I won't last—"

"I'm so close! Don't stop!" she begged.

He reached between their bodies, swiping a slick thumb

over her sex, causing her back to bow as an orgasm tore through her body like a roaring storm of shivers and convulsions.

She screamed as she felt her body grip his length impossibly tight. Coll bent backward, clasping her hips, making a tight seal between their bodies. He shouted her name. She felt every jerk of his sex as he pumped inside her.

Cat felt tears prick her eyes at the momentous ... thing, they'd just done together and never so thankful that she'd saved herself for him. This was sex, yes, but it was everything else too.

As he curled over her body, resting his head against the armrest next to hers, she loved that he stayed inside her. She began to massage his scalp. His rumbles and neck kisses showed that he liked the attention.

His hips shifted, allowing his softening penis to begin its retreat.

Her eyes suddenly popped wide, and her fingers stilled. Coll must have felt the tension stiffen her limbs because he lifted his head and looked at her in question.

"I don't think the Catholic Church taught us well enough after all." He looked confused for all of three seconds, then it was his turn to panic. He shoved off her body and went to stand, forgetting he'd taken his leg off after they'd made it to the couch. He swayed on one leg, which only made him look even more alarmingly dazed.

His mouth opened and closed a good number of times before his jaw snapped shut, and his face turned red. The sweat beading his brow was a nice touch of panic.

She slid from the couch and stood on his right side. She slipped her arm around his waist to steady him. Despite his obvious discombobulation, he reacted to her nearness and used both arms to pull her tight, lightly touching her back and sides.

"I'm going to help you sit on the couch. Then you are going

to sit patiently while I go pee and flush out all your baby-makers. Sound good?"

He looked at her like he was guilty of murder. "I'm sorry, Cat. I told you I would pull out, and then the first time we're together ..."

"I'm just as responsible. If you'll recall, I might have strangled you if you'd left my body before I orgasmed. Now, will you sit and stay?"

He looked solemnly down at her and pinched her ass. "Woof," was his only response. At least he didn't look like he was going to throw up anymore—most women wouldn't find terror on their partner's face after intimacy a confidence booster.

She got him settled but still stood between his thighs. It was a wonder to stand in front of a man naked without thinking she should cover her body. She trusted Coll with every part of herself. More than her own self-worth discovery, she was preening inside that Coll finally seemed comfortable with his residual limb—and perhaps more open to a real relationship.

She was about to back up when his hands on her outer thighs stopped her. "You are all sleek muscles, lovely angles, and slight curves. I can barely stand to take my eyes from you."

He stared so intently at her face that she began to fidget. She broke eye contact and looked down because she could feel his seed seeping out, the warm, sticky cum dripping sluggishly down her inner thigh.

He noticed too. If his thickening shaft meant anything, he liked what he saw.

"I know I shouldn't, but seeing my cum drip from your body ... fuck, baby ..."

He lifted her easily and held her suspended over his hardened sex. He waited for her moan of assent before sliding her down his length. Penetration was swift, and the sudden fullness had her gasping and moaning, "Coll, God." The thinking part of their brains was clearly compromised by the thought of further sexual gratification.

He sucked one of her nipples into his mouth as deep as it could go while simultaneously pumping her body over his, hitting so deep and hard she was one big quivering mess—she wasn't thinking of consequences then.

She grasped his head and moved his mouth to her other breast, holding him to her chest like she never meant to let him up for air. For his part, he was a machine. His hands had moved from her hips to her ass cheeks. She'd definitely have finger bruises. The thought made her sex clench.

"You keep squeezing me like that … I'm already close."

Cat began to grind and twist her hips, creating the best type of friction. Coll's moans grew louder, her pants deafening in the still office.

"I'm—"

"There!" She threw her head back, and they both rode the ecstasy wave together. Their breaths sawed in and out, muscles quivering, and spines drooping.

After another few minutes, she couldn't help but ask. "You told me once that you regretted sleeping with that Alvarez woman for two reasons. What were they?" Why his admission flashed in her mind after they'd just had sex, she couldn't explain. It struck her then that he'd been so specific that it was two reasons.

"I'm still buried deep inside you, and this is what you want to discuss?"

"Yes."

"You're a menace, Catriona MacGregor," he sighed in defeat. "The first reason was that I felt I let Thomas down and my team. My actions put our family in the crosshairs of a killer."

"The second?"

"That night in South America, it was only a few months

after that dinner where I got angry when I found out you were dating. I ... I imagined Amaru was you."

"You wanted me over two years ago? I wasn't alone in my feelings?"

"I wanted you," he admitted through gritted teeth.

She gently kissed him. "I'm glad," she spoke against his lips, kissing him once more. "Now, I better go use the toilet. Coming in me twice hasn't improved our odds, Colly." Honestly, it isn't how she would choose to start a family, but the simple fact was that Coll was it for her.

His next words ruined her warm and fuzzies. "No worries. I'll take you home and run uptown and grab a morning-after pill and some condoms."

25

Dear Brother,

I can forgive you many things, but not this. You took that whore in every way that you swore was mine alone.

I saw you.

I saw everything.

That whore is nothing like me. How could you do this?

Can we get past this? I pray it's so.

While you were fucking to your heart's content, I lured a man to his death. In your name. For you. Always, only for you. He was number six.

When I kill the redheaded slut, will you care?

When you had your face between her thighs, did you think of me? Did you taste me? Will you promise to never touch her again?

Two more days of meditation and prayer. Two more days of cursing her body. Two more days until the beginning of her ending.

The man whose throat I ripped out. I fucked him in that dark alley, Inti. As his cock tried to create life, I took his.

Forgive me.

You hurt me, and I wished to hurt you. I know you are suffering in the in between. You used your new body because you needed to feel ... something.

But please, brother, wait for me. Wait until the transfer is complete—until it's me beneath you.

The Guardian of the Gates has taken notice of my sacrifices and tithes, of my hours and hours and days of meditation. Papa Legba will surely open the gate between our worlds when the time is right.

Nothing is lost, Inti. There is only life to be gained.

Your beloved,

A

26

As soon as the words were out of his mouth, Coll knew he'd screwed up. The look on her face ... like he'd slapped her.

"Cat." She shook her head no and slipped off his lap—he'd still been inside her when he'd treated her like ... like she didn't mean everything to him.

I'll grab a morning-after pill. Cat didn't do casual anything. She'd slept with him because she had genuine feelings.

Without a word, she walked to her desk and gathered her clothes before going to the restroom. He quickly put his leg on and got dressed. He began tidying her desk and righting the throw pillows on the couch. His nervous energy wouldn't let him settle.

Why had he done it? Why in the hell had he come in her twice? Never in his life had he done such a thing—and then twice in a row.

The door opened a few minutes later, and she walked out looking put together. Stunning. He was afraid the blush on her cheeks wasn't an afterglow but from embarrassment.

"Cat—" He tried again, but she started speaking at the same time.

"Everything's fine, Coll." She waved a hand in front of her. Everything was fine between them? The room? "You and I are in two different places. I love you, and you can't bear the thought of my brother or anyone else knowing that you even like me. As more than family," she clarified.

I love you. Did she mean it? He felt his knees go weak.

"We are two consenting adults who chose to have sex without protection. I think we both can agree with that. You want me to take a morning-after pill. I understand why, and I'll do it. Please go get it and leave it in my kitchen. I'll take it when I'm done working here. I have some tinctures that need to be finished."

"Please." He closed the distance between them and took her hands. "It came out all wrong. I came off as flippant, and that's the opposite of how I feel."

"I know you didn't mean anything by it. As I said, our feelings are not the same. If you were only someone that I planned on hooking up with a few times on the down low, I wouldn't have gotten bothered by the pill thing.

"You didn't do anything wrong. I do think it's best that when you drop the pill off, you gather your things and head out. I think we both need a breather after today."

He felt his heart pound painfully in his chest. "I don't want a fucking breather. We don't have to live together or have sex, but that doesn't mean I don't want to see you." The feeling churning through his intestines was definitely panic.

"Listen, I didn't expect you to shout our status from the rooftop. I also knew you would dread telling Tommy. What I didn't realize, and should have after lunch today, is that you *never* want to tell anyone. You were pretty clear, and it's on me that I chose to paint it in a different light.

"You said you just weren't ready to tell your bestie about us, but I think if you were being honest, you never saw yourself revealing anything. And before you try to argue, I'm telling you that I need this break. Get me the pill, Coll," she said in a resigned voice. "Text me when you're gone."

He watched as she disappeared into her workshop, sliding the door closed, effectively shutting him out.

He berated himself on the walk to the cottage. The thing was, Cat was right. They were in two different places, though he was beginning to realize that the difference between those places wasn't as far apart as he might have thought.

The pill was weighing on his mind. Why in the hell had he ever brought it up? It should have been her call to make. He was the dumbfuck who didn't pull out like he said he would. Twice. He acted like her taking the pill was a given. Neither of them had discussed anything as significant as whether or not they wanted children—they did have sex, though, so he should have had the conversation instead of spewing presumptions.

It only took ten minutes to throw his shit in the back of his truck. The bottle of ginger massage oil was carefully placed in his center console. He sat in his truck for thirty minutes, debating on what to do. Leave without another word or stay and fight to see her again. To put off making a decision, he called his sister, Aileen, who was presently in the States with her boyfriend, Charles, and her daughter, Mirren.

She answered on the first ring. "I was just thinking of you, Coll." Her sweet voice filled the cab of his truck.

"Just checking on you and Mir." He couldn't share his dilemma over Cat with his sister, or she would fly straight home to kick his ass.

"We're grand, thank you. Now, tell me what's happening. You sound off."

Damn sisters. Did they always need to know their brothers

so well? "Nothing's happened. I know Tommy already called you and let you know the South American woman has been spotted and you and Mir can come home. I was just checking in about that."

That was the truth. The whole truth was that he really just needed to hear her voice. He and Aileen had always shared a close bond. God knows they didn't have one with their parents — the judgmental fucks.

"I was relieved to hear it. It won't only be me and Mir, though."

Damn Charles Morrow, Mir's birth father. He sighed in resignation. There was no getting rid of the bastard. "I know."

"Don't sound so overjoyed," she teased.

"I'm not."

"Coll."

It was her disappointed tone that got him. Sighing, he told her about what he'd done so she hopefully wouldn't be able to stay cross with him. "Mom and Dad sold the farm to me. I'm going to build a house on some of the land closest to Thomas, but I thought ... I hoped you might consider remodeling Mom and Dad's place for you and Mirren ... and the other guy."

"Charles," she reprimanded him.

"Charles." He spat out the name through gritted teeth.

"Oh, Coll. I can't believe you bought it. I didn't even know they were thinking of selling. To stay close to you and Tommy would be a dream. I can put my house up for sale and give you the money from that, and I also have some savings to add as well."

He couldn't help his smile. He liked that his little sister was so pleased. After her cancer scare, he was desperate for her cheerful nature to return in full.

"You aren't paying for anything but for what you choose to do to the old farmhouse."

"I'm not a bloody charity case, Coll Alexander Barr!"

"You're right. You're my bloody sister that I love, and I'm not taking a pence of your money. I don't care how many names you call me." There was silence for a solid minute. He could imagine Aileen choosing her next battle words. So, he was surprised when she finally replied.

"Thank you, brother. I accept your gift with my whole heart. If ... if anything were to ever happen to me, with the cancer again, or whatever, I would be greatly relieved that Mirren had her uncle and father close."

And just that fast, tears pricked his eyes. "Nothing will ever happen to you," he demanded fiercely.

"Of course not," she soothed, "but it does make me happy nonetheless. Thank you. Now tell me what is bothering you."

So stubborn. Just like Cat. "Nothing. Come home as you like or not. It doesn't matter to me." He knew he was being an ass, but he wasn't going to discuss his personal problems with his sister.

Unfazed by his mercurial behavior, she simply said, "I will. I'll give you my flight details once they're made."

"Fine."

"Fine." Her fine sounded suspiciously amused.

He texted Thomas next, not wanting to call him during his honeymoon. He was cognizant that he was putting off making a decision about buying the "pill."

> Aileen and Mir are coming home soon. She agreed to take our folks' house.

> I'm grateful. Between the two of us, we'll be able to keep watch over them.

> And Charles?

> And fucking Charles. You moved out of Cat's?

>> Yes.

> Guards called off and paid from Grandma's?

>> Yes. What job do you need my time on most?

> Littleton. Security breach. Ask Don for details.
> They need fresh eyes.

>> Fine.

> You'll need to fuck off to London for at least three weeks.

>> No problem. Cheers, then.

> Cheers.

Coll stared at his phone, wishing there was at least one more person he needed to check in with. No such luck.

Sighing, he did what he always knew would be the end result. He texted Cat.

>> I'm out of your house. No pill.

She replied within seconds.

> You mean they're out?

>> No.

> Coll! Don't you flipping dare to one word answer me.

Catriona

> I don't want to do the pill.

Okay?

> I may be a coward with your brother, but if we made ... something today ...

A baby?

> Yes.

???

> We'll figure it out.

Fine.

> I'll be gone for up to three weeks on a job. London. When I get back, we'll talk.

Maybe.

> No maybe. We will.

27

Cat tried not to think of Coll, so of course, she thought of nothing but him. He'd been gone for several days. It felt like months.

She did what she did best and worked. She did her best not to look at the security cameras because Coll wasn't even trying to hide that he was watching her.

He would text her if he thought she was working too late. He would ask if she had time to eat with all the clients coming in and out. She didn't try to tell him to stop. He wouldn't, and if she complained to her brother, Thomas would side with Coll's overprotectiveness.

At least there was no concern that she had a squatter on the farm. Catriona had recognized the intruder in the video Coll showed her of the person sneaking into the shed. The video had been dark and there was never a shot of the person's face, but in the early morning hours, moonlight had glinted off a headscarf. Réka.

She spoke with her gardener who came clean instantly, apologizing profusely. She admitted her elderly cousin wasn't the most pleasant person to live with, and she'd only wanted an evening away but didn't want to use any of her savings on a motel room.

Cat made her promise that if she needed another evening away from her cousin, to let her know. She was welcome to crash at the cottage with her. It's not like she had a man living with her.

And just like that ... Coll invaded her thoughts again. He texted her two days after he'd left to ask if she was pregnant.

> Do you know?

> What?

> Are you pregnant?

> Jesus. I don't know. It's only been a hot second.

> When?

> I'm supposed to start my period the end of next week.

> I miss you.

> I miss you, too, but don't say things to me that you aren't willing to back up.

He didn't respond. She knew he wouldn't, but she'd hoped. Damn foolish hope.

∽

A week later, Réka called in sick. Cat had offered to bring her medicine and some food, but she had flatly refused. That's why she found herself loading the day's deliveries with Stanley and Dean's help. Coll had vetted the two new hires, who also happened to be best friends.

They were in their forties, had gone to school together, had always lived together, and had worked every job with each other. They were a package deal, and Cat was very thrilled to have them. Since she'd lost another one of her older gardeners who had originally worked for her parents, it was great to have two more sets of eager hands.

She only had to remember not to ever ask if they had a good evening or weekend for that matter. She got stuck twice listening to an epic saga of an intense Lego build while watching a movie themed after the build. It was next level torture.

No matter their quirks, her new employees were all making a huge difference to the farm. Production levels were strong and getting stronger. It was time to take her lotions, tinctures, and oils to the next level. She needed to find a facility that would manufacture her products, using her recipes, and only her plants.

There was a company she'd been looking into for a while out of Glasgow that she had an appointment with next week. Thomas and Jo were coming home in a few days after extending their honeymoon, so her brother would be here to oversee the farm in case the new hires had any questions, though she didn't imagine they would.

She was giddy about having so much more time to create in her workshop, and now that she'd discussed overseas shipping with Feodor and his parents, she felt confident on that front if she chose that route. Manufacturing was the last big hurdle—and the new website.

She'd have to ask Coll how it was coming along. He was probably almost done except for adding pictures of her products, which she wouldn't have until she had them professionally manufactured and packaged.

Her mind whirled with the huge laundry list of things still to be done. She believed in her products. One day, she wanted to see her creations in health food stores, spas, high-end boutiques, and posh department stores.

Her brother happened to marry a woman with more contacts than God, and Cat planned on picking Jo's brain at the first opportunity.

One day, she hoped MacGregor Farm would be a household name.

In the meantime, she had flowers to deliver. She was looking forward to seeing some of her regular customers. Since Réka had taken over the duty, Cat hadn't seen them in a while.

She was parked in an alley behind the last of her stops and was grinning as she exited the shop using the back door. Mrs. Whitcom was old and ornery and one of Cat's favorite people. She got a good butt chewing for not coming in sooner before being made to eat a cookie that had been baked at least twenty-two minutes past overbaked and then got to wash the briquette down with cold tea filled with at least eight spoonfuls of sugar.

Mrs. Whitcom hadn't run the shop in years, her great-granddaughter, Mel, did now. Mrs. Whitcom insisted she still needed to drop in two to three times a week. Cat was glad she's been in today. Mel had looked at the tea and cookies set before Cat and mouthed a silent "Sorry."

With the lingering taste of charcoal in her mouth, Cat went about closing up the back hatch of the truck. It was at that moment she spotted a dark van parked in front of her truck. "What kind of dodgy bullshit is this?" Backing out of this alley would be a real bitch, and all because some asshole decided to block her way.

She was about to walk to the van to see if maybe someone

was sitting inside. As she approached the back doors, rough hands grabbed her from behind. Her mouth was covered, and her body was slammed into the back of the van, pinning her easily.

She tried to thrash and scream but the man holding her only gripped her tighter. There were two, maybe three men. They all were speaking Spanish, which she recognized but didn't understand. The man holding her barked what sounded like an order. He wedged his shoulder between her shoulder blades, which freed his other hand.

Through the tint on the back glass, she saw the image of a hand coming closer with some sort of rag in its fist. The hand closest to her face took it.

Panic, true panic, flooded her then. These men meant to kidnap her. Traffick her, maybe. That rag was bad news. She knew that if it covered her face, she would never see her family again. Cat knew that as sure as the sun would rise tomorrow.

As the hand covering her mouth let up, she didn't bother trying to scream but took a deep breath before the rag was slapped over her mouth and nose. She struggled but barely. Pretending to breathe. Was it chloroform? Like in the movies?

Before she was forced to take a breath, she let her body go limp. The man, still pressing her body into the dirty van, removed the rag. Sweet oxygen. She was careful to take slow, steady breaths in and out. She didn't know how an unconscious person behaved but they would definitely be dead weight. The man picked her up like a baby, and she let her head fall against his chest.

The voices were becoming easier to differentiate. Definitely two men. The one holding her said something in rapid-fire Spanish. Her eyes were closed, but she could hear that they were opening the back doors to the van.

She wasn't expecting to be tossed into the air and almost

gave herself away by screaming. Her body landed, presumably in the van's back hatch. As soon as the doors closed, she opened her eyes to take in the surroundings. She was right about the back, and blessedly, there was a third-row seat shielding her from the men climbing in the front.

She was trying very hard not to panic, though the feeling was riding her hard. She wasn't about to end up another casualty of the illegal skin trade. The van idled for a moment while one of the men placed a call on speaker. She couldn't hear anything. The voices were muffled, but the one who answered also spoke Spanish and was a woman.

The van started to move forward. She heard a blinker. They were definitely about to pull onto the main thoroughfare. She would only have one chance to get out of this, and it hinged on her jumping out of this van into traffic and hopefully finding help.

She was panicked enough that she couldn't tell what direction they were going or when a stoplight might be coming. It was now or never. It was close to noon. Bright. Lots of people. She just had to get out of this van.

Now, Cat. Now, damn it!

She knew an alarm would sound the moment the door opened, and she would need to be prepared to jump immediately. She carefully pulled the handle toward her, praying it opened. It did. She threw the door wide open and jumped ... in the middle of oncoming traffic.

She screamed as a car hit her.

28

Cat's eyes flew open, heart pounding and disoriented. She was lying on the ground, and paramedics were on either side of her shouting orders to ... who knew.

Kidnapped. Jumping out of a moving vehicle. Hit by a car. *Ahh, it was all coming back.*

Ouch.

"Miss. Miss." One of the paramedics leaned over her. "Are you with me?"

If 'with me' meant I hurt like a sonofabitch but was lucid, then "Yes."

She was placed on a gurney and loaded in the back of the ambulance. Her hip was tender, and her calf was on fire. She could only see out of one eye—that worried her the most. She had to force pictures of herself with an eyepatch out of her mind. *Argh! Fear the mighty wee Pirate Kitty Cat.*

The paramedics took their place on either side, taking her vitals and whatever else. "I think I'll be fine. Just maybe a few bruises," Cat offered in a hopeful voice.

"More than a few," the woman paramedic replied dryly.

"Can you tell me what happened?" the woman's male counterpart asked.

"Two men abducted me during a flower delivery and threw me in the back of their van. I think I need the police called."

"Holy fuck," said the young male paramedic.

"Exactly."

∽

Hours upon hours later. "I may be pocket-sized, Officer, but I can assure you that I am well into adulthood. Most of my family is due back within the week. I will inform them of what happened then. I'm safe. I'm sure I'll only have to stay in the hospital overnight.

"I've given you all the information I have. I hope there were cameras in the alley, but we both know that's unlikely. A couple of my employees picked my truck up from the alley once you cleared the scene and took it to the farm. I'll get a lift home in the morning."

The police officers were very kind, and she didn't want to make an undo fuss or cause them more work, but she wasn't about to call her brother during his honeymoon. He would lose his shit and simultaneously ruin the end of their time away. Grandma would never let her leave the farm again. Her parents lived too far away to make a difference. Coll ... no.

"Fine, Miss MacGregor," the older of the two cops relented. "We'll be in touch if we find anything. Your detailed description of the van will help.

"The car that hit you said the van cut off several vehicles fleeing the scene, and they were so worried about hitting you that they didn't pay any attention to the van's number plate. We will be checking whether the intersection's cameras picked up anything."

She thanked the officers profusely. They had been gruff but kind. Finally, she was alone in her hospital room. She took out her compact mirror from her purse to have a better look at herself.

Stanley and Dean, the sweethearts, dropped off her purse and cell phone at the nurse's station with a message that they would come to collect her on the way to work tomorrow.

She caught her wobbly lip between her teeth at their kindness.

She groaned at what her reflection revealed. One side of her face was black, purple, and swollen, and the right eye was swollen shut. "Damn. Damn. Damn." No hiding that eyesore—pun intended.

The car that hit her tried to brake, but no one was expecting a person to jump out of the back of a van in oncoming traffic. She hoped whoever hit her knew it wasn't their fault.

Her right side took the brunt—bruised ribs, bruised hip, and a decent sized laceration on her calf.

All she could think of was what a miracle it was that Thomas and Coll were both out of town.

First things first, she called Grandma. She answered on the first ring.

"How's my Catriona, then? I have a roast simmering on the stove with your name on it."

Cat winced. She hated lying. She really hated lying to Grandma. "That's why I'm calling, Gram. I'm so sorry to cancel dinner plans, but Feodor asked me to eat with him and his parents. We're going to finalize some of the shipping costs for my lotions and sundries."

And sundries ... Was she auditioning for a nineteenth-century period film?

"Oh, how exciting. I'm so proud of you. Don't you worry about the stew. I'll bring some over to you tomorrow. It will make a hearty lunch. Coll mentioned you weren't eating enough."

Kill me. "No need to go to the trouble. If you'd freeze some, I'd be grateful. I'm meeting a client for lunch to discuss wedding arrangements."

"Oh. I see. Of course."

"Okay, I'll talk to you tomorrow. Love you, Gram."

"Love you always, Cat."

Cat felt tears prickle her eyes at the familiar farewell.

She kept a charger in her purse, so she was able to plug her phone in. She put the damning mirror back in her purse and then just kind of ... broke down. She felt her lips quiver, and her eyes began to sting.

It finally hit her. She'd been abducted. Those men had tried to drug her. They'd thrown her in the back of a van. Her body began to shake, and heaving sobs wracked her chest.

It's how a nurse unfortunately found her. Having a breakdown on the downlow while in a hospital wasn't in the cards.

"Miss MacGregor. Here now." The nurse rushed over to plump her pillows and straighten her bedding. Really, there wasn't much else to do for her battered body, but she did appreciate her kindness.

"My name is Patty, and I'm pleased to take care of you while I'm here tonight. I have news that might turn your frown upside down, little miss."

In Nurse Patty's defense, she was as old as God and taller than Big Ben. Any woman under sixty and shorter than six feet were little misses.

"It looks like you'll only need to be with us one night!" She clapped and did a little jig.

Swallowing down a second go-round of tears, she forced her head to bob up and down in encouraging agreement. One night only. In a hospital. All alone. Definitely good news.

"Thank you, Patty. I appreciate how kind everyone's been." This seemed to please the woman to no end.

"Dr. Hoss is doing rotations now and should be in to see you soon. Then, I suggest you rest as you can. I'm sorry to say you'll be getting poked and prodded the rest of the night because of that nasty concussion."

With that joyous announcement, she smiled again and left the room.

And she thought Coll pulling a 'kiss and don't you dare tell' was the worst thing that could happen. Turns out, attempted kidnapping was worse. She dreaded her family finding out for several reasons, but if there was any whiff, a micro-nano of a possibility that it might be connected to the South American woman, Thomas would place her in a backpack and tote her around until she was thirty. Never mind that a gazillion people spoke Spanish. "Bullheaded man."

Earlier, when she'd been wheeled into the emergency room, she was asked all sorts of questions. Name, age, address, allergies, was she pregnant. The nurse had long braids tipped with metal balls that almost created music as they swung and clicked about her hips. She was a no-nonsense woman, so it made it easier to answer the baby question honestly.

"I could be, but I sure as hell hope not."

The nurse snorted in amusement. "We've all been there, eh?"

Eventually, she was wheeled into a curtained bay and told a doctor would be in to see her shortly. It felt like she was lying in the curtained cocoon for days, listening to patients moaning and crying. Cat gathered from the nurses speaking around her that there had been an accident involving a bus, cars, and pedestrians. Horrible.

Eventually, she was seen by a doctor, given something for the pain, and taken to a room on the floor above.

It had given her time to think. Not about the two men in the alley, but about the last time she'd seen Coll. She was still thinking about that hours later.

She should have insisted on taking the morning-after pill. Instead, she threw a tantrum and made Coll feel like he was being flippant about having sex with her. She practically guilted him into not getting it.

Making love to Coll—it was love for her, most likely opportunistic sex for him and maybe a bit ... more—felt like the beginning of a forever. When he so casually mentioned the pill ... she didn't know ... it cheapened the moment.

Regardless of how it made her feel, she'd dismissed his feelings, and that had been wrong. Tears squeezed out of her one good eye. An icepack soaked up the other eye's leakage. The thought of her bruises and aches and pains made her cry harder.

Rock Bottom, meet Catriona MacGregor.

She leaned over to grab her phone from the bedside table, wincing as her body complained about the movement. If this was day one, she shuddered to think how miserable she'd be tomorrow. She was sure the drugs were working as best they could, but it still hurt like hell.

Since Stanley and Dean already knew to pick her up in the morning, she texted Réka to let her know what had happened and to also let her know that Stanley and Dean had no problem working a few extra hours until she and Réka were back on their feet.

She responded immediately with an appropriate amount of horror. Kidnapping certainly tipped the horror scale.

> The police took my statement. I had a description of the van but not much else besides that. There were two men, and they spoke Spanish.

> Are you able to go home soon? I can come sit with you unless Mr. Barr will be staying with you.

> I have to stay overnight because of the concussion. Mr. Barr is out of town, but I'll be fine. Plus, you're sick. Getting better is the only thing you need to worry about right now.

> I'm much better this evening. I had planned on working tomorrow. Let me cook your dinner tomorrow night. Cook. Clean. Anything. Then you can relax and heal faster. I would be honored if you let me help.

Well, jeez, put that way, how could Cat say no? This was definitely a new level of friendship for them. She'd been wanting to get to know Réka better, and this was the perfect opportunity. Well ... perfect would be if they hung out without being run over by a car first.

> That would be really great. Pack a stay over bag and bring it to work. I really appreciate it.

She asked Cat to text her tomorrow morning once she got home before signing off. She set the phone down on her stomach and sighed deeply—that hurt her ribs. "Jesus Christ."

She wanted to call Coll desperately, just to hear his reassuring voice, but they weren't in a relationship, and more, she didn't have the energy to explain ... anything.

Her phone rang, startling her and ripping another curse from her mouth at the jarring movement. Looking at the screen, she moaned. This time, it had nothing to do with her bruises. Thomas. She couldn't not answer. He'd only keep trying.

Deep breath. Upbeat tone. "Hey." Her normal way to answer his calls. *Check.*

"What are you up to tonight?"

Did he sound odd? "I did deliveries this morning. Réka's out sick. Been running around doing errands since. Are you and Jo going to extend your honeymoon again?" she half teased but prayed they were.

"Are you at the farm?"

Deep breath. Keep your cool. "No, I'm still in town. Why? Do you need me to do something for you?"

"I checked the farm's camera feeds to make sure you were at the office before I bothered you. Your truck was there."

Brothers were bad enough. A brother who ferreted out lies for a living was a nightmare. "I ... I ..." *Don't you dare fucking stutter, dumbass.* "I'm actually going out with Feodor. Jo knows him," she was quick to add. "And Coll." She knew she'd need to tell him what happened, but why ruin the end of his special time with his new wife. Not happening.

Chuckling, in what she hoped sounded natural, she added, "A few weeks ago Feodor and I had a double date with Coll and his date. They really got to know each other."

Silence. Cat started to squirm. "Coll agreed to a double date?" His skepticism was warranted.

"I'm sure it was purely to irritate me." That sounded better than the truth. That she'd orchestrated the whole evening out of a disgusting amount of jealousy and then turned it into a way to make Coll jealous. She was really batting a thousand in the bad decision department lately.

Thomas grunted. "Sounds like him. I'm happy to hear he actually asked someone out. If there was ever a man that needed to get laid, it's that stubborn bastard."

"Don't make me vomit by talking about his sex life, or I'll start talking to you about mine." Too late. Thomas' comment about Coll having sex with some rando made her see red, and she spoke without thinking.

"You better not—" She heard Jo's voice in the background. She must be listening to their conversation. "We'll discuss this when I get home."

"Actually, big brother, we won't."

"I can see Grandma's worry was misplaced. You're as cranky as you ever are."

"Grandma called you because I had to cancel dinner plans?" *What the hell, Gram?*

"She said you sounded off."

"I'm fine." *Or I will be once I can move without pain and have the use of both eyes.*

"Okay," he sighed, which made her feel bad for barking at him. "I can't help but worry, Wee Cat."

"I know. Love you."

She was about to hang up when Thomas said, "Hang on, Coll just texted."

And that was when the shit hit the fan.

"Why the fuck are you in the hospital?"

29

Dear Brother,

I need your words of wisdom more in this moment than any other. Our most trusted men have failed us. They had that redheaded bitch that dared to touch you in their grasp—and they let her escape.

I had to punish them. They deserved far worse for tipping our enemies' heads in our direction. The bungled kidnapping will make them put a defensive line around her.

Forgive my rage.

I had planned on playing with her for hours. She would have regretted ever turning her attention in your direction ... to what is mine.

I have never been more thankful for the nursemaid you insisted our parents hire for me. It is due to her diligent teaching as a Brujas that I will not let this setback waylay our victory.

Unfortunately, not all of the coming trouble will stem from the botched job. I was prideful—too sure of myself.

I made a tactical error by sending the demon a present

for her family to find once she went missing. In consequence, I had to call off the man following you, or your body, in London. He was to pick it up after the demon was in my hands.

Now, now, now. Oh, Inti. If I am the cause of prolonging your agony, I will take my life and count it as justice.

There is no longer a way to perform an appropriate bloodletting. The timeline had to change.

I will have to kill her where she feels the most secure.

Home is where the heart is—and where hers will stop beating.

You will be reborn, my love.

Your beloved,
A

30

There was no left turn or right turn, only a walk off the plank. Stanley and Dean were hovering at Cat's elbows as she signed her hospital release forms. She made a mental note to buy them some retired badass Lego set with an appropriate movie to complement it. She'd had to put on her dirty clothes from the day before. It was that or a hospital gown that showcased her ass cheeks.

She had to do a bastardized version of relaxed yoga breathing since she woke up. Her body hurt everywhere. Thomas had been so furious he could barely speak yesterday, eventually handing his phone to Jo. She'd given her new sister-in-law the short version of her kidnapping ordeal, assured her that it was not a situation requiring her brother hulking out on her behalf, and reminding her to tell her brother that she didn't need security.

To which Jo said, "Bitch, please. Thomas is already bellowing at whatever poor security staffers made the mistake of answering their phones. He's back on with Coll, and that asshole is worse than your brother. You'll have security on everything, including your vagina, within the next ten hours."

"For crying out loud, Jo. I'm a little banged up. I wasn't *the* target ... just *a* target that happened to be accessible." She hoped. "The police even believed it was some sort of trafficking bullshit. They were too kind to say, but I do probably look like a 'tween when I wear work clothes, and my hair is in a ponytail."

"Cat, my dear sister, pull your head out of your ass. You know very well there is no reasoning with Thomas when someone he loves is hurt or in danger."

Cat appreciated Jo's bluntness ... most days. Today was not one of them. "My head is completely anus free. I assure you."

"Don't get testy with me. I'm a MacGregor by marriage. You and Thomas are the ones chopped off the 'ole ancestral MacGregor block.'"

Cat couldn't help but snort in amusement at Jo's assholeyness. Feeling her ribs scream in protest sobered her immediately. She was right ... day two was going to be a bitch.

Jo must have heard her moan of pain. "Catriona," she whispered in concern.

She didn't whisper quietly enough because her brother's bellows could wake the dead.

"What the fuck happened, Jo? Tell me, goddammit. How bad is she?" That question must have been meant for his wife. "Christ, Coll. Where the fuck were you? You left my sister alone." And then, "Fuck you. No one made you go to London."

Five minutes of slamming and cursing later—Jo, bless her, was clearly holding the phone out so that she could hear the Tommy show—a Scottish telenovela.

"I know I sent you ... it's Cat, though. Had the bastards managed it ... fuck me ... we might have never seen ... no ... yes ... I've already called the fucking doctors, asshole. They won't tell me a goddamn thing over the phone. I need you there now. Helicopter ... Yes. I want her records from the hospital before I fucking land."

Annnnd, that's where her fight or flight kicked in. *Hello. Pregnancy test!* "Jo," she whisper-screamed, hoping not to alert her maniac of a brother, "I don't want anyone to look at my records. Period. Please."

True to Jo's nature, she didn't waste time on questions. "Thomas," Jo shouted to get his attention, "Neither you nor Coll will access Cat's records without her permission. Don't even try it."

"Why the fuck not?" her brother rejoined.

"What Cat chooses for you to know will be all that you get to know. A woman has the right to privacy. Are we clear?"

"Fine." Back to Coll, he said, "I want to know what we're dealing with. Get the police report, brother, and get to Cat's as soon as possible."

Thomas was having two conversations at once. It killed her that her predicament had ruined the end of their honeymoon.

"Jo. Would you hand the phone back to Tom?" She must have because it was like a bellows of wind hitting her eardrums. "Tommy?" she said with what she hoped was a steady voice.

"I'm here."

Oh God, oh God, oh God. She heard his voice crack with emotion, and that set hers off. Cat had to pinch the bridge of her nose and tip her head back to stem the flow of tears that desperately tried to break free.

"Thomas. Brother mine. I am fine. It scared me. I admit to that, but you taught me well. I didn't panic. Much. I kept my head. I heard your voice telling me what to do. I'm fine," she repeated.

"The thought of—"

"If the worst had happened, you would have found me," she interrupted. "Keep Grandma off my doorstep for a few days, and I will do your yard work for a month." She tried to tease him out of his mood, but she heard his breath hitch once more. Her heart squeezed painfully at her beloved brother's anguish.

Any sibling worth their salt would rather cut off a limb than see a brother or sister suffer. She had to put her frustration with the whole damn situation on the back burner and focus on smoothing Thomas' ruffled feathers.

"I promise I'm fine. You'd barely know a car ran over me. In fact, I plan on working on a new—"

"Shut up, asshole."

"The fuck?" So much for ruffled feather smoothing.

"I was talking to Coll, not you, Cat. Coll is listening to you and didn't know a car ... hit you."

"You can hang up with Coll now. You'll barely know I've been in ... a thing. I held my breath forever, so I didn't even breathe in any of the chloroform," she ended lamely. "They just threw me in the back of the van without tying my hands or anything because they thought I was unconscious. See," she tried for a bit of cheer, "it could have been so much worse."

"Fuck you, Coll. I'm the one who wanted to teach her self-defense and weapons training. You're the one who said she didn't need it because we'd always be there. Well, we weren't there, were we?"

Her reassurances fell on deaf ears. It was still the Thomas & Coll Guilt Show.

"No, damn it. I didn't mean that. I'm sorry."

Men ...

∼

"Ow, ow, ow, ow, ow! Damn it!" Cat's feet were off the ground, and her very sore body was currently smashed against her brother's chest.

"Thomas. Sweetheart. Let your sister down. You're hurting her," Jo said gently.

He didn't let her down. Instead, he picked her up the rest of the way, cradling her in his arms like a baby. Cat looked toward Jo, who just shook her head and shrugged.

Her ever-helpful sister-in-law waved a hand in front of her own face and did a quick swipe down her body before widening her eyes and mouthing, "Yikes."

Yeah ... Cat understood the mime. She looked like hell or like she'd been run over by a car, and her brother didn't like what he was seeing. She'd only had an hour of peace and quiet once she'd gotten home before Thomas had practically torn her front door from its hinges.

She'd been in the kitchen getting some water to take another naproxen-acetaminophen combo for the pain. The doctor would have given her stronger pain meds for a few days, but unfortunately for her, most pain medicines made her extremely nauseous. This particular pain management combination wasn't doing too bad.

She'd hoped to be in bed when her brother storm-troopered his way into the cottage, but no, luck was not currently riding. At all. She was in a sleep tank and shorts, which showed off enough of her injuries to freak her brother out and why she was currently in his arms.

She was about to try again to reason with him when he, honest to God, began to rock her. *Too far, bro.* "Thomas," she began sharply, only to be interrupted.

"Coll is almost here. He's coming straight from the police station where he spoke to the officers that ran your case."

"What?" she squawked. She knew Coll wouldn't stay away, but she'd foolishly hoped he might give her a few hours to herself—maybe she hoped her face wouldn't look like it ... did.

Her face heated, thinking about their exchange last night.

He'd tried to call her twice when she was at the hospital, but she couldn't chance crying when she heard his voice. He began texting when she didn't answer.

> Call me. Now, Cat.

> Everything is fine. Thomas is already ruining the rest of his honeymoon to fly home. I don't need both of you hovering over me.

> Call me. Now.

> Coll! I want to go to sleep. Talk tomorrow.

> Please.

Coll saying please slayed her but not quite enough to put herself through another ass chewing.

> Good night.

> Call me, or I'm calling Grandma.

The asshole left her no choice. She called, damn him.

"Cat." He sounded breathless like he was running. "Talk to me."

And just like she knew would happen, her eyes started to leak. She tried to speak nonchalantly. "I'm fine, Coll. Really."

"Catriona."

His voice shook. He was terribly upset, and that made more tears fall. "Nothing that a good night's sleep won't fix," she lied.

"You're crying, baby. Don't cry. Christ!" He yelled before she heard a thump. He'd hit something.

She heard a slam. It sounded like a truck door. "Despite

what my brother said, you don't need to come home, Coll, seriously."

"The hell I don't. I'm driving it. There wasn't a goddamn helicopter to rent. Some big fancy premier is happening in London and every bloody one of them is in use for either celebs making a grand entrance or the paparazzi. I decided not to waste any more time looking. I'll want my truck anyway because I'll be staying home."

He was making her aching head spin. She stayed quiet, letting a few straggling tears drip from her eyes into her hair. She wouldn't admit it, but just having him on the line made her feel better. Still, he couldn't be allowed to run roughshod over her wants.

She took a deep breath and wiped her eyes. Before she could say anything else, he said, "I know you're still crying. It's killing me. Please just talk to me for a bit so I can hear your voice and calm down."

Okay. "How has the job in London been going?"

"It was a security breach at one of London's poshest clubs. Some of the elite clientele's personal information was stolen before the alarm was sounded, and the hacker was ousted. I was able to find who did it. The police have the scammer in custody now. He was planning on attempting to hack the client's bank accounts. It's what he does. He's very good."

"Not as good as you."

"No."

"I assume the club will be installing MacGregor Security's software."

"Yes."

Back to one-word answers. He must have calmed down to be able to go back to his normal, irritating ways. She refused to say another word. The silence was nice anyway. He was there, and that's all she needed.

Minutes later. "I've missed you."

Cat was taken aback. He was speaking about feelings, out loud and not just through text. To lie or not? Shaking her head at herself. She didn't want to lie. "I've missed you too." His relieved sigh made her smile.

"You'll let me comfort you when I see you."

He didn't phrase it like a question, but she knew the man well enough to hear the uncertainty. There was nothing she wanted more ... but ... "Thomas." She didn't say more. She didn't need to. If Coll showed her attention differently from a normal, concerned family member, her brother would notice. He noticed everything.

She knew it. Coll knew it.

His silence said it all. He still didn't want anyone to know. She was suddenly so exhausted ... and sad. "I'm tired, Coll. Goodbye." She heard him begin to say her name as she hung up.

Now, here she was, cradled in her brother's arms like a newborn, when the front door crashed open for the second time in a quarter of an hour.

"Lord, save this poor sinner," she lamented.

Coll looked like a trainwreck. Not as bad as she did, but his bloodshot eyes and rumpled menace spoke of a sleepless night. His eyes fell on her, taking in her half-bruised and swollen face, contusions, scrapes, and the stitches on her calf.

His eyes went wide with shock and horror. Thomas held her so that her right side was out. Good thing Coll couldn't see her ribs or hip.

He didn't acknowledge anyone in the room. Jo watched in wide-eyed wonder. Thomas just kept patting her back and jostling her up and down in a parody of rocking comfort.

Coll stalked within two feet of them before demanding, "Give her to me."

31

Coll wanted to weep at the state of Catriona. Her body was so battered and bruised, and she was clearly in pain as her behemoth of a brother—Coll was the same size, but still—crushed his sister in his giant arms. Coll could see her wince each time Tommy's paw tried to smash her head to his chest.

"Give her to me," he repeated. Stepping close enough to smell the sweet, earthy plant smell that was Cat.

"Fuck off. I clearly have her. She's my sister," Thomas growled. Territorial as usual.

"She's my ..." Oh shit. She was my what? "She's my ... family too." He pretended not to see the hurt in Cat's eyes. Damn him for the pathetic, non-committing coward that he was.

Thomas was about to hand her over, but Cat put a hand up, stopping the exchange. "Thomas. Set me on my feet."

"You shouldn't be walking around."

Coll could see a storm brewing on Cat's face. Tom wasn't reading the signs.

"I appreciate your opinion, Dr. MacGregor, but I most certainly can walk."

Thomas clasped her tighter to his chest. A small moan

slipped out of Cat's mouth. He was moving to intervene, but it wasn't necessary. Thomas heard her and looked stricken at hurting his sister.

"I'm sorry." Thomas grimaced, glancing at his wife with a look of horror.

He carefully set her on her feet, but Cat was too loving to let her brother feel bad. She took his hand in both of hers, making him look at her.

"Thank you for loving me, Thomas." At his sigh of relief, she asked Jo to sit on the couch with her.

"Before we talk about anything to do with yesterday, I'm dying to hear about all the fun things you guys did on your honeymoon. Though from your gorgeous tans, I'd say it included a lot of lying about that gorgeous resort."

Thomas and Jo spent their honeymoon at a luxury resort in Athens, Greece. Even Coll felt some envy at the stunning views from the pictures they'd sent the family. When he'd spoken to Thomas on occasion, Coll could tell that the time away had been exactly what the newlyweds had needed.

Neither of them had an easy path to the aisle. Coll could understand why Cat hadn't wanted to tell either of them about her near abduction. She wouldn't have wanted to overshadow their honeymoon.

Jo spent half an hour describing the sights, activities, and their explorations. Jo was giving Cat the momentary reprieve she'd asked for. Coll would rather categorize each and every bruise and scrape on her body, but it was clear Catriona needed to talk about something happy before discussing police reports. He would give her whatever time she needed.

"The food, Lord Cat, the food was divine. I don't know if it's the mini MacGregor I'm growing, but if I hadn't gone there already sporting a bump, I would have left with a food baby anyway." Jo grinned at Thomas.

It was fascinating for Coll to see a man he'd known his entire life, who rarely smiled, full-on grin at his wife.

"Oh, I almost forgot." Jo started, clapping her hands in excitement. "I may have met your future husband, Cat. Thomas and I met the family that owns the resort during dinner one night. It was a special chef's table evening, where the resort's chef cooked several courses for a few guests under a pavilion that looked out over the stunning Aegean Sea.

"Anyway, Lucas and his family own resorts all over the world, but they're all from Greece. Lucas is a commercial lawyer who handles the family's legal business."

Coll would chip his teeth if he ground them together any harder. He was sitting on an old, rickety wooden chair that was set to the side of the couch. It creaked loudly as he adjusted his weight forward. Cat was studiously avoiding looking his way. He glanced at Thomas, who didn't look thrilled as Jo waxed on about all of Lucas' amazing qualities.

"He's got dark wavy hair and lovely olive skin. He smiles and laughs a lot. The whole family does. They're all lovely. I'd place him at around five feet nine or ten inches, which would be a fine height for you. He's athletically built, all smooth muscles. I saw him one day at the pool. Let me see, what did I forget?"

Josephine tapped her lip in thought. He was so annoyed listening to the Lucas' Greatest Hits Show that he was perspiring. He looked at Thomas, who met his glance. Coll gave him a 'what the fuck is this, and why aren't you shutting this shit down' look. His friend only shrugged in defeat. Useless.

"Oh, right!" Great. Jo remembered more. "Lucas is twenty-eight and single. I told him about you and even showed him a couple of pictures from our girls' night out. He was very interested then. But the best part is that his family has a personal greenhouse that he personally helps to tend. A lot of the flower arrangements seen around the resort are ones he's grown.

"I told him about MacGregor Farm. Luckily, Thomas had some pictures. Well? What do you think? He gave me his number to give to you if you'd like to meet. He said he'd fly here anytime."

That was it. All he could take. He wanted to give Cat time to relax, but instead, he stood, grabbing everyone's attention. "Why would Cat be interested in some playboy from Greece? Christ! The man looks at a couple pictures, which I personally don't think you should be sharing with strangers, and he wants her number. What the hell is that?" He throws his arms wide in exasperation, hoping he's made his point clear.

Jo and Cat looked at him like he'd lost his mind. He felt like he had. In his unhappy, growly voice, Thomas admitted, "I thought the same. I researched the family and Lucas specifically that night. They were clear." He sounded disappointed. Not as disappointed as Coll was.

"What the hell, Thomas? Is that the night you said you had some work to take care of?" Jo was not happy.

"It was work," Thomas defended.

"No more discussing my personal life, please. Send me his number, Jo. Thank you for thinking of me." He and Thomas were about to protest, but Cat shook her head. "Thomas, I warned you that if you didn't stop overstepping, I would make you listen to my sexcapades."

Coll felt his body stiffen in shock at her pronouncement. Her eyes clashed with his briefly before turning to Jo.

"It would be nice to meet a man who isn't embarrassed to acknowledge interest in me."

His chest seized. He'd pushed her to this. He had to look away and out the window to regain his composure. He was seconds away from grabbing her off the couch and *acknowledging* his interest.

"I'm glad you guys had such a great time. I'm just so sorry you had to rush home for me."

"Nothing is more important than family. Don't apologize again. Plus," Jo smiled, "Thomas and I would both have kicked your ass if we hadn't known to come home."

Cat attempted to roll her good eye and smiled back. "I'd like to hear what you learned at the police station, Coll. I wouldn't think they would have been able to tell you anything about it since we aren't related."

Coll felt his face heat as her attention focused on him. "They know Thomas and I from when we helped Interpol on a case." He refused to bring up that the Inverness officers helped him and Thomas bag the man who had assaulted Jo years ago and who'd planned on kidnapping her. He would never do or say anything that would trigger bad memories for her.

Jo's trauma made Thomas extra tetchy and protective with all the women in the family, and he'd already been borderline obsessive. Coll considered himself to be the more reasonable of the two men.

"If our acquaintance hadn't worked, your brother instructed me to tell them that you and I are handfasted Pagans."

"The hell? Why would you suggest such a ridiculous thing?" Both women were eyeing the men like they were dropped from another planet.

Thomas defended himself. "It's true. If you claim you're Pagan, couples can have a handfasting ceremony, and the damn country accepts it. I didn't make up the law."

"No, you just would have the citizens of Inverness believe Coll and Cat are married heathens!" Jo choked on a laugh.

"Jesus, Tommy, if Grandma ever found out you even considered fake besmirching our good Catholic name, she'd take a belt to your ass." Cat shook her head in wonder.

Coll was glad he shared that bit. It was worth seeing Cat

smile. "They don't have much more to go on," Coll explained. He then went over the little information they did have.

There were no cameras in the alley where she was taken. "They knew from Cat that there were two Spanish speaking men involved. Cat did have a good description of the van. They found a van matching that description early this morning in the parking lot of a derelict hostel. It had been drenched in petrol and set on fire.

"No prints or anything else for that matter were left. That leads to more questions. If they were traveling traffickers, just opportunistic men on the lookout for easy marks, why burn the van? They could have just as easily put a considerable amount of distance between them and Inverness and stolen another vehicle down the road."

"They may have thought their number tag was made as well as a description of the vehicle," Thomas thought out loud.

"Or ..." Coll began.

"They are locals," Thomas finished.

"The detective I spoke with mentioned another big case they were currently working on, and Cat's case was stretching them thin."

"They wouldn't have been able to tell you anything about the other open case. Damn," Thomas cursed under his breath. "Until this is resolved in some way, shape, or form, lass, you can't live on your own."

Coll watched as Cat's hackles rose. He was only thankful it wasn't him who brought up the obvious. "I can move back in." He tensed, waiting for her reaction. From her stiffened shoulders and curled fists, he knew he wouldn't like her answer.

"Thank you, but it won't be necessary. Réka is feeling better and came back to work this morning. She brought a bag of her things to work and will be staying with me for a few days." Thomas was about to disagree, but his sister spoke over him.

"She's not in a great living situation with her elderly cousin. Living here would help me and her. It's a perfect solution. Plus, Coll installed cameras over the whole farm."

Coll couldn't gainsay her reasoning. It was sound, but he wanted badly to live together again. He was aware of how selfish that was.

"I'm actually so tired, guys. Would you mind if I kicked you all out?" She chuckled dryly. "Réka is coming here straight from the farm after work. I hope to make it into the office tomorrow morning to at least open the mail and move some appointments around."

Jo instantly stood and leaned over to kiss her sister-in-law on the cheek and give her a hug. "Thomas and I haven't been home in a while, and I'm not too woman enough to admit this pregnancy is wiping me out."

Josephine O'Connor MacGregor was not even close to being wiped out, but she knew Catriona needed a moment and wanted to give it to her.

Coll looked toward Thomas to gauge his reaction. He barely moved his head in the negative, but it was enough.

"I don't want you by yourself all day, Wee Cat. I won't budge on it." Thomas crossed his arms over his chest, clearly bulling up. Catriona knew arguing would be futile. "Coll will stay the day and come back every day until your case is closed."

It was almost exactly what he wanted. He wanted the days and the nights, but again, he was too much of a pussy to make his real feelings known. He was smart enough not to comment. He would let the siblings fight it out.

Thomas would win.

With a world class eyeroll, Cat spit out, "If Coll has nothing better to do with his days, and you are committed to bullying me, then there isn't anything else to say."

"I am a bully," Thomas confirmed.

"I don't have anything better to do," Coll added.

32

Cat was hurting and tired and desperately wishing Coll's strong arms were holding her. She'd maintained a brave face as long as she could. The last twenty-four hours had taken a toll. She needed a dark room and a box of tissue.

Her brother and Jo left with promises to call later. Thomas warned her to expect Grandma on her doorstep sooner rather than later. She didn't even whine about it. Grandma knew something was up from the get-go. It was honestly shocking that she wasn't there now.

She'd been staring off into space when Coll's deep voice startled her. "Catriona. Will you let me sit by you?"

Here come the waterworks. She nodded, not trusting her voice not to crack.

"Cat, Cat, Cat." He repeated in a thick voice. His emotions were as raw as hers were, and he was letting her see them. He bent over gently and scooped her into his arms.

Right where she needed to be.

He sat back on the couch and cradled her so that her left side was touching him, giving her bruises room. The warmth of his body gradually seeped into her muscles, and she was able to relax.

He finger-combed the knots out of her hair and massaged her scalp as he went. It felt like Heaven.

He finally spoke, and it broke her heart to hear the emotion. "I wish you had called me."

"I wish I had too." He seemed satisfied with her answer, gently running his thumb across her lips.

With one arm, he snuggled her to his chest, stood from the couch, walked a few feet to the front door, and grabbed a bag off the floor. She hadn't noticed him bring it in earlier, but then she only had eyes for him.

Without a word, he went to her bedroom and laid her down on the bed. He went to the closet and turned on the light, closing the door until there was enough light to see but not enough to blind. Just like she'd done for him the night she'd given him a massage. Next, he shut and locked her bedroom door. Cat felt her brows wing up at this but continued to stay silent to see what he had planned.

He grabbed a pair of sweatpants from his bag and tubes of ... something and a paper bag and put them on the foot of the bed where he was standing. Pulling his pant leg up, he took his prosthesis off and then his jeans.

Cat's body was miserable, *but damn*, Coll in boxer briefs had interest stirring in her body. She sighed as he sat on the bed, putting an end to her ogling. He slipped his sweats on and took a moment to roll up the bottom half of the right leg.

He stood like he was about to walk, shook his head, and sat back down. "No crutch," he admitted ruefully.

Cat swallowed any emotion with even a hint of pity. He'd forgotten for a moment about his injury. "I got you a knee walker." She could feel her cheeks burn and nervously cleared her throat.

He slowly looked over his shoulder at her. "Did you, now?"

"The forum I'm a member of suggested it. Along with a few other things." Her voice became quieter as her embarrassment grew louder in her head.

His hand enfolded her left foot. "Thank you. What is the name of this illustrious group you're a part of? I'd like to join."

No way in hell. "Oh, no. I'm sure there are a million other groups that you would like better. It's mostly women in mine."

"I want to be in yours. What's it called?" When she remained silent, he doubled down. "I have your phone tracked, lass. I can get into it anytime I want and find the group all by myself. Or you could just tell me."

Cat was gearing up to tear him a new one for tracking her, so he assured, "I would not invade your privacy unless it was a matter of your safety."

"Oh really? How did you find out I was in the hospital?" He'd turned on the bed so he was completely facing her, and that's how she caught his grimace. "Spill."

"I sometimes pull up the cameras at the farm. Not all the time," he defended as if she'd spoken. "You were gone a long time and then Stanley and Dean brought your truck home late and you weren't there ... I ... worried."

"What exactly were you worried about?"

"That you might be on a date. With Feodor."

Cat might have felt bad that he still believed she and Feodor were interested in one another, but finding out he'd been watching her on the damn cameras negated her guilty conscience.

"I shouldn't have looked at your phone," he growled grudgingly, "but I'm glad I did. You were hurt and by yourself."

She knew she'd scared everyone, so she couldn't argue his logic. Well, she could, but she wouldn't. "Fine. This one time. We'll talk about your camera privileges later."

"What's the name of the group?"

Good night, the man was relentless. "Military Wives of Amputees." Her blush was severe enough to make her swollen eye throb. "I told the ladies immediately that I was not your wife or ... or anything else," she stammered. When he started to chuckle, she kicked his hand off her foot. "Don't you dare make fun of me."

He spun on the bed and crawled close to her body, careful to stay on her unbruised left side. Ignoring her protests, he took her hand and placed it against his chest. "I would never. It's only that I'm amazed at the lengths you've gone to help me. You are a marvel, Kitty Cat. That's all."

That soothed most of her feathers. "Okay."

"Where is the walker?" He looked around the bedroom like he might find it hiding in the small space.

"Everything's in my workshop. I didn't expect you home yet. Not my home," she corrected, flustered, "but home to Bunchrew." Wanting to change the subject, she asked what he'd put at the end of the bed.

"Right." He reluctantly let her hand go so he could reach for the stuff. "I stopped by Boots before I came here and picked up some ice packs and Arnica cream. You told me once that Arnica is good for bruising. I knew you made your own, and it's surely better than this, but I didn't know where to look, so."

He was rambling. Coll wasn't a rambler. He was nervous. "That's very thoughtful. I should have thought of it myself. Help me sit up, and I'll put—ouch."

"Damn it, Cat. Don't move. I planned on putting it on."

He touched her face with such tenderness that moisture tickled her eyes.

"I'm going to take your clothes off. You said most of your right side has bruises."

He was trying to act like it was every day that he suggested getting her naked, but his hands kept flexing on his thighs. She heard her soft breaths turn into shallow pants. Coll must have heard because he swallowed deeply.

He didn't say anything while he took the straps of her night cami from her shoulders and slowly drew them down her arms until she could pull free. Instead of taking it over her head, he pulled it down. Her breasts were freed as he slipped it further south. She heard him whisper, "Christ." Her nipples were so painfully erect that she almost begged him to touch them.

He never broke the glide of fabric over her skin. Her shorts were snagged as the shirt went over her hips, and from one blink to the next, he was pulling both garments over her feet.

"Oh, God, baby. You must be hurting. I wish I could take your pain." He hovered his fingers over the worst of the bruises. "I won't be as good as you at massage, so you'll have to tell me if I'm too rough."

She was hurting, uncomfortable, and exhausted ... despite all that, she found her mouth suddenly too dry to swallow just thinking about having Coll's hands on her flesh. She watched as he squeezed some cream into his palm and worked it between his hands like he'd seen her do.

She'd been expecting him to ask if she was pregnant. He would probably like to know, and because she felt so guilty about the pill debacle, she wanted to put him out of his misery. She touched his arm, stilling his movements. "They took blood at the emergency room for a pregnancy test."

His eyes snapped to her stomach. "Are ... are—"

"They would have told me if I had been," she cut him off. "I just ... I didn't want you to worry. I'm sorry I didn't get the pill when you wanted me to. It was selfish."

"No," he denied, shaking his head. "I did sound like I took what we did lightly. Like it was just sex. That's not how I felt."

When he set his warm hand briefly on her flat stomach,

something warm passed between them. Perhaps the tiniest bit of regret.

"I'll start with your face, lass." He adjusted his knee, kneeling close to her left side, and started dabbing Arnica carefully around her eye and cheek. "When I'm through, we'll get an ice pack on your eye, and hopefully, you'll be able to see better out of it tomorrow."

Cat could only nod. Coll Barr nursing her with such care left her speechless. His hands were always warmer than her own, and by the time he'd moved from her face to her shoulder, shoulder to ribs, then ribs to waist, she was all but a limp bit of flotsam floating in an ocean of content.

Her hip was particularly sore, especially over her hip bone. Coll's strong fingers were firm, but his ministrations were a perfect blend of soft to medium. He was careful not to intrude too close to the four stitches on her calf so by the time he reached her toes she was melted wax ... melted stimulated wax.

She knew she looked like a trainwreck. For heaven's sake, half her body was a discolored mess, but Coll had magic hands. He didn't need the five months she'd taken to receive her School of Massage degree. He was a natural.

Her body felt as pliant as butter and as sensitive as a woman denied pleasure for weeks, which she was.

Coll cleaned his hands and leaned back, stretching his back and shoulders—massage was hard work. He never took his eyes off her naked body, and in consequence, her back arched, and her legs widened.

"Cat," his whisper was pained. He knew exactly what she wanted, and if the bulge in his pants was anything to go by, he wanted the same thing. "You're hurt."

33

"Please, Coll. Your massage has made me halfway to coming already. Just go slow. I need you," Cat begged.

Coll had already been losing control from his body's reaction to touching her bare skin—

coupled with the panic that had been riding him hard the whole night ... his resistance was barely registering.

"I want you naked so I can see your gorgeous body. I want your mouth on mine. I want you inside my body."

This was a side of Cat he'd never dreamed existed. He should have known she would vocalize her wants. She never held back in any other part of her life. Why would sex be different?

Holding her eyes, he pulled his T-shirt over his head and tossed it to the side. Pushing up to a kneeling position, he pushed his sweats and boxers over his hips until his erection bobbed free, its glistening head already covered in precum, swollen and throbbing.

It was quick work to pull one pantleg over his stump and then the other. He hadn't even tossed the pants away before Cat used her closest hand to stroke his length.

"Christ, baby, that feels good." When she flicked her thumb over his slit, playing in his moisture, he released a deep groan, the rumble vibrating his chest.

"Spread your legs as best you can. I want to see how ready you are for me." Her left knee dropped, red curls sat perfectly above her smooth, damp slit. "So wet." He brushed fingers over her folds before sliding one and then two fingers in.

She tried to lift her hips, but he saw her wince and placed a staying hand on her abdomen. "No. You do nothing," he demanded.

She raised her brows at the order. He didn't stop pumping in and out of her body. Her breathing was turning more frantic. She kept her eyes on what he was doing to her body while she swiped her thumb over his head again, gathering some cum before bringing it to her mouth and licking her thumb clean.

His dick jerked at the erotic vision. She told him, "I've dreamed about us a lot."

"Were we having sex?"

"Every type of sex. Everything."

Coll grunted as he felt her channel grow tighter and wetter around his fingers. She liked thinking about her dreams. "We'll try everything you've dreamed of. I need a list. As soon as you're well. We'll start ticking them off."

"Coll, please. I'm close. I want you."

He maneuvered between her legs, taking his fingers out of her sex. He leaned over her body and placed them next to her mouth. "Help me clean up first." Even with her battered face, he'd never seen a woman more beautiful. There was no hesitation when he slid his fingers past her lips. As her tongue curled around his digits, her soft panting moans would be his undoing if he didn't get inside her soon.

He had to calm down, or he would never last. He cupped

the non-bruised side of her face and took her mouth. Their tongues languished together, twisting and licking and sucking, so slow, sensually gentle.

He searched the bed around him until he found the box of condoms he'd picked up when he was shopping for Cat's Arnica. Technically, the condoms were shopping for her too. She watched in fascination as he fisted his length and rolled the rubber on.

"I've never seen a man do that. It looks … restrictive."

Coll grunted in amusement. "Bare is better. You're … I've never had sex without a condom. Before you."

"As soon as I don't look so scary, I'll make an appointment with my gyno. I want it to feel good for you," she added quietly.

"Oh, baby." He grinned at the red-haired goddess spread naked before him. "I'll take you any way I can get you, and trust me, Kitty Cat, it all feels good. Better than good." On his knees, he rested his ass on his angled left foot. Not having two feet to lean on was slightly awkward but doable.

"I'm not going to lay over you. I don't want to risk bumping your bruises," he explained. They shouldn't be doing this at all, but he couldn't deny her anything, and his body was screaming at him to take, take, take.

Slowly, he cupped her ass, sliding her up his thighs until they were sex against sex, skin to skin. They both moaned. She tried to rub against his erection. "No, Cat. If we do this, I'm the only one who gets to move. You'll take what I give you. Only."

"Fine," she said breathlessly as he began arching his hips, rubbing his hardness between her folds. "Fine," she said again, the husky quality to her voice making his skin pebble in gooseflesh, "but just know that my sexual position list is long and varied, and I definitely won't be a silent partner in those."

"God, baby, your imagination is more than I deserve and

everything I plan on taking advantage of," he said as his big hands gripped her ass to anchor her center where he wanted. He rubbed himself in long, sure strokes through her hot, wet folds and across the bundle of nerves that made her suck in air at each caress.

"Coll. Please."

"No need to beg, baby. I've wanted back inside you since the second I pulled out over two weeks ago." He'd lost count of the times he'd jacked off in his London rental with thoughts of her hot, little body.

He stopped teasing them both, finally lining their bodies up and gradually pushing. Her tight sheath had his molars grinding and the veins on his neck throbbing. It was pain and excruciating pleasure.

Christ. His whole body was shaking. Watching himself disappear inside Cat MacGregor's body was a hedonistic experience. Give this up? Never.

He went slow, so slow. In and out and in and out again. The sweet drag of his dick, the clenching muscles of her core ... he wanted to move in her like this forever.

There was something at the periphery of his thoughts that made him bury himself to the hilt before stalling out. Her eyes popped open at his stillness.

"Coll?"

His chest heaved with sensation and stuttered with emotion. "Are you dating Feodor?" He had no right to ask. No right to this debilitating jealousy. None.

He hadn't claimed her publicly. He hadn't claimed her privately. He *had* claimed her in his dreams ... *Jesus, man. You can't claim her.* Not yet.

She watched him with eyes that saw too much, but she was always one that could keep her own counsel when she chose.

"No," she sighed heavily, barely pumping her hips to get him to move.

"No?"

"He knows it's you I love, Coll Barr. Now fucking move before I make my tender skin impossibly worse by moving for you," she warned.

She'd told him that she loved him before. They'd always loved each other, though, as family. She didn't mean a brotherly type of love. Of course, she didn't. That would be disgusting, and what they were doing was far from that. She loved him, loved him. He should feel trapped. He didn't.

"For fuck's sake. My vagina can hear your brain trying to work overtime. I'm not asking for a damn marriage proposal. Move, or I'll take over," she threatened.

He shook his head like a dog, shaking water from their ears. He resumed his patient in-and-out draw, bringing them both back to moaning messes.

"God, baby, I want to wreck you, but ..."

"I'm already wrecked. Just not in a good way," she teased.

He flattened his palm against her sensitive flesh and continued to fill her body with his own. Even with the relaxed pace, his cock was swelling, sending signals of finishing.

"Not long, baby," he warned.

"Just a little harder." She panted, grasping his thighs to pull him harder, faster.

He shouldn't, but he complied. In, out, in, out, harder, then harder again, bodies slapping in an age-old rhythm ... clap, clap, clap until ... her body climaxed, milking him until he lost everything ... the time, the place, his name ...

He filled the condom with pulse after pulse, wishing it was her womb he was flooding.

Cat was his lodestone. His way home. His true north.

Seconds, minutes, maybe hours passed with him still holding her ass—with them still connected. Finally, he reluctantly pulled out and peeled the condom off, tying his cum unto a ball to be disposed of.

He would rather it be sitting in Cat's body, and wasn't that a dick thing to consider when he wouldn't even acknowledge their relationship.

Silently, he dressed Cat back in her PJs and straightened the covers around her body, carefully tucking her in, attempting to ignore the fact that he'd just had sex with a woman who was almost drugged and abducted twenty-four hours ago.

Now, he stood by the bed, carefully hunched over her upper body. "I could have lost you." His breath caught in his throat as he pressed his face into the crook of her neck. "If you'd been taken ... if that car ... If you'd died, Cat, I don't know if I could have recovered. I would be in that grave with you," he whispered, like he was in confession, she a priest to his sinner.

Cat ran her hand down his right thigh until she could grasp the stump. "If you hadn't come back from this ... if you hadn't come back to me ... I would never have been whole."

His truths seemed awfully close to an admission of love. Commitment. Forever. Publicly claiming one another.

He shook his head at his tangled thoughts. It was good he was leaving her side because there was no clear thinking to be had while he looked into her bright green eyes.

"Grandma will be here in thirty minutes, and if I don't get this room opened and aired out, she's not too old to have forgotten what sex smells like."

"Oh my God, Coll. Don't even threaten the possibility."

Cat's blushing cheeks made him grin as he put his prosthesis on. "Oh, so you want me to fess up to your brother, but telling Grandma has you tucking your tail and running," he teased.

Her smile dimmed, and he felt his chest tighten. *What a stupid fucking thing to say, Barr.*

"Tommy doesn't need to know. After my accident yesterday, I've been doing a lot of thinking."

He could tell he wasn't going to like her revelation. "Oh?"

"Yeah. We can keep our …" she hesitated. Had she been about to say relationship? It felt like one. "We can keep what we do together a secret. I only want to be with you, Coll. Whatever way it looks like is enough for me."

He should feel relieved.

He was pissed instead.

She was settling, and he didn't want her to. He situated her icepack, giving himself a moment to consider her words. He walked to the closet, shut the light off, and opened the bedroom door. He leaned on the jamb and crossed his arms over his chest. She contemplated him from her one good eye while he broodily looked at her.

"I don't want us to be a secret," he finally managed. "You mean more than that to me."

"I know I do, but we are new."

"I've wanted you for over two years."

"And I've wanted you for much longer. Let's agree to discuss it. Maybe when my accident isn't fresh in our minds."

As suggestions went, it was sound. Still … He cleared his throat, suddenly nervous. "We can discuss things, but," he shifted his weight and smoothed his hands down his T-shirt, "I'd like us to have an understanding."

"About?"

Cat was trying not to smile. She knew very well he was struggling. "I've dated. Before." That took the smile from her face. Discussing feelings was clearly not his forte. "What I meant to say was that I've never been serious with anyone. While we work ourselves out, I want us to at least know."

"Know what, Coll?"

He sighed and looked at the ceiling briefly before returning to her slightly bemused yet confused face. "Until we figure out if we are going to tell people or when, I should have said." Her crestfallen look was there and gone again. *Idiot, Coll.* "Jesus, Cat. I only meant to be saying that I want us to know that we are a couple. A couple who only sees each other." He thought to tack that last bit on.

"If you're sure."

She didn't look sure. More skeptical than anything. He didn't blame her. "I'm sure."

"Then ... we are ... together."

"Yes." He moved back by her side of the bed to give her one more kiss goodbye. It was supposed to be a gentle sealing of the pact they'd just made. It became dirty and desperate. "Christ, Cat. What you do to me." He reluctantly pulled back, adjusting his hard-on as he retreated.

"Take a nap, Kitty Cat, and text me when you wake up. I'll be around."

"Should I text you something on my list?"

He had to swallow a moan. "You aren't helping my dick go down, baby, and I hear a car. You wouldn't want Grandma to catch us in a compromising position."

Her eyes went comically wide before whisper-shouting, "Oh my God. Get out, get out. Get out! And take the damn condoms with you, neanderthal!"

He'd already slipped them into his pocket. He chuckled as he left her room, grabbing his duffel as he went. He was startled to see the gardener who always wore head scarves slipping out the front door. What the hell had Réka Farkas been doing in the house?

He was about to chase after her even though Cat would kill him when he noticed a small, scuffed-up suitcase by the door.

The skittish woman was dropping her things off and probably planned on checking in with Cat. Still, he didn't like someone coming into this house without his knowledge. He needed to be more vigilant.

He also needed to do a more thorough background check on the woman. He was just thinking that he and Thomas could work on it together that evening when Grandma burst through the door. A dozen sacks of groceries and pots and pans hung every which way from her body.

Her eyes landed on Coll. He would have sworn her eyes flicked to his duffel. The woman didn't miss a thing.

"Oh good, you're still here. I've a crockpot in the backseat. Fetch that for me. I left dinner warming for you, Tom, and Jo. You can take that over as soon as you leave here."

His marching orders given, she began filling Cat's kitchen with enough food and snacks to feed half of Inverness.

He ran out and grabbed the pot and was in time to see Réka round the corner of one of the greenhouses. "Odd woman," he said to himself.

He took the crockpot to the kitchen for Grandma to plug in where she would. He found the older woman standing still, her hands threaded together and shaking. "Gram?" He sat the pot down and took her hands in his.

She shook her head and took a deep breath before looking up at him. "I'm fine. After what Thomas told me ... I just have to keep reminding myself that my wee girl is safe."

He understood. "She looks bad, but you know Cat. She's tough. Your food will set everything else to rights. I got her Arnica cream, and that seemed to soothe her skin, and I have an icepack on her eye now."

"Good. That's good." She went back to organizing the kitchen.

"I'm taking off now. That Réka woman is staying the night, but I'm not sure about that."

"No worries, lad. I'll be staying late. I won't leave if I think she needs me."

He pulled open the door and was about to leave when Gram spoke again. "Oh, and Colly. Your shirt is wrong side out, sweetheart." He whipped his head around, but she was already turning. He swore he saw her smile. *Oh, shit.*

34

> I'm going to my workshop this morning. Réka spoiled me with breakfast in bed, but I can't look at this depressing excuse for a bedroom another minute.

Wait another day.

Coll's unsurprising response.

> Not a chance. Thomas is on his way to carry me to the office. That was not a joke. Make him stop.

No one can make Thomas MacGregor do anything he doesn't want to do.

> Last time I checked, Coll Barr falls under the same classification.

I miss you.

Cat felt her heart squeeze, and giddy 'new relationship'

bubbles fizzed through her bloodstream. She was embarrassingly in love with Coll. She believed he had finally accepted that her love was much more than familial, but he was clearly still wrestling with his feelings.

She'd been working through her emails and orders since early this morning and had already sent Réka off with the daily delivery schedule. She was dressed and sitting at the kitchen table waiting on her damn brother.

The Arnica had done wonders. She was less achy this morning, and she could see out of her right eye again. She reapplied the cream, not nearly as well as Coll had. She still looked like crap, but she was optimistic that the worst was behind her.

> Come see me. I miss you too.

> I have another hour and a half of work, and then I'll be there.

> I think Grandma suspects something is going on between us.

> She does.

Christ, kill me and incinerate my body. Cat knew it. She flipping knew it. Grandma had been cagey. All secret smiles and winks. After she cried over Cat's bruises for an hour ... but still. Cagey AF after that.

She decided it was best not to think of Grandma.

> I'm going to pretend you didn't say that. Wear something that gives me easy access to your legs.

> You want access?

> Mmhmm. Bring the ginger massage oil. Oops. Thomas is here. Gotta go.

She grinned. Coll would struggle to work thinking about the massage that was waiting for him. She'd just dropped her phone and laptop in a tote when her brother waltzed in—without bothering to knock. Brothers took tremendous patience.

He walked to the table where she was sitting and gently touched her chin to lift her face to his. He cleared his throat and swallowed. "It's a little bit better, I suppose."

She couldn't wait for the bruises to be gone. Mostly so Thomas would stop getting upset by them. "It is. I feel better today.

"How's Jo feeling? When I spoke with her last night, she said she'd been struggling with indigestion." She switched the topic to one of his favorites. Josephine.

"Nothing worked that the doctor said to do. I'm thinking of getting a new one," he grumbled.

Cat tried to cover her chuckle by clearing her throat. The problem with her brother was that he was serious. "I thought of something this morning that might help." His eyes lit instantly. "Grab my tote, and I'll tell you while we *walk* to my office."

He opened the door, but the moment she set a toe outside, Thomas scooped her up. He even had the nerve to say, "Up you go." He obviously parked at her office to make sure he could carry her. He was trying to get a rise out of her, one of his favorite things. She didn't say a word.

Doing her best to ignore the indignity of her employees seeing her being carted around, she explained what she'd thought of for Jo. "I did flowers for a grand opening last year for a woman who opened a quaint little baby shop. Tera is in charge of the baby clothes and gadgets, but her sister Tara makes sweets for pregnant moms.

"She also has a line of suckers for anything from nausea, heartburn, indigestion, constipation, and whatever else a pregnant woman might have. There was a write-up a few months ago on Facebook. Moms swear by her suckers. I should have thought of it sooner.

"Grab my phone out of my tote, and I'll give the store a call and tell them you'll be stopping by." If there was a chance he could provide his wife with something to make her feel better, Cat knew he'd be out the door as soon as he settled her behind her desk.

As soon as her phone was unlocked, a text from Coll was waiting. She swiped it off the screen, deciding not to chance big bro reading over her shoulder. She found the number and by luck, Tara answered. She explained that her sister-in-law was in need of her suckers.

She put the phone on speaker. "My brother is with me now," practicing his baby-holding technique, "and he'll be the one coming to see you."

"We'll get his wife fixed up in no time! My stock is full. When he gets here, we'll go over any and all of her symptoms and go from there."

"This is Cat's brother, Thomas. I'll be there shortly. I appreciate it."

"Of course, Thomas. No problem. And maybe when she's feeling better, Cat, you can bring her by the store. Tera has a whole new line of uber soft cotton baby blankets she won't stop going on about, plus a million other lovely things."

"I will. Definitely. Talk to you soon. Thank you."

"She seems nice. I hope it works."

"Tara knows her way around health and healing." They'd arrived at the office, and Thomas said he'd already remotely turned off the alarm and unlocked the front door. She gritted her teeth so that a snarl couldn't escape.

Coll and Thomas, the Kings of Overstepping. *They mean well. They mean well. They mean well.* Chanting that to herself over the years had saved a lot of confrontations. Tommy had better stay out of her texts, though, unless he wanted to overstep into his sister and best friend's sexting.

"Just set me down and put my tote on the desk, please. You'd better run to the baby shop. Tara's expecting you."

He set her down, fiddling with her chair's height. "Where do you keep your blankets?"

Endure, Cat. "I don't need a blanket." Or to be tucked in. "Let me know if the suckers work for Jo, please."

"I will, but I'll be coming back later. Coll wants me to walk over the farm to see if I notice any blank areas with his cameras and lighting. We also need to discuss Réka with you. Coll and I investigated her past last night. There are a few red flags."

"What? Why would you do that?"

"Coll doesn't like that you let her stay in your home. I'm not crazy about it either. None of us know her."

They mean well. They mean well. They mean well. "Okay. I can assume she isn't a serial killer since you've not had her arrested," Cat replied with heavy sarcasm.

"She is not, but if she's going to stick around, I think you'll need to let me speak to her."

With that ominous announcement, he thanked her again for the sucker lead and promised to see her soon.

"Oh, I almost forgot." He paused outside. "Coll put a quiet alarm on your phone. It only requires you to swipe a pattern on your screen and he and I will be sent your location."

They mean well. They mean well. They mean well. "I'm surprised you two didn't opt to chip Josephine and me."

"Jo refused," he said matter-of-factly before shutting the door.

Cat sighed deeply. "This must be what saints feel like." She opened her heavily tracked and managed phone to see what Coll had texted earlier. "Asshole," she said with a giant grin. He'd sent several camera screenshots of Thomas carrying her from her home and across the property.

On the floor by her feet was her mailbag, fetched by one of the men in her life. It was pure luck that her father was out of the country, or she'd have had three men to dodge.

Not that she wanted to dodge Coll. She picked up her bag of mail and was about to begin to go through it when her front door opened to her tall, dark, and handsome secret boyfriend—an hour early.

"Decided to piss off from work early, Colly?" she teased.

"Tommy texted me. He didn't want you by yourself today."

He walked over and sat his ass on her desk next to her unopened laptop. "I was about to open my mail." To this, he took something out of his pocket and set it beside her hand.

The ginger massage oil. She raised her brows. Two could play. She stood and stepped between his legs. His hands instantly gripped her hips, mindful of the right one. "I woke up with my fingers between my legs, needing and wanting. You were nowhere to be found."

"Cat." He hissed while lowering his head.

When his tongue swiped her lips, she opened, wanting him inside her mouth more than her next breath. And then ... her door opened suddenly, startling her and Coll apart.

It was Dean. He didn't acknowledge what he had to have seen. "Cat, damn it, I'm sorry to bother you when you're hurt."

She took another step back, but Coll, damn him, gripped her left thigh and kept her close. "It's not a problem at all. What's happened?"

"It's the gardenias. Damn, the finicky bitches all to hell. They're yellowing. Stanley is staying with them. We hoped you could come."

"No, no, no. I've got a huge order for them in three months. Damn it!" She rounded the desk, but Coll caught her hand.

"Thomas and I didn't want you working in the greenhouses today. *I* don't want you to overdo it," he admitted.

He looked so concerned. She couldn't help but melt under his stern gaze. She touched his cheek briefly. "Come with me then. The gardenias are my archnemesis. A few bruises, and they think they'll pull one over on me."

"I'll carry you then."

"No, the absolute hell, you will not. I tolerated my brother babying me. You … you won't get away with that bull."

"Tom will be notified when you leave the office."

They mean well. "I'll deal with that cyclops when the time comes. All I need right now is to see those damn moody flowers … and you."

35

Cat needed him. Whether it was to be her significant other, bring her to orgasm, or watch her back while she inspected a gaggle of noxious flowers ... he would be there.

Watching her work, where she took charge and exuded confidence, was a total turn-on. They went to one of the smaller north-side greenhouses that held several varieties of 'difficult' flora. Cat immediately started inspecting the yellowed gardenia leaves and asked Stanley several questions.

Coll took that moment to edge closer to Dean. "It would be best if you never mentioned anything you think you might have seen in the office." He wasn't threatening the man so much as advising him.

Dean was made of stronger material than Lego, clearly, because the man didn't even flinch.

"Stanley and I have never worked for anyone better than Catriona. We love this job. We already love her. She is like a sister to us. *She* has our loyalty."

Noted. Their loyalty to Coll was TBD. Fair enough.

Dean wasn't finished. "I would be more concerned with her brother than Stan or me if I were you."

He could only nod his head in reluctant agreement. Dean had read the room and understood who the biggest baddest wolf in the story was.

When they joined Stanley and Cat, she was going over a plan of action. "The yellowing leaves aren't due to under or overwatering. We've confirmed the roots are healthy, so no rot. Which means the problem has to be low iron. Let's add an acidic nitrogen fertilizer that contains micronutrients. We'll try that twice a month at first. Get Réka's opinion. She loves these damn diva blooms. She'll 'talk' to them if nothing else."

Coll finally got Cat herded back into her office, but he didn't lead her to her desk, instead he grabbed up the massage oil and much to her amusement, led her to her workroom where she had an old ratty loveseat shoved into a corner. He knew from Thomas that when she first took over the running of the farm, she occasionally slept on it.

It was barely long enough for two people to sit comfortably, especially if they were his size, but the depth of the cushions was perfect for what he intended.

"Do you have a sheet to put down over this?"

She nodded toward the low cabinet sitting on the floor to the right side of the couch. "What exactly do you have planned, Mr. Barr?"

"You promised me a massage." She pulled out an ancient white sheet that looked beyond well-used, along with a blanket and pillow. He covered the couch with the sheet and placed the blanket and pillow against an armrest.

"Sit sideways and carefully lean against the pillow. See if that doesn't bother your bruises." She was moving more freely today. Her aches and pains were giving her less trouble. Of course, he didn't have to see her to know that. Had Thomas seen so much as a wince on his sister's face, he would have refused to let her out of the house.

She took her boots off and sat down, twisting to lean against the pillow. She pulled her knees up to give him room to do the same.

"This couch is comfortable to sit on. Try sleeping on it, though," she laughed. "This is not how I usually position myself to do a massage."

"I've thought it all out. It'll work. Plus, you're too injured to do a full-body massage like last time. I'll give you one of those tonight if you can stay quiet for your houseguest." He smirked. Before she could reply, he pulled off his tennis shoes and unzipped his jeans.

"What are you doing?" she asked as he pulled the jeans off, folding and setting them on the nearest workbench. He didn't try to hide his body's reaction at the thought of having her hands touching him. When her eyes widened as they landed on his crotch, he was deeply satisfied to see her interest.

Innocently, he asked, "How can you massage my leg with them on?"

"You realize Thomas plans to come back here, and from all appearances, you have more on your mind than ginger oil and my skillful hands." She circled her finger in the air, indicating his arousal.

Coll casually adjusted himself. She tracked the movement, making him want to tease, so he ran his palm firmly against his length. When her little tongue darted out to flick her lower lip, it was him that felt teased.

He sat opposite her and was about to take his prosthesis off when she shooed his hands. "Let me do it. I've only got to do it once before."

She was efficient like she was in all other aspects of her life, detaching it all like a pro. "Have you told the other wives on your forum that you've been massaging more than my leg?" He loved that she blushed.

"I have not," she replied with a slightly offended tone. "Lean back and put your knee in my lap. Your left can rest on the floor. I assume that's what you had in mind."

Before he complied, he admitted, "Honestly, Cat, I didn't think this through. I don't really need the massage, and you are still recovering. This was really just an excuse to see you, and then my plans became elaborate and convoluted. Maybe we should—"

"No way we're stopping now. It was a perfect idea because I want to touch you as much as you want me to. Give me your leg, Coll."

"I wouldn't go so far as to call that thing a leg," he corrected as he swung the residual limb over her lap.

~

"Hand me the oil." Cat had just about enough of Coll disparaging himself. It was always said in a joking manner, but he'd already admitted before they slept together that first time that no woman had seen it since the accident. She frowned, thinking he might not believe that she didn't see him differently.

She warmed up the oil in her hands, not that it took much. Ginger was potent. Her fingers were already tingling with its effects.

The first few strokes against his scarred flesh had Coll moaning in pleasure. "Feels so good. Unbelievably good."

She didn't stop working his flesh as she said, "I've asked you before if you would look at me differently if my body changed ... like now. If these bruises and swelling on my face were permanent ..." She left the thought hanging, hoping he would understand.

"You'd be beautiful to me no matter what. Forever."

Cat just raised her brows. *Do you see what I see?* The massage got deeper and deeper and warmer. Their eyes never severed contact.

"Your body is a wonder to me, Coll. Every dream. Each fantasy. A wonder ... never diminish yourself to fit into some type of normal box.

"Haven't I been clear enough for you? Don't you trust me?"

"Yes." He hissed, and his back arched as she worked over a particularly tender spot.

"I will want you forever and a day."

The look Coll gave her had her sucking in air from its intensity. She'd never seen him look so vulnerable or hopeful. Cat felt her throat grow tight.

And then ... "Forever and a day. No matter what."

Coll might not have realized it yet, but his words were a promise—most definitely a commitment. "No matter what," she echoed quietly. The massage went on longer than it should. Her hands were nearing his groin. They were both feeling pleasure pinging between them. He wasn't the only one swallowing moans.

"Touch me, Cat. Please, God."

"I have been, you brute," she huffed as she dug and dragged her hands over his muscles. If her knuckles nicked the heavy balls between his legs, who could blame her?

Without a word or warning, he tugged her top off. The bottoms quickly followed. The massage was over—at least the traditional massage was. She pulled his boxers down, not bothering to take them all the way off.

He gripped his shaft, stroking his hard length. "Is this what you want, baby?"

"Every chance I get." Why lie? She bent over his chest where he was perfectly propped to kiss. As she took his mouth, he grasped her hips, careful of her bruises, and slid her up until she straddled his thighs.

Breaking from the kiss to lean back, she demanded, "Lift me up. I need you inside me." She ran her hands down his muscular chest and over the ridges of his stomach. She grasped his sex as he easily lifted her body—a perk of being slight.

Once aligned, he began the slow descent. "Christ, Cat. I wish you could see your body swallow mine from this angle."

Cat was just as fascinated with her view, watching all that hardness disappear inside her. The fullness was pleasure and pain until she was fully seated and adjusted to his size. Then it was all pleasure. Without lifting, she moved her hips in a few leisurely rolls that made them both moan.

He covered her stomach with his hand so that his fingers brushed the underside of her breasts, and his palm pressed firmly to her sensitive flesh. He firmly clasped her left side, encouraging her to ride him up and down. The sensations were almost too much. Her body shook with need and want and fire.

Through gritted teeth, Coll growled something that sounded like, "Christ, the ginger."

Oh shit! No wonder her body was a weeping, oversensitive inferno. Her hands had been covered in the oil when she'd touched his body ... and now that body was inside her.

Ginger massage oil—the new orgasm maker.

She might have giggled at the absurdity of the happy accident, but she was too busy ... "Oh God, Coll ... I'm already ... right ... there!" She exploded—a ginger oil eruption. And then it was his turn. She'd never heard Coll shout so loud ... her ears might ring for a week. Add that to the list of things currently making her happy.

Coll pulled her chest down to his and fondled her ass as she melted in a boneless heap on top of him.

"Kitty Cat," he whispered against her scalp.

"Colly Barr." She breathed against his nipple before nipping the distended tip.

A notification went off on his phone three times, which had him palming the device and flipping through screens.

"Thomas is pulling up."

The panicked note in his voice got her ass in gear. She slid off his still semierect sex and stood by the couch, naked and heart pumping. As she bent to pick her clothes up, she felt a warm trickle of ... "You came in me again. Jesus, Coll. If you wanted a baby this bad, just say," she said part exasperated, part teasing, part hoping.

"Fuck me, Cat."

"I did."

"Cat."

"Get your naked ass up and get dressed. For the love of God! I do not want to witness the trainwreck of my brother seeing his sister naked with his best friend."

"Cat, Christ." His pleading tone stopped her in the middle of fastening her bra. He was standing on one leg looking ... dazed.

"Coll. Seriously, snap out of it, man. Thomas. Incoming. Make an excuse and run get me a pill. I'll go to my gyno for birth control as soon as I can. Stop freaking out. It's freaking me out."

"It's ... I ... It's just that I lose my mind when you touch me. I didn't mean ... Jesus, babe. I don't want you to think I don't take your body seriously."

She sidled up to kiss him, taking a brief moment to run her hands over his chest and shoulders. "Stop overthinking, Barr. Get your leg on. Get dressed. Get me a pill."

He quickly pulled his prosthesis and pants on. As he buttoned things up, he said, "I'm not getting a pill." At her questioning look, he added, "If we ... if what happened between us created a child ... I would want it."

His look of wonder and worry gripped her heart in a vise. If her damn brother wasn't incoming, she would have loved to discuss his epiphany further. As it was ... "Fine, babe. You're willing to be a dad. Good on you, just please get dressed, man," she hissed, ignoring her swoony heart over his declaration.

36

Cat sat at her desk while Coll and Thomas sat on the couch discussing ... something. She was struggling with her concentration—because her vagina was a hundred degrees warmer than it ought to be. *Damn that ginger.* An old nursery rhyme surfaced in her mind.

Scotland's Burning, Scotland's Burning.
Look out, look out,
Fire fire, fire fire,
Pour on water, pour on water.

Her only consolation was that Coll was shifting his private bits each time her brother turned his head. She'd been biting her cheek to stop herself from giggling. She didn't dare make eye contact. Subterfuge had never been one of her strong suits.

"I'm so thrilled the suckers worked for Jo." She wasn't just trying to keep her brother's sharp-eyed gaze from his squirming family. She was truly happy for her sister-in-law. Pregnancy must be a total bitch.

Thomas beamed, much more relaxed than he had been this morning. "She said it was like a switch flipped on her insides. There was instant relief. Setting up her new hospitality training program for people rescued from trafficking has been consuming her days, and getting little sleep from feeling miserable has taken a toll.

"She put her work aside for the rest of the day and said she planned on taking a nap since she felt so much better."

"So, if I'm reading between *your* lines, you demanded she not work and forcibly carried her to bed with orders to sleep." Coll's snort confirmed that Cat's version of events was probably spot on.

"That isn't true at all," he sniffed like an offended Victorian miss.

"You didn't set your bedroom alarm before you left. So that you'd know when she left the room?" Coll asked. His silence was answer enough.

"Jesus, Tommy. Really?"

Thomas twisted on the couch and punched Coll in the stomach before she registered any movement. Coll's huff of expelled breath was startling.

"You love someone besides Grandma and our sisters and Mir, then you can talk to me about protection," Thomas thundered.

"Calm down, bro," Coll placated. "There isn't anything I wouldn't do for our women. Nothing I wouldn't do."

"Obviously," Thomas agreed.

And just like that, the bromance was fully back online. Men were simple creatures.

"Réka Farkas." Thomas began. The change in subjects gave her a side of whiplash to go with her overwarm nether parts.

These two had decided her employee needed further investigation, which meant Cat had no say in the matter. "Yes?" Her phone notification vibrated. Looking at the screen, she saw that it was a text from Coll.

> That oil is keeping me with a semi. When does it stop working?!?!

Cat flicked her eyes to Coll before quickly focusing on her brother. "I hope you didn't find anything alarming. I really like Réka," she replied dryly while texting Coll back.

> Get rid of my brother, and I'll bend over my desk and let you work the last of the heat from your body.

Coll's moan-cum-throat clearing made her thighs clench. She didn't dare look in his direction, but out of the corner of her eye, she saw him adjust his privates again.

"She didn't lie on her application, but Coll found information on a broken engagement. Apparently, her fiancé was a cheater and abusive. Réka didn't have any social media herself. We tracked her family by her name and the past address she used on the application."

Coll picked up the story. "Both sides of the family posted on social media platforms. Most of the comments were in her ex's favor. They made her out to be dramatic at best and a liar at worst. It looks like she comes from a rough family that lives in a small rural farming town. They seem like the type of people to know about her abuse and not care."

"Her skittishness around men suggests she was telling the truth," Thomas finished.

She sighed, hating that the kind, hardworking woman she'd been coming to know was dealing with personal trauma. What Réka must have endured, what she was still enduring, put her own minor woes into perspective.

She'd known Réka was dealing with things, but she hated to think she'd been abused—and by someone she'd trusted. Then to be made out as a liar by people who should have sheltered and comforted her. Unthinkable.

"I'm sick that she went through that, but she isn't being hurt by that man anymore. She's making a new life for herself, and I have to admit, I'm uncomfortable that I know something so personal about Réka without her consent."

"We knew you'd feel that way, sweetheart, but with the attempted abduction, well, nothing trumped your safety, including someone's privacy."

Coll probably didn't realize he'd just called her sweetheart, and not in a familial way. Thomas didn't appear to notice, thank the heavens. If they were committed to a relationship and coming clean to family, it would need to be done with the precision of a well-planned out campaign. Accidental slips would not help their cause.

"Neither of us believes she's a threat to you, but will her ex come after her? We don't know that. We're willing to let her employment ride for now, but the sooner she opens up to you about her past, the better. Your brother and I can make her ex wish he'd never so much as sneezed in Réka's direction."

"With her permission only?" Cat wanted confirmation.

"Yes," Thomas agreed.

"Maybe," Coll replied with his typical brash honesty.

"I don't need her to stay with me since I'm doing much better, and my kitchen has enough food stocked to feed an army thanks to Grandma, but I don't want to ask her to leave. Her living situation with an elderly cousin sounds horrible."

> If she stays living with you, I won't enjoy hearing you scream my name when I make you come.

> True. And when I make you come with my body, or hands, or my mouth … you'd have to hold back too.

Coll's smoldering look after he read her text had her squirming in her seat. "Maybe we should ask Grandma what she thinks about having a houseguest for a few months while I help Réka get her finances figured out. I can help her find her own small home. I'd even help with her down payment. After all, helping her is like making an investment in the farm. She has the potential to be a huge asset to MacGregor's. More than simply a gardener."

"Not a bad idea. Grandma loves to look after people." Thomas was thoughtful for a moment. "It's highly doubtful Réka's ex-fiancé will bother trying to track her down, and according to her phone records, she is not in contact with anyone from Hungary. Her number is new. She didn't get it until she moved to Inverness, so it's unlikely her family even has it."

"Oh my God, did you look through her phone? Jesus, you guys. That was too far." They shrugged just to rile her up, she was sure.

"I already told you that your safety trumped a stranger's privacy." Her brother's insouciance was grating.

Looking at the two men sprawled over her dainty couch, she shook her head. One light and one dark, both believing that everything that left their mouths was brilliantly logical. Annoying.

It was a good thing she loved them.

"I'm for home to check on Jo. If she feels up to it, let's meet at Grandma's and see what she thinks about being a house mum."

"Fine. I'll stay with Cat. If we go to Gram's, I'll bring her with me."

"Good. I'll bring my property maps so you can compare them with yours and decide where you'll be building. Oh, I almost forgot," Thomas began, his blush getting both her and Coll's attention. "When I told Aileen that I'd hired a contractor to start renovating your folk's house for her and Mirren, she told me to cancel. And then she hung up on me. What the hell is her problem?"

He was clueless for such a smart man. "I know why. Mir called me this morning. She told me that Aileen wants Charles to be involved with the project since he will be living there with them. Mir said, 'Tell Dad to slow his roll before Mom cuts his balls off.'" Thomas' shocked face was comical. She wished she'd recorded it to show Jo later.

Coll stood looking for all the world like an avenging angel. Avenging devil might be a better description with his furious expression and bulging muscles. "If she thinks I'll allow for one goddamn minute my sister to move in with a man, and one she isn't even married to ... in front of my niece. No."

He did not just say that ... Cat looked at Coll with surprise and her own rising fury. "Are you suggesting that your sister, who lived like a nun for sixteen years while she was married to my brother, is not allowed to have sex with a man she isn't married to? I know that can't be what you meant."

She was satisfied when Coll's eyes widened. He must have forgotten for a moment that Cat was currently sleeping with a man she wasn't married or engaged to—hell, their relationship was still a secret.

Coll's desperate look of 'Help me' he sent to Thomas didn't go unnoticed either. Her brother, who thankfully recognized this wasn't an argument he'd win, let alone should even be a part of.

"I ... I," Coll hesitated, "misspoke. She has every right." He crossed his arms over his chest in a pout before tacking on, "I just don't like the fucking bastard."

Are you testing me, Lord? "Well, Aileen and Mirren do, so that's the beginning and end of it, then. Isn't it?" Without waiting for his agreement, she went on. "I suggest you begin with a good-faith gesture, Thomas. Smooth Aileen's ruffled feathers by *asking* if she would like you to help her and Charles get started on the house once they get back to town, which I think will be in a few weeks.

"To help get Tommy out of the doghouse, Coll, you can tell her that he wrote down a list of contractors for her and Charles to look over."

Her brother looked relieved to have a plan. Coll looked like he'd swallowed something bitter, but he did nod his head in agreement. "Okay then." She patted her desk, signaling to the other occupants of the room that it was time to get on with the day.

Coll had already told Thomas that he would be staying with her. The lingering heat between her legs sent shivers of anticipation zipping from her core to her breasts. As Coll walked her brother to the door, she pretended to be busy with sorting the mail.

She kept her head down even when she heard the door firmly close—even when Coll stood at her elbow, she kept her eyes averted. Why she felt shy at that moment was ridiculous. She *had* texted him some racy comments, and they'd already *done* some racy things.

Silently, he dragged his fingertips over her shoulder and down one of her arms. Chill bumps erupted wherever his heat traced.

"You have two choices. I bend you over this desk and take you where anyone might walk by and see us, or you take me to your workroom where I can bend you over one of the tables back there."

Her body wasn't just warm, it was on fire again, and it had nothing to do with ginger and everything to do with Coll's deep, gravelly voice talking dirty.

She did look at him then as she stood and took his hand. She was about to lead him to the back when he tugged on her hand to stop her. With no warning of what he intended, he picked her up, her arms wrapped around his neck and her legs went around his waist.

Their kiss was savage moans and greedy tongues. "I can't get enough of you, Cat. Christ, I want to live in your tight, little body." Even in the midst of their furious lust, Coll was careful of her healing injuries.

"Take me to the back." She would have confessed that she could think of little besides their bodies sliding together had she been able to take more than a single breath before his mouth was back on hers.

Coll closed the sliding door after they entered the darkened interior of her workshop—the same shop where they'd just come together barely an hour ago. And yet, there was something frantic in their movements.

He let her legs slide down his body, quickly turning her toward one of the rough wooden tables. She gripped its edges as he slid her pants down her legs, taking her shoes with them. Whimpers escaped from deep in her throat. Her body was shaking and needy.

When she heard the sound of a zipper releasing behind her back, she hissed, "Yes, Coll." She expected to feel his sex nudging from behind. Instead, she heard, "Shit."

Spinning around, she immediately knew what the problem was. He was ginormous, and she was ... much smaller than that.

"Step stool." It's all the instruction she gave before running to the sliding door where she kept several of the 'height helpers.' Running back, she dropped it at her feet, giving herself only a blink to appreciate his engorged length proudly waving above his jeans that were only dropped to the middle of his curved ass. She stepped on the sturdy wooden box and turned her back on the mouthwatering sight.

"Bend over more, baby. I've been picturing how you'd look open to me this way."

She did as he asked. Not shy or embarrassed in the least. Only desperation and need were riding her now.

"This is going to be hard and fast," he warned.

She felt Coll's blunt sex at her entrance and could only moan and bend deeper, arching her hips as high as they would go.

"That's it, Cat. You want me as much as I want you."

That was true. Completely one hundred percent true. "I do."

No more words were exchanged. None were needed. It was hot, hard, relentless, and ... divine.

37

Dear Brother,

 Tonight.
 Tonight.
 Tonight.
 I am finally going to get rid of the last obstacle between you and your new body.

 I have been pleading every hour of the day with Samedi and Legba to allow you to leave Death behind and to open the Gate back to the human world, letting your Spirit find me.

 I am on my knees all night pleading the same.

 I hope you recognize me. Part of the sacrifice was my hair. The witch elder used a sharp razor until nothing but my bare scalp remained.

 I am ashamed to tell you that I mourned its loss. My beauty felt diminished, though I believe that once you are restored to your body, my body will be made whole again as well. It's only ...

 You loved my hair when I was a little girl. When you

taught me how to please your body, you always loved how it felt skating over your naked skin.

Sometimes I wish I was that girl again where we lived in a secret world of our creation. It was simple. It was love.

But most importantly, you were alive.

I almost forgot, Inti! The package I sent to the demon who flaunts herself for you, never opened it. I have seen it through the cameras. Still unopened. I still have to act quickly, but at least they won't be alerted that I am after her.

She is never without company—your body included.

I forgive you as you have had to forgive me.

Night is my best, my only chance to get to her.

We're down to hours until our forever begins again.

Your beloved,

A

38

"Of course, the poor lassie is welcome to stay with me," Grandma assured them. "We'll figure her out in no time."

"She'll barely speak to you in the beginning, and that's if she agrees to it," Catriona warned.

"I'll talk enough for both of us," Grandma reassured. "She's had a tough go of it, but I'll make sure she understands that the boys will take care of anyone who might try to threaten her. Eventually, she'll realize she has the right to happiness."

Coll looked at Thomas and shook his head in amusement. Grandma MacGregor was nothing if not her boys' biggest fan.

"She was hurt by someone who should have loved her above everyone else." Her head shook back and forth with disgust and sadness. "I don't want her to think this is about charity. This is about a woman giving another woman a helping hand."

"I hope she agrees, Gram," Cat smiled fondly at her grandmother.

"I'll have her teach me some of her Hungarian recipes, and I'll teach her some of mine. She'll like being closer to work."

"Do you know if she needs anything? Bathroom essentials?

Clothes?" Jo asked. "Now that I'm feeling human again, thanks to these suckers," she made a popping sound as she pulled one of the anti-morning sickness suckers from between her lips, "I'll have plenty of time to gather what she needs. Plus, I'm working from home for the foreseeable future."

Thomas had told Coll that after Rome and all the shit that went down with Percy Donovan, the scumbag that had assaulted Josephine when she was only a teenager and tried to kidnap her eight years later, she wanted to stick closer to home for now. If Thomas had his way, his wife would never step foot out of their well-protected fortress, which had more security than most government buildings.

Jo was working on a project with some billionaire philanthropist that would help people who had been rescued from trafficking. She reminded Coll of Catriona. Both women were honest, loyal, and passionate.

It still haunted him that Cat could have been one of those stolen women. He could barely sleep at night worrying about her now. The sooner Réka Farkas moved out of Cat's, the sooner he could move in.

As soon as the thought occurred, he remembered why he wasn't free to do that. *Damn it.* He tried to envision telling Thomas that he was ... seeing his sister ... sleeping with his sister —the fallout had his ass clenching.

When people say things like, "What's the worst that could happen?" or "It's not like they'll actually kill you." Yeah ... those people hadn't met Thomas MacGregor.

He wanted to sit by Cat at Grandma's dinner table, but it would have red-flagged that something was up faster than announcing it. Until he spoke with Thomas, secrecy was the only option.

He glanced toward Cat, who was speaking animatedly to Jo. Without pausing, she gave him a blank look before her eyes moved away. That was for her brother's benefit. She was doing her part to not bring any attention to their interest in one another.

He didn't like that she was acting as though she hadn't just screamed his name when she came, his body buried deep inside her.

If he had any balls, he would speak to Thomas, take the beatdown, and move on. And there would be a beatdown.

His phone pinged.

> Stop brooding.

Cat didn't even look his way when he read it.

I'm not.

> Fine. I swear I can still feel you sliding in and out of me.

Now it was his turn to ignore the flame-haired imp across the table, or he wouldn't be able to get up anytime soon.

I need you.

> Again?

Every hour of every day if you'll have me.

> I'll have you.

"So anyway," Cat continued speaking to Jo, "I doubt if she'd allow any charity from us. It's going to take all my charm to convince her to move in with Grandma, even though we all know it's the very best thing for her—sluffing off the past and beginning something new."

When Cat's brother snorted in amusement after she mentioned her charm, Coll knew Thomas had stepped in deep.

"Did you have something to add, brother?"

Coll didn't always like to be right ... but ... Jo was already silently laughing behind her hand at her husband's gaffe.

"No. No." Thomas shook his head in the negative, pretending to be flummoxed. "I agree with you, Cat."

"Mmhmm." Cat didn't look the least bit convinced, but it was clear that she was going to let it slide.

He'd like to believe it was because he left her so sexually satisfied. He really needed to stop thinking about sex with Cat.

Coll was considering how long it would be before he could get her naked and under him when her comment to Grandma finally registered.

"... No, I think it's best that she stays the night with me. I'll speak with her when I get home, and then we can come up with a schedule."

"So ... so you'll have her another night at your place, Cat?" He thought his query sounded normal. However, their grandma's raised brow and chuckle had him wincing. Another bit of commentary from him in that vein, and he'd be announcing to the entire table that he'd prefer Réka elsewhere so he could screw Cat's brains out with no worry of keeping the volume down.

"I mean, wouldn't it be easier to move her here immediately? Tom and I could run into Inverness to fetch her extras."

"Nah. Let's leave her be for now. I want you and me to look at our property lines to see where you plan on building." Thomas didn't have a clue he was cockblocking Coll from his own sister.

Coll was going to hell.

"Sure. Sounds good. We still don't know who tried to take Cat in that alley, but if you feel secure about her safety without any evidence to prove it was a one-off, then I'll concede to your opinion."

Mentally, Coll was punching himself in the nuts, but damn it, no one could protect Cat like he could—and it damn well wasn't all about wanting her naked in his arms.

"I suggest you keep your opinions to yourself, Mr. Barr."

Cat was being snarky like she usually would when she felt he was getting out of line. It was also clearly meant to warn him that he was being too involved. He was showing his cards.

"You agreed with me that Farkas checks out, Coll, so I know you don't think she's a safety issue. The police seem to think that Cat's kidnappers took off after she escaped, and I agree. Wrong place, wrong time.

"The statistics of how many women and children are kidnapped daily all over the world are shocking, and I'll be thankful until the day I die that my sister wasn't one of those statistics. Is there something bothering you about the police investigation that you've not mentioned? If there is, I'll listen."

That's why he and Thomas had been friends for so many years. Coll knew Thomas would listen. They'd both learned to trust their instincts in the military, and it still served them well in their security business.

Sighing, he decided it would be okay to be honest ... partially honest. "The kidnapping scared me. It scared all of us. I'm still struggling with her living alone." He glanced at Cat. Her eyes were softened in understanding.

Until her brother ruined the moment.

"I feel the same way." Thomas' deep baritone rumbled. "But you know Cat, she won't be told what to do—"

"She also doesn't like being discussed as if she isn't sitting right here." Cat threw her hands up, clearly exasperated.

Thomas continued as if she hadn't spoken. "... which is why I am constantly surveilling the farm and her house. I have my notifications turned on for any movement, animal, human, or vehicle."

"Grandma!" Cat's outraged wail as she stood had the table gearing up for fireworks. "Tell him to stop watching me. Jesus Christ!"

"Do not take the Lord's name in vain, young lady. There's no telling your brother anything, and you know that very well."

"Unless you're me." Jo added before poking her husband in the shoulder. Thomas only grinned at his wife.

Grandma continued, used to dealing with ruckus family dinners. "Cat, you'll just have to invite Coll to your cottage more often. As soon as Tommy sees that you're well-tended, he'll stop watching. Simple."

Cat's face turned beat red when Grandma winked at her. If he and Cat needed confirmation that the older woman was on to them, they just got it.

"Ha. If those two could be in the same room with each other for longer than a few minutes without Cat scratching Coll's eyes out—tell me where to place my bet." Thomas' guffaw would have been insulting if it weren't true.

It used to be true.

Now, the thought of Cat being out of his sight irritated the hell out of him. He'd suppressed his feelings for her for two years. He didn't want to do it anymore. Getting off to fantasies of Cat in the shower weren't going to cut it any longer now that he knew what she felt like, tasted like.

He should just say it. Tell everyone now. *Do it. Do it. Do it.*

He was gutted when he realized Cat had been watching him war with himself. She knew exactly what he was struggling with. Did she know why? He didn't.

Cat and Josephine began gathering dishes from the table effectively putting an end to his dilemma of 'should he, could he.' Within twenty minutes Grandma was giving everyone hugs goodbye and he was driving Cat home. In silence.

"I can cancel the meeting with Thomas at his place and stay with you." Her response was that it was no big deal and that she needed time to speak with Réka. They parked outside her tiny cottage. Before she could open the passenger door, he placed his hand on her arm to stop her.

"I want to tell Thomas. Tonight. I don't like lying, and neither do you."

"No, Coll."

"What? Why the hell not?"

"I saw you tonight, Coll. You looked like you were going to puke all over Grandma's table. You were thinking about telling Tom, don't deny it."

Cat was so still. She wasn't angry, or shouting, or crying. She was resigned. "I was thinking about your brother, I admit, but I've changed my mind."

"Listen. We agreed to be us, whatever that looks like. I admit that it's harder than I thought to lie, but you and I agreed to see how things go first."

"I'm not saying any of this right." Coll groaned at how immature he'd been these past weeks. Scrubbing a hand over his face, he tried again. "Hold my hand, Kitty Cat."

"The cameras," she started.

"They can barely see inside the cab, but I wouldn't care even if they did. Now give me your hand." She shook her head like he'd gone crazy, but she did lay her palm against his on the seat, twining her slight fingers through his.

Coll thought he would be more nervous, but he wasn't at all. Finally, somehow, he'd started using his purportedly high IQ to realize what he should have known months ago.

"I love you. Not just as family, but as my ... my ... what are we? My girlfriend. That doesn't seem like a big enough thing, but regardless, I love you, Catriona. I'm desperate to tell our families. I can't believe I ever thought I wasn't ready. I'm totally ready."

Cat had started to cry at some point during his mangled declaration, but she had picked up their linked hands and now held them against her chest. Her heart was beating wildly, a match for his erratic pulse.

"You're serious?" she asked in wonder.

"Completely. I should have always put your feelings and thoughts above anything else, including your brother. I'm done screwing up with us. I let my age, and then your brother, and my leg all become roadblocks to admitting my feelings.

"The thing is, I've never considered myself a coward, but I have been. You deserve better, and I plan on giving it to you."

Cat leaned across the seat and cupped the side of his face. "You might have been hesitant, but you wouldn't know how to be a coward if someone handed you a manual. If you're sure I'm it for you, Coll Barr, just know that I've been all in for you from the moment you looked at me like you're looking at me now."

When she closed the distance between their lips, there was no mistaking the promise. "I love you, baby. So much," he whispered. Louder, he said, "But if you don't want Tommy to rip off your favorite body part of mine, you'd better scoot back."

Her burst of laughter made him chuckle. "Second favorite, asshole."

"Really now? What's in the number one spot, then?"

"Your broody dark eyes. When I was a little girl, I would think about your beautiful eyes for hours—all those long, inky lashes ... yeah ... your eyes, Mr. Barr." As she moved to put space between them, her hand brushed his groin. With a wicked grin, she added, "This is a close second, though."

"Kitty Cat. You're playing with fire. I'm supposed to meet your brother."

"And I'm supposed to speak to Réka."

"The house I'm building," he started.

"Yes?" Cat cocked her head in question, her hundreds of perfect ringlets shifting at the movement.

"I want us to build it together. For us. I've been thinking ..."

"Yes?"

"Your Hungarian employee of the year can rent this cottage once we have our own place. She would be able to take over some of the running of the farm easier if she lived here—helping her and helping you." Coll loved watching Cat mull over his suggestion. Her clever mind was intoxicating.

"You might be on to something. I would have a lot of opinions about this house of ours," she warned.

"You were born with opinions, lass. Do your worst." He tweaked one of her curls, earning him a slap on the wrist.

Her jovial expression dimmed, and he felt his muscles tense. "Truly, Coll. Is this happening? It's just ... I hoped, but I kept telling myself not to get my hopes up."

"I love you, Cat. Yesterday. Today. Tomorrow."

She blinked rapidly and swallowed, trying to stem tears. "Who knew? You're a poet. My boyfriend is a romantic poet," she said in wonder.

"That's reaching." He poked her side, and a laugh burst from her.

"Go talk to my brother, and I'll talk to Réka. The sooner we figure out our people, the sooner we can have hours of uninterrupted sex."

"Tomorrow morning we tell him." Him being Thomas MacGregor.

"Tomorrow. Oh, Jesus."

39

Dear Brother,

Do you hear that, Inti?
Tick.
Tick.
Tick.
When the last of the seven dies. When that demon dies, jump with every part of your spirit through Legba's gate.
Find your new body.
Then find me.
Find me.
I feel as lost as you must.
Find me.
I am weak.
My knees bleed from kneeling. Begging for your new life.
This is our only chance. The witch warned me.
The only and the last.
I have written your letters in my blood. A vow and testament. A love letter to last an eternity.

Find me. I beg you.

Our parents and brothers have been circling me for days. They tread across my blood.

They taunt me. Haunt me. Laugh at my pain and weakness.

They don't want us together. They never did.
Find me and finally make their voices stop.
Tick ... It's time.

Your beloved,

A

40

Cat hadn't stopped smiling since Coll dropped her off at home. Even when she found that Réka was holed up in the extra bedroom, Cat still had trouble suppressing her grin. They were announcing their 'couple' status in the morning. *Holy shit!*

She knocked softly on Réka's door and heard a faint, "Come in." Her employee was dressed in a long nightgown and robe. Her hair was twisted in a small towel. She must have already showered.

She had a book in her lap that almost slipped to the floor when she sat up in bed, along with two disposable icepacks she'd had draped over her knees.

"Oh my God, Réka! What in the world happened? Are you hurt?" Cat rushed over and was about to lift one of the packs, but Réka flinched when her hands got too close to her body. Cat was instantly contrite.

"Sorry about that," she backed away toward the door. The woman was still skittish about people touching her, probably because of her bastard of an ex-fiancé. That man needed his own beatdown so he could see how it felt.

"No, no." Réka shook her head, clearly embarrassed by her reaction. "I only tripped on the walkway leading into greenhouse five."

Cat instantly began to mentally walk the path leading to that particular greenhouse. The raised pavers her dad had placed there years ago were rough and wonky. Cat had skipped across them for so many years that there wasn't a crack or crevice hidden from her, but someone new ... dang it.

"The path is crap. Damn, Réka, I'm sorry you were hurt. I'll get to work on replacing them first thing in the morning."

She waved away Cat's concern. "I'm embarrassed to say, but when Stanley and Dean found out what happened to me, they fixed the walkway before close this afternoon." Her pinkened cheeks showed she wasn't used to having people care for her.

"Those two are the best." Cat needed to remember to thank them both tomorrow.

"Did you have a good evening?" Réka quietly asked.

"Amazing, actually." Cat could feel her grin come back in full force. "It's why I wanted to speak with you tonight."

"I'm moving back to my cousin's in the morning," Réka rushed to say as if Cat was about to kick her butt to the curb.

"Oh, no. That's not what I meant. I have a proposition for you. I know we don't know each other well, but I hope that continues to change." Cat leaned against the doorframe and tried to relax her body. This woman was free to live her life however she chose, but it was important to Cat to offer her something—a light in the dark, an ear to listen ... hope.

"My brother, Thomas, and I spoke with our grandma tonight. About you, actually." Réka's wide eyes showed alarm. "All good things, I promise. Here is my proposition—I admit that not all of my family know all the details I'm about to share —you move in with Grandma for the next few months."

When Réka began to instantly protest, Cat held her hand

up. "Wait, please. Just hear me out." At her nodded consent, Cat dove back in. "Before I get into details, you should know that Gram is beside herself at the thought of you moving in with her for a while. She loves to cook. You love to cook. She plans on you teaching her some traditional Hungarian recipes, and then she can show you up with her Scottish ones." Réka's lips twitched in amusement at that. Good so far.

"You haven't told me everything, but I know your life hasn't been easy, and living with your old-ass cousin is surely an insult to injury. Live with Grandma. Save money. Create a life strategy, and plan, plan, plan.

"You're important to me and MacGregor Farm. I have big plans for you if you intend on sticking around."

"I do," Réka quickly interjected.

"Good. Then let's work together. Give yourself a break. This isn't a handout, Réka. This is me investing in a woman who I believe will eventually be one of the farm's backbones. There's more, but Grandma and Thomas don't know about that part yet." Cat damned her fair, red-headed complexion when she felt her cheeks burn.

"Is this about you kissing Mr. Barr whenever you think no one is watching?"

Cat's mouth dropped open at Réka's rare show of cheekiness. "I ... oh, God," she shook her head. Good thing she was a gardener and not attempting espionage. She hadn't exactly been careful with her relationship with Coll, but she didn't think she'd been that obvious.

"No one else at the farm knows. Or they aren't saying," Réka tried to assure her. "It's just ... you know I try to stick to ... less traveled routes." Her grimace was less confession and more chagrin.

Cat asked, "Is this a good time to admit that my brother and ... boyfriend are ex-Royal Marines who now own a security firm? I won't say anything more than this—if you have something in your past that you want to make sure stays there, you only need to ask. They are both exceptional at their jobs and extremely protective of anyone they consider under their protection."

Réka was silent for a moment, possibly considering Cat's roundabout offer of making sure her dead-beat ex never darkened her door again.

In the end, she simply dipped her head in acknowledgment of the offer. Cat decided to move on to a happier topic.

"Back to it, then. Grandma's house. You will not be a guest. You'll be a renter. Grandma will set the terms, which means it will almost be free, but you'll have to cook and help with chores. Doable. Right?"

With great hesitance, Réka nodded. "Yes."

"This is the part that they don't know about. Yet. Coll bought his parents' farm, which shares property lines with my brother's. He's building a house near Thomas. We are actually going to be building a house." Cat felt a surge of nervous excitement zip through her veins. Saying it out loud was fantastical as if she were living in an alternate universe.

"My thought, or my hope rather, is that once Coll and I move in together, you might be interested in leasing this cottage. You could do anything you wanted to it ... well, besides, painting it a crazy color. Brilliant colors are for flowers.

"Seriously though, I hope eventually you'll be open to taking on an even more important role at the farm than you already are. My dream is to be able to create my oils and soaps, and to do that, I need someone I can trust to run the rest of the farm."

It was a few minutes of uncomfortable silence before Réka found her voice—it wasn't the response Cat expected.

"Have you thought ... that is, have you considered that ... Mr. Barr is not everything that you, ah, believe he is?"

Cat could tell Réka struggled to say anything negative. It wasn't meant as a snark but as a warning from a woman who had suffered at the hands of an untrustworthy man.

"I appreciate you caring enough about me to ask. I truly do, but I've been in love with that man for ten years. I'm not letting go of him now that I have him. Plus," Cat grinned, "Coll is my brother's best friend. If he steps out of line, he'd be answering to Thomas, and no one wants to answer to my brother."

Réka gave a shy smile. "I accept. Everything. This job ... you ... It's all more than I dreamed for myself. I won't let you down, Catriona."

"I won't let you down either."

Réka looked at her, determination in the slight uptilt of her jaw. "I believe you."

Cat was honored. Trust was the hardest earned belief a person could bestow on another.

"Thank God. Now that we've settled that, let's discuss tomorrow. I don't know if you're a praying woman, but Coll and I are telling Thomas in the morning. No pressure, but if you see windows breaking in my office, call ... Gram," Cat chuckled. "I'll give you her number. She's probably the only one who can talk those two out of a row, and by row, I mean a full-on fist fight."

"Should I get my things from my cousin's tomorrow after work?"

"Actually, why don't you go do that first thing. Thank your horrible cousin for her hospitality and assure her that you will never need it again." Réka smirked at that, but she seemed pleased by the idea. And when you get back, maybe you would take mercy on me and help me go through the mountain of mail and parcels I've been putting off opening and organizing since my accident." Accident sounded better than attempted kidnapping.

"I'll come straight to your office. If I don't see your brother's car." Réka grinned and widened her eyes with an exaggerated grimace, making them both laugh.

When Cat left Réka's bedroom, she felt giddy with promise. This was the path her life was always meant to travel.

She went through her nightly bathroom routine and then grabbed a notebook to write down some new ideas for massage oils before climbing into bed. A bed that she really wished was already occupied. Sex for hours in a comfy bed sounded pretty damn good.

Once she settled against the pillows, she unlocked her phone and pulled up Coll's number.

> Why aren't you naked and in my bed?

She knew she was being a shithead since he was still probably at her brother's place.

> Don't start. At Tommy's.

She snorted. She wanted to do something that she knew Coll would love, but he'd spank her ass later for. That didn't sound like a terrible thing.

She scooted up on the pillows and adjusted her night tank to just below her breasts. They were small, but knowing how much Coll loved them made her love them too. She snapped a picture of just her uplifted boobs, no face, which was good because her grin was so big it would have ruined the whole sexy vibe she was going for.

Send.

COLL WAS GOING to strangle Cat when he saw her in the morning. He was having a beer with Thomas, sitting at his best friend's kitchen bar, and sporting a semi ... over his sister. Thank God Tom went to the bathroom. He needed a minute to calm his body.

His phone dinged again. "Don't look, you idiot." He looked.

"What the fuck, brother. Is a woman actually sending you tit pics?"

Coll was so startled by Thomas' booming voice behind him that he threw the phone in the air, barely managing to catch it before Thomas could.

"Christ, man," Thomas chuckled, "I thought we stopped getting naked pictures from ladies in the military."

Thomas' laughter died when he spotted Jo. *Thank God.* A distraction.

She just raised her brow at her husband. "What did the woman's boobs look like?"

Cat could never, ever, ever, never know this conversation took place.

"Umm, I'm not—"

"Come now, Mr. Detail." Jo interrupted while she slowly walked to stand in front of Thomas, who looked like a naughty schoolboy caught with a porn mag.

Coll would be laughing if they hadn't been discussing ... this. *Don't cave in, Thomas. Don't speak about your sister's breasts.*

He did. "Small, round. Nice. I like yours way better. I *only* like yours," he quickly corrected.

Jo smiled at Thomas, letting him know she wasn't truly pissed. She wrapped her arms around her husband's waist and smiled up at him. "You lied about not getting naked pics since you were in the Marines, though." Coll watched Thomas' face turn a horrible shade of red. "You're pretty handy with video, too, baby."

Jesus Christ, Coll did not need any visuals of Thomas videoing ... no. This whole conversation had evolved from TMI into gag territory. At least they weren't talking about Cat's nudity anymore. He was too hasty in celebrating.

Jo turned in and grinning, asked, "So, do we get to meet Miss Perky Tits?"

Take me to Heaven, Lord. I'm ready.

41

Cat had been drumming her thumbs for thirty minutes, waiting for him to respond to her breast text. "What the hell, Coll?" she growled low, beginning to feel like she'd made a huge mistake. Then her phone finally pinged.

> Christ have mercy, babe. Sorry just replying. Your brother's been sitting on my shoulder all night.

Cat let out a relieved sigh.

> I thought maybe you didn't like the picture.

> I didn't fucking like it. I loved it. I almost came in my pants over it.

God, his dirty mouth turned her on. Knowing he liked what he saw was everything.

> Réka agrees with the plan. All of it.

> You told her we were building a house together?

> Yes. We still are. Right?

> It kills me when you question this. Us. You've known me your whole life. When I say it, I mean it.

Cat's heart hammered. She never meant to question his intentions, and he was right. If he said he would do something, he would.

> I'm sorry. I trust you. I love you. Tomorrow XOXO

> I love you. You're still going to pay for sending me a picture of your tits while I was with your brother. Tomorrow …

Cat held her phone to her chest and drummed her feet on the mattress, silently squeeing in absolute glee. How did she go from being a young, no-dating workaholic to relationship goals?

Coll was big, sexy, and all hers. She knew Thomas would kick up a fuss at first, but eventually, he would give in. He loved both her and Coll, after all. To cover a few more bases, she texted Jo earlier to come by with Thomas in the morning under the ruse of plantings around her home, discussing the baby's room, and shopping. Josephine's love language.

She spent an hour writing down a few formulas she wanted to try out in her workshop. Lately, she'd been dreaming about perfumes, specifically Bayberry and Bee Balm. The leaves from both plants' leaves had a unique, lovely smell when crushed.

She wanted to grow Bee Balm first. She smelled their leaves

once years ago. The citrusy scent had entranced her. It would be unique in the perfume market.

She reluctantly set her notebook aside, knowing she could doodle out ideas for several more hours, but the sooner she went to sleep, the sooner she got to see Coll.

∼

WHAT SEEMED like eight hours later but couldn't have been more than three or four from the moon's lighting outside, Cat was still awake. She might have dozed a few minutes here and there but inevitably, she was checking the time on her phone.

Telling herself that on the day she and Coll were going to announce their relationship, she should look well-rested, fresh-faced, and gorgeous—not sleep-deprived with smudgy under eyes and asylum hair.

One thing about knowing a man since birth ... he'd seen you at your best, worst, and everything in between—that list included diapers.

Huffing in irritation, she rolled to her back once again. She'd already tried to sleep on her stomach and both sides and managed to nod off here and there but jerked to wakefulness every time. Every. Time. "Jesus, Cat. Sleep for the love of God."

She finally touched the screen on her phone to see the time. "Threeee," she whined to the darkened room.

Cat grabbed her phone again and was about to turn on a sleep music app. Desperate times ... but then she ... smelled something.

Like boiled eggs. What the hell? She sat up in bed, too quickly, obviously because her head swam. Her eyesight was blurry. She grabbed for the side table to steady herself. She took several deep inhalations. Her nose burned with ... sulfur.

She was trying to figure out what was going on when she

realized she was lying flat on her back again. When had she done that?

Her head was spinning worse now and she could feel her stomach rolling like she might get sick. The smell was so strong, she really needed to get up and see if she could ... locate ... locate what?

Something was wrong. With her. She felt like her body was weighted down by boulders. Panic finally got through her foggy lethargy. Help. She needed help. She was too weak to pick her phone up. She managed to turn her head to the side and almost cried when she saw that she'd dropped her phone face up by her side.

It took every bit of her waning strength to roll toward it. She propped the phone on her arm and, after five tries, unlocked it. Two more touches, and she was in her contacts and pressing Coll.

Tears leaked freely when she heard his raspy voice. "Catriona." When she didn't answer quick enough, he shouted, "Goddammit, Cat. Answer me."

She heard banging, and Coll yelling her brother's name. His breaths were heavy, panicked.

"Cat, baby, Cat. Please."

"Help." That one word was all she could manage, and Cat wasn't even sure it made it past her lips.

"I'm coming. I'm coming, Cat. Hold on, baby. Tommy! Where the fuck is she?"

Her brother's voice barked over the line. "Home. She's home. Jo, call the police. Ambulance. Cat's house. Lock up. Set the alarm."

More door slamming. Her eyes were closed even though her mind was screaming at her to stay awake.

"Coll. Need ..." Cat lost the fight with sleep and let it take her under. Coll was coming. He would always come for her.

"Cat!" Coll screamed into his phone. "She's not fucking answering. You're sure she's still at home?" Coll had never felt such debilitating fear. Even when she'd almost been kidnapped.

Now ... Now she wouldn't fucking answer him even though they were still connected. "Tommy." He clenched his jaw at the whimper he heard in his voice.

"I can't think ... I can't bear to ... to ... my Wee Cat. Coll, Christ, I will never forgive myself."

Thomas' anguished voice burned through the hollow ache of the phone's silence. Cat was there. She had to still be there.

Her cottage was in sight, and Coll had just muttered a "Thank fuck," as Thomas tore the steering wheel clean off the column. "Jesus, Tom," he yelled as the truck came to a stop in the middle of a pasture. Tom had been driving offroad when he could and clearly gripping the wheel way too tight.

"Fuck!" Thomas roared as he opened his door and jumped out, running full speed to Cat's. Coll was right there, eating up the quarter mile like it was nothing. He heard the distant wail of an ambulance and prayed they were not too late.

Both men hit the front door at the same time. Wood and hinges cracked and flew into the living room.

"Gas. Fuck, Tom, it's gas!" His best friend had already torn Cat's door from its frame and thrown it like it was a piece of trash behind him.

Coll almost dropped to his knees as he heard Thomas screaming his sister's name over and over. "No, no, no, no, no." Denial was his prayer. No. No. No. God. God. God.

Thomas had Cat in his arms before Coll could take another step toward her bedroom. "Get Farkas. Let's get them outside. Now Coll! Fucking now!" Thomas screamed. Panic was riding them both.

Every cell in his body wanted to grab Cat's limp form from her brother and crush her to his chest, but Thomas was right. There was another woman that needed saving.

He kicked in Réka's door. The skittish gardener was already sitting up in bed, wide-eyed from the ruckus and holding a knife. There was a lot to unpack here, from the mound of towels and spoons on the floor to the knife-wielding woman with bald patches covering her scalp.

He held his hands up in peace. "Miss Farkas, the house is full of gas fumes. Catriona called for help. She is … not awake. Her brother took her outside. The ambulance is almost here. Please," he held his hand out, "come with me. The house isn't safe."

He watched as she smelled the air. The miasma of rotten eggs must have convinced her that he was telling the truth. The clothes and towels she'd stuffed beneath her door must have kept the gas from permeating her room. The spoons were obviously a rigged security trap. Her past probably saved her.

She nodded and followed Coll without a word, only grabbing her headscarf on the way out. He saw the lights of emergency vehicles approaching and jogged the rest of the way to the front porch, where Thomas still cradled his sister.

Cat's eyes were fluttering. "Thank you, God," he whispered.

"Go around back and shut the gas off from the house. We'll deal with the source once the sun comes up."

Coll only nodded. They couldn't risk turning on any lights in case of an errant spark igniting the cloud of gas in the house, though leaving the front door open would already be helping to dissipate the danger.

When he reached the porch again, an emergency medical team was checking the women's vitals.

"Sir. If you would allow us to take your little sister to the ambulance, we could check her easier."

Jesus. They thought Cat was a primary school lass. She would be so pissed. Thomas, of course, was escalating ... everything.

"You aren't taking her a good goddamn, any-fucking-where, out of my arms. Fix her. Right where she is. Now."

And then ... "Tommy, you big brute. Set me down." Her voice was weak and scratchy, but she was awake, God be praised.

"No."

Coll knew his best friend well enough that he would become violent before he let Cat out of his arms. "Tommy, brother, sit on the porch stairs. It will be easier to take Kitty Cat's vitals. Let them see her. Please."

He watched Thomas' big body shudder. He didn't want anyone to touch his sister, but he knew he had to. What no one said, but most knew, was that Thomas and Cat's parents were good people, loving parents, but they loved themselves more than even their children. Coll didn't think Mr. and Mrs. MacGregor realized they'd always put themselves miles above their children. The family was extremely close. It was just ...

Thomas had been Cat's true father figure for years. It was the biggest reason Coll had shied away from Cat. Thomas was more dad than brother to her. He always had been. In Thomas' mind, there was little difference between his daughter, Mirren, and Catriona.

Cat's tiny hand touched her brother's cheek. "I feel much better. Truly, Tom. I love you, but you can't hold me forever."

"The fuck I can't," he barked back.

Cat's sniffle was barely audible, but it brought tears to choke his own throat. He wanted to hold her just as desperately as Thomas did.

"Réka," Coll startled the timid woman, "would you sit on the steps and let Thomas sit Catriona next to you?"

The woman stood taller at the request, immediately walking to the porch steps and sitting down.

"I will not leave her side during the examination, Mr. MacGregor."

Thomas wasn't happy, but he knew he needed to let her go. He finally relented and set Cat next to Réka, taking the shy woman's arm without permission and tucking it around his sister. She let him have his way without a word, only nodding at his gruff, "Careful with her."

It was another hour of checking the two women's vitals and securing the house before the group was able to move to Cat's office.

Detectives were on site now. The gas had been tampered with. Coll's blood turned to ice in his veins.

This was no accident.

42

It wasn't an accident ... Someone tried to kill her. Cat's body shuddered. Thankfully, she'd been sleeping restlessly. Otherwise, she might never have woken up. Thomas and Coll wore identical thunderous looks, clenched jaws, and straining fists.

"Whoever it was hacked into the security cameras and froze them until they were out of range."

Well, that was even more worrisome. *Dang* ... Cat couldn't have a normal old killer after her ass. She had to get a tech-savvy asshole.

Poor Réka just finished being interrogated by the detectives. Cat thought they were treating her like a suspect because she'd blocked her door with towels that didn't allow hardly any gas into her room.

It had been painful to listen to her explain that she always put towels under the door with spoons, marbles, or anything that would make a noise when they hit each other or the floor when the door was opened.

"It's only that locked doors didn't always keep out ... my ex," she hesitated before quickly adding, "fiancé. It helped if I was awake when that happened."

Cat saw Réka touch her headscarf. Coll had told her the state of her hair. She probably suffered many worse things living with that bastard, but it had to have been devastating.

Cat looked at her brother with a pleading look. She didn't want Réka to have to explain anything else.

"Surely that's enough detectives," Thomas began. "My security firm fully vetted Miss Farkas. Otherwise, she wouldn't have been allowed to be close to my sister."

They didn't look inclined to stop their line of questioning until they received a call from one of the forensics team going through the house now that it had aired out enough not to be a danger.

Detective Harvey looked grim after the call. "There was a slow-burning fuse wedged under the stove's range. It went out halfway. Whoever did this meant for the house to explode."

"Catriona. Come here." Anyone would have thought her brother was angry at her, but she knew he was upset at the news.

She didn't say a word but went to stand close to his side. He promptly wrapped a thick arm around her waist. She didn't even bother to tell him that her feet were dangling above the floor.

Coll glanced in Cat's direction before speaking to the detectives. "I know they hacked into our cameras, but they surely weren't capable of hacking every bloody camera between here and town. Surely, their home base is Inverness since that's initially where they tried to take her. Bunchrew is too small for locals not to notice if strangers were lurking about.

"They might not know their plans didn't work yet. If you find a vehicle coming and going from this area, the cameras might lead to where these people are hiding."

"We are already looking, I assure you," the detective said.

"Good. MacGregor Security has helped police and other law enforcement agencies with several cases over the years. I'd like to extend our resources to your people to assist in sifting through the camera feeds."

Harvey nodded thoughtfully and pulled a card from his front shirt pocket, writing a name and number on it before handing it to Coll. "Have your people call Jonas immediately. I'll text him now to expect the call. I don't need to tell you that time is critical."

Coll nodded, already speaking to one of MacGregor's teams.

The sky was just brightening. Dawn. This morning could have ended so very differently for her. She could have died, but so could the sweet woman currently sitting at Cat's desk going through the mail. Cat wiggled out of her brother's arm, giving him a pat on the chest before placing a chair near the desk.

"You do not have to do that." Cat nodded toward the giant pile. "I think it can safely wait another day after what we've been through."

Réka smiled softly. "I find it helps me to keep my hands and head busy. I don't mind."

"Réka," Cat said her name softly, getting the woman to look up and make eye contact. "I can't tell you how horrified I am that you were almost hurt because of me. I would have never asked you to stay if I'd even thought for a sec—"

"No, Catriona. No. Never blame yourself for what someone else does to you. It took me a long time to understand something so simple, but once I did, well … I found you and this farm. Everything will work out for you in its own time as well."

It took Cat a minute to process the words of wisdom, and then … "You're a badass, Réka. Don't ever let anyone tell you different." Sighing, Cat reached for a pile of what looked like hospital bills. Finding out what she owed for almost getting kidnapped would be the cherry on top of this lovely day of attempted murder.

"I'll open these depressing ones first. You start on the packages. I'm expecting some Bayberry and Bee Balm seeds. I was working on some new ideas last night, and I'm dying to get those seeds planted." Réka's eyes lit up at the prospect of new plant varieties. She loved caring for the farm's plants like Cat did.

After opening the fifth hospital invoice, she felt her pulse thrumming faster and faster. "Christ Almighty. I think they billed me for flipping breathing and using the damn toilet." Réka snorted in amusement but didn't comment.

She was about to set down the last invoice when one item out of the hundreds in the list caught her notice.

"Oh my God," she barely whimpered out of suddenly numb lips.

Réka went still across the desk. "What is it?" she whispered. When Cat didn't respond, she said more sharply but just as quiet, "What?" She must have known that whatever Cat was looking at, it was nothing for anyone else in the room to know.

She forced herself to slide the piece of paper across the desk, swallowing bile down her throat as Réka's eyes went side to side, scanning the list of blood results. Cat knew what she was about to see.

Pregnancy test.

Positive.

Réka's eyes went wide, and her mouth dropped open. She gripped the results tighter before meeting Cat's gaze once more.

"They didn't tell you?" she said, moving her mouth with as little sound as possible. She understood the assignment.

Top Secret.

Cat sighed, taking the paper back. "I remember there was an accident of some sort that day. A bus, maybe. The emergency room was crazy, and they barely had time to work me in. I'm sure the test got put aside in the chaos."

"What do you think ... he'll think?" Her eyes flicked toward Coll, who was on the phone and pacing by the bank of windows in the sitting area.

As if he knew Cat was watching him, his eyes met hers. Thomas was deep in conversation with the detectives, so he missed Coll mouthing, *I love you.*

"I guess that answers my question. The timing is not ideal."

Cat wasn't sure what held her attention more. The ruggedly handsome man of her dreams or how surprisingly well sarcasm fit comfortably around Réka's shoulders. "Yeah ... the timing could be better, but ... is it wrong to be excited? I mean, someone tried to kill me last night, but I'm only feeling excited. Slightly overwhelmed but hopeful and excited too."

"I'm happy for you. I promise to help out as much as you need me on the farm."

"Screw the farm. I'm going to need you to hold my hand. Stanley and Dean can take care of the farm," Cat laughed.

"Don't get me wrong, but Stanley and Dean love Legos more than plants. You know that, right?"

Cat giggled because it was true. She was about to answer when Detective Harvey came over. "Miss MacGregor—"

"Catriona please, Detective."

He nodded with a grim smile. "Would you mind answering some more questions for me?"

"Of course." Cat stood and led the way to the sitting area, where Coll was still pacing. Once they were seated, she asked, "What else would you like to know?"

"Unfortunately, or fortunately, if you're the detective on the case, we can rule out a crime of convenience where you're concerned. So that means we're dealing with a person or persons targeting you specifically. They know your schedule and where you live. They have the means to break into your security cameras.

"Mr. Barr disabled all the cameras the moment we found out the cameras had been breached. We've looked at the saved data and several breaches have occurred over the last few weeks. Early this morning at one-thirty this morning was the last one. So, unless they have someone hiding under a wheelbarrow reporting back, they might not know yet that you survived.

"Our window to find them is closing with every minute. They will find out you lived, and they will run. Those are the facts. Have you considered my earlier question? Is there anyone you are acquainted with that might be holding some sort of grudge against you?"

"I've been thinking about who might not like me or, I don't know, someone I've offended, and honestly, I live a very ... small life. I work. I make deliveries. My social life barely registers as social." Cat shrugged her shoulders, almost embarrassed at the lack of potential killers she might know.

"I'll need a list of past and current boyfriends."

Cat's face flamed red as she studiously avoided Coll, who she noted had become as still as a statue. Before she could say anything, Thomas butted in.

"There isn't any list," he growled, causing the detective's bushy eyebrows to wing up in question.

"I will write down the few men I've dated for you, Detective."

"What the hell do you mean by "men" as in multiple? I've only done a background check on the one college boy and your high school prom date."

Thomas was clearly all up in his feelings if his affronted brother-stance looming over her head was anything to go by.

"Talk about a cockblocker," Detective Harvey's partner mumbled. Unfortunately for him, Thomas heard.

"I suggest you shut your partner's mouth before I shut it for him," Thomas warned.

Coll ended his call and walked closer to Thomas' side. Ready to intercede if necessary. Her brother getting thrown in jail for assaulting an officer wouldn't make this day better.

"Thomas," Coll admonished.

"Don't Thomas me, Coll, when that motherfucker just suggested our sister gets around when he should be worrying about who's trying to fucking kill her!" he roared.

Detective Harvey quickly stood, holding a hand out to stave off Thomas from going after his partner, who now looked as white as a sheet. Having two pissed off gladiators looking at you like their next meal would shake most men.

"Wallace," Detective Harvey barked, "step outside."

As soon as the object of her brother's wrath was out of sight, Cat stood and grasped two of Thomas' fingers in her grip, something she'd done since she was a little girl. She instantly had his attention. "Brother, please. They're only doing their job. You know that. The list can fit on one hand, and the dates were extremely uneventful. Nothing to get worked up over. You're just upset about the gas. Calm down. For me."

He brought their hands to his chest and exhaled. Looking at Cat, he said, "I apologize, Detective."

War averted. Coll touched her back, and she couldn't help but look at him and smile softly. She couldn't wait to tell him her secret. When she turned back to Detective Harvey, he had a strange look on his face, which was glued to where Coll's pinky twined with her own before falling away.

Before she could attempt to deflect the detective's attention, a gasp from behind them had everyone turning. Réka was standing by the desk holding a small open box. Her face was white with a look of horror marring her beautiful features.

43

Where are you, Inti?

My men never came home from killing the demon. I don't think they even tried. They abandoned our cause.

They abandoned us.

I am surrounded by my blood and rotting corpses. Specters circle me. I'm afraid to close my eyes.

If I die—when I die, they will take great enjoyment in tearing me limb from limb.

Maybe ... maybe I've been going about this all wrong. Instead of bringing you back, I should have been coming to you.

I've failed you. Failed. Failed. Failed.

If I could just drag myself to the laptop, I could check the camera's monitoring the demon and your body.

I told you to come back, but if she still lives ...

What have I done?

Inti.

Inti.

Inti.

If I can kill her myself, you'll remember who I am.

I just need ...
If I could ...
Get up, Amaru.
Get up.
Inti ...

44

Coll knew Detective Harvey had seen him touch Cat. Having his name added to Cat's short list of boyfriends would not improve Thomas' mood, but it looked like that might be how their news came out. *Damn.* He wanted to be the one to tell his best friend about dating his sister. The timing was shit.

A gasp from behind them dragged him from his thoughts. Réka was standing with a small box in her hands, her whole body shaking, and she was staring right at Cat.

He and Thomas were by the woman's side, and each reached for the box when Harvey shouted, "Don't touch that box." He strode over while fitting latex gloves over his hands. "Miss Farkas, I'll take that from you."

The detective's jackass of a partner must have noticed the excitement through the office's glass windows and let himself back in.

They all stood around Cat's desk and watched as Harvey removed a ... doll. Thomas gave Coll an alarmed look over the top of Cat's head. Coll hadn't seen the front yet, but when he did. "Christ."

He didn't know anything about voodoo besides what a

person saw on television or read in *National Geographic*, but this was clearly a voodoo doll. It had six sharp, bloody pins stuck through the stuffed body and one stuck through the head.

There was a message written in what appeared to be dried blood on the inside of the box. *You are dead, Demon. He is mine.*

"Oh my God." Cat's voice warbled with emotion, and tears were squeezing out of her eyes. "Is that ... oh God, Tommy. Is that my hair?"

In horror, Coll finally realized that the red fluff on the doll's head was red and curly. "Catriona," he murmured, taking a step toward her.

"Miss MacGregor," the detective began in a stern tone. "Are you seeing a man that might have a jealous ex attached to him?"

Coll watched as Thomas realized the same thing he did at the same time. "Christ, Coll. It's Alvarez. She did follow you to Scotland, brother. Sonofabitch, that fucking bitch has been here all along. Why would she target my sister?"

Detective Harvey looked sharply at Coll, waiting for him to explain. He filled the detectives in on what had gone down in South America and exactly who Amaru and Inti Alvarez were. He despised bringing up that he'd had a one-night stand with the crazy drug lord, but he did it. He would divulge anything and everything if it would help them catch the woman terrorizing Cat.

Not a whole lot was making sense, so all Coll could do was go over what they did know. "She knew MacGregor Security had a hand in putting her brother behind bars where he was murdered. The DEA agent that she kidnapped and tortured gave up classified intel.

"It's why we believe she sought me out at a local bar. From things I found in the room, she'd performed some sort of witchy bullshit then, so this doll tracks. Thomas believes I was drugged at some point during the ... encounter." He briefly let himself look at Cat and sighed in relief. It didn't look like she hated him.

"If Amaru is behind Catriona's attacks, then she is clearly unhinged and trying to take out someone who is close to me like Inti was close to her. An eye for an eye sort of thing."

"Wallace, send everything we have so far to the DEA. They'll be interested if one of the biggest South American drug lords is holidaying in Scotland." Harvey turned back to Coll. "Why target Miss MacGregor?"

"It's simple. Her incestuous brother died, and she blames us. Cat is like a sister to Coll, so she's fair game in the woman's deranged mind."

Coll's chest thumped painfully. Thomas truly believed he felt for Cat like he felt for his true sister, Aileen. What a mess.

"She sent this doll to gloat. It's postmarked close to the date of the failed abduction. It was only luck on her part that Miss MacGregor was too injured to keep up with her post. We would have known someone was specifically after her, then."

"Coll placed our best trackers on the farm's security system. We've shut the camera's down on our end, but the moment Alvarez or whoever is behind this bullshit tries to hack into the system, we'll be notified immediately and be able to provide you with an address where the hacker is pinging from," Thomas explained.

Detective Harvey set the doll aside and told Wallace to get a forensics bag from the car. They would need to run tests to see if it was blood coating the pins and, if it was, who it belonged to.

Harvey set the doll to the side and pulled out a couple pieces of paper. No, not paper, but grainy, black-and-white photos, and Coll felt nausea rush up his throat. He looked at Cat, whose face showed her horror, before switching back to the detective, who was holding two pictures of Cat.

One where she was naked and bent backward on her desk. Coll's face wasn't visible because it was between her legs.

The other picture was of Cat riding him on the couch in her office. His hands were grasping her ass. Her hands were clasping his head to her breasts.

Both had *Whore* scratched over them.

He brought this to Catriona's door. He was responsible for her almost dying twice.

"Oh, Christ. I'm so sorry, baby," was all he could manage. The violation of their privacy was gut-wrenching. Thomas was back on the phone and hadn't seen the pictures. Yet. Never if Coll could manage.

"Please, Detective, I'm asking you not to let her brother see these." Thomas was moving back to the table. Coll was about to snatch them out of the officer's hand and destroy them, even though he would probably be arrested for tampering with evidence.

Just as Thomas loomed over the tense trio, Harvey put the photos back in the box, placed the doll on top, closed the lid, and shoved it in the clear evidence bag his partner had just handed him. Coll exhaled in relief. Cat's eyes closed briefly in thanks.

Having sex was nothing to be embarrassed or shamed about. He was furious to think that Cat's first time was violated in such a way. That was bad enough, but now she had to worry about her brother potentially seeing something so private ...

"Miss Farkas, Cat," Thomas growled, probably scaring the shit out of Réka. "You both will sleep at my house tonight."

Cat must have caught the stiffening of Réka's shoulders at the order. "Thomas." Cat said quietly, raising her brows and rolling her eyes toward the quiet woman at her side.

Thomas huffed in irritation, but he had never been a man who could stand to see a woman in any type of distress. "Umm, Miss Farkas, moving into Grandma's house instead of mine is a second option. I would ask that you choose one of them to ease my mind about your safety."

Jo had clearly made Thomas a lot more diplomatic. For Réka's part, her posture loosened. She was intelligent enough to see that Thomas wanted to protect her just like he did his sister.

"I would be very grateful to move in with Mrs. MacGregor. I will leave now and go gather the rest of my things from my cousin's and Catriona's."

"You aren't going anywhere alone. I mean," he caught himself, "I would prefer you take someone with you."

If Coll hadn't been watching the quiet gardener, he might have missed the slight lift of amusement on her lips. "I'll ask Stanley or Dean, Cat, if you don't mind."

"Great idea. I'll gather my things too and stay at Grandma's with you."

"No, you won't," Coll said sharply and regretted the tone instantly when Cat's chest and neck flushed red—a sure sign she was irritated but leaning toward pissed. "I should have said that Thomas and I would feel better with you staying in a well-secured house."

"You two are both so annoying. You know that, right?" When they both shrugged their broad shoulders in a way that they knew would piss her off, they grinned when she threw her hands up and stomped over to where Réka was seated.

"Coll, would you stay close to Cat today?" Thomas asked. "She'll get mad at me if I hover, and you two seem to be getting along better than usual."

Coll felt that damn squeeze of guilt. He had never been a liar, but here he was, lying to Thomas' face. "Of course."

Detective Harvey ended a call, announcing, "Your team, Barr, already tracked a small, blue van seen going toward Miss MacGregor's property with two occupants around one-thirty and was picked up again, leaving fifteen minutes later. They drove straight through Inverness, eventually exiting on to A9. We've got eyes on them now, and a team is gathering at the M6 toll.

"Whether they are working on their own or for Alvarez, I hope to know within the next hour."

Coll felt some relief that the case was seeing some results. He was about to gather Cat up and head to her house when an alarm went off on his phone. "Fuck! Harvey, I'm sending you an IP address now. Someone just tried to hack back into the security system." Harvey didn't ask questions but was instantly calling the Inverness precinct.

"Tom, I'm going to keep monitoring the signal. Call Dean and have him send the video and stills that Janice created. Make sure the camera on Cat's house shows the AI-generated image of the destroyed, smoking cottage." Tom was already speaking to Dean before Coll finished.

"Cat, you and Miss Farkas order food and drinks for everyone, please. We'll be at this until arrests are made and neither of you ladies has eaten a thing." When she started to argue, Coll cut her off. "I'm hungry too, baby. Do this for me. Plus, we both know you're an absolute bear when you're hungry."

"Hmph," Cat scoffed. "I'm calling Grandma for food and drinks. If I called in for delivery, she'd tan my hide."

"I should have thought of that." Coll said as he walked toward his obsession. He knew he shouldn't, absolutely should not, but he placed the flat of his hand on her lower back and bent down to whisper, "I love you desperately, Catriona MacGregor. Tell me you forgive me for all of this." *This* being Amaru Alvarez.

"I might need you to beg me on your knees," she whispered back.

"Baby ... I want to take you in my arms so bad. Getting on

my knees for you would be the least of attritions I would perform for you."

Detective Harvey's voice was an ice-cold shower on their brief, intimate moment. "I hid those pictures, but that act of kindness will be in vain if you two keep groping one another in front of Mr. MacGregor."

"Understood. My apologies, Detective." Coll responded while surreptitiously, he prayed, adjusting his manhood.

Harvey announced to the room, "They have a location. Wallace and I are meeting officers there now."

As the detectives rushed out the door, Coll said, "Thomas, stay here. I'm following the detectives. I want to see with my own eyes that this is over." Thomas nodded, understanding. Cat looked like she wanted to say something but settled for nodding as her brother had.

45

The demon's house is a smoking ruin.
I did it, Inti.
Find me.
Find me.
Please.

46

Coll stared down at the emaciated woman lying prone on an ambulance gurney. They had only just lifted her from the garage floor that was attached to the house she'd commandeered. The pale concrete bore streaks and smudges of blood, as did her filthy t-shirt. The only clothing besides panties that she wore. Water bottles and plates of what was most certainly cocaine littered the room.

Amaru was unrecognizable. Her shaved head had patches of dark fuzz where it had tried to grow. Her eyes were sunken and dark, her lips cracked and bleeding, and her legs and arms …

"Christ," he whispered. They were bruised and crusted. Hundreds upon hundreds of cuts had been made by the sharp, metal kitchen knife they'd found under one of her hips.

She'd cut herself everywhere, using her blood to write letters to her sick brother. Dirty pens were scattered about as well. She'd used them like quills to dip in her bloody ink. The detectives found piles of the letters around her body as well as a laptop with a cracked screen.

The coroner's office had already removed the three decomposing bodies from one of the upstairs bedrooms. They belonged to the poor family that had lived there.

The paramedics were trying to start an IV, but her veins were impossible to find. Dehydration had shriveled the woman like a mummy.

He briefly squeezed his eyes closed, sickened once again that he'd brought this insane killer to his family's door. To Cat.

The garage door had already been raised. The ambulance was backed up and waiting. The EMTs moved the gurney past where Coll stood, sickened and in shock, when Amaru's eyes suddenly opened wide, and she sucked in a deep breath, startling them all.

The pitiful woman found Coll and locked gazes. Her dead eyes burned with life for seconds only. Long enough to force words through her raspy, dry throat.

"Inti. You found me."

She died as the last word left her mouth. Her body still once more.

Coll felt just as empty. He looked at his right leg ... and wondered. He remembered tracing Catriona's bruises, smelled her cottage filled with gas ... and wondered.

What kind of man slept with evil?

Could that man ever be worthy again?

47

TWO WEEKS AFTER AMARU ALVAREZ WAS FOUND.

Cat still felt physically ill after reading the former drug lord and her potential murderer's incestuous love letters to her brother.

It was abhorrent. It was desperate, sad, and sobering.

It was ... awful.

She was gutted that Coll had been there to see the poor woman take her last breath. He hadn't told her. Coll confided in Thomas, who then told Cat. It sounded straight out of a horror movie. She tried to comfort Coll, and get him to talk about how he was feeling—how he was doing. He refused.

Amaru Alvarez was a product of abuse. How could Cat hate a woman who had once been an innocent child? She was groomed to become that person. The woman was a child laborer and a drug-producing killer who had come to Scotland to kill her.

Amaru was destroyed before she ever stepped foot in Scotland. She was a shell without a moral compass. To expect compassion from such a woman was a fool's wish, and Cat was no fool.

Amaru told her brother, Inti, in one of the letters—that had all been written in blood—that she had drugged Coll and asked him who he loved. He'd said, Catriona MacGregor. Of course, Thomas thought nothing of that, only that Alvarez had misunderstood the type of love Coll meant. Catriona understood though, and her heart thundered at each remembrance.

Was she saddened that the woman had died from a diet of cocaine and delusions? Yes and no. Amaru was a victim, but the woman had also created a legion of her own victims. Rehabilitation for someone that far gone ... Was it even possible?

The Drug Enforcement Agency, along with state, federal, and local agencies, raided the Alvarez facilities—all of them this time thanks to Amaru's personal laptop. She hadn't meant for it to happen, but because of her, one of the biggest drug-producing families was gone, and hundreds of men, women, and children were saved from forced labor. Without their true leader, her soldiers fled or surrendered. They destroyed millions of dollars worth of product and arrested several top leaders under Amaru.

The two men who had first attempted to kidnap Cat were apprehended. They admitted to working for Amaru. There had been one other man, but he'd left days before. Out of loyalty to the woman, they did everything she asked until her sanity, or lack of it, could no longer be ignored.

They knew if they stayed, they would die with her. Their plan was to kidnap a woman in London that resembled Amaru and use her as a ticket to board the Alvarez's private jet that was currently hidden in a rented hanger. They gave up the pilot's location, and he was arrested as well.

Forensic testing proved that the hair on the voodoo doll was, in fact, Cat's own. The brush that had gone missing all those weeks ago ... The pins were dipped in two of Amaru's brothers' blood, as well as a family of three whose house she had commandeered in Inverness, and the last was from a victim left crumpled in an alley. That was one of the murder investigations the detectives had been working on at the same time as her case.

Cat was meant to be the seventh in some twisted witchcraft ceremony, all in an effort to resurrect Amaru's dead, pedophiliac brother.

Inti Alvarez was filth. Amaru Alvarez had right from wrong taken from her as a child. The letter that she had so painstakingly written for her brother would haunt Cat.

She would never wish death upon another person, but in all honesty, it was a relief that Amaru did die. She had died of blood loss, malnutrition, drugs, and a broken heart. A horrible, sad way to go, but it was over. The threat to her family was over. The guards and the worry were over.

She had believed that after the whirlwind of Amaru Alvarez died down, she and Coll would have announced to the family that they were in a relationship. Not only had they not taken that next step, but they had taken three steps back.

Aileen, Mirren, and Charles had arrived the night before, and it was proving to be one more roadblock between her and Coll. She was thrilled that her ex-sister-in-law and niece were back in Scotland, but damn it, it felt like Coll was using any and every excuse to keep their relationship a secret.

First it was giving information and statements to the Inverness detectives. Then it was getting Réka settled into Grandma's. Then it was helping Aileen and Charles hire contractors to remodel the old Barr family home. They planned on living at Aileen's old house while the farmhouse was renovated.

Next came fixing Grandma's washing machine, Zoom meetings with MacGregor Security team leaders, going with Thomas to pick out a car for Mirren, and a hundred other minor things that Cat eventually stopped listening to. With every excuse Coll had for not spending time with her, her spirits drooped a little more.

She threw herself into work, creating in her workshop and finally meeting with the production and packaging company in Glasgow. She'd had to cancel her first appointment because of the kidnapping thing. Black and blue mottled skin wouldn't have made a great first impression.

She ended up signing a contract with them, and they were currently in the process of label design. She would have loved to discuss her exciting news with Coll, but if he ever gave her a moment, she wanted to tell him about the baby. MacGregor Farm could wait.

A hundred times a day, she thought of forcing Coll to stop and just listen to her. She was bursting to tell him he was going to be a father. They hadn't had sex since before the gas leak. Secret touches, brushes to her back or hands, and certainly kisses were few and far between.

Talking about their feelings ... nonexistent.

The more he pulled back, Cat began to wonder if maybe he'd changed his mind. Maybe he didn't want to be with her after all. If she'd told him about the baby now, he would have done the right thing, but she didn't want that to be the only reason he committed.

She missed him, worse even than when he would be gone for months at a time on security jobs because now she knew what it felt like to be wrapped in his arms.

What it felt like to have him say "I love you."

In the end, she and Réka had gone to see her new obstetrician together. Her shy, introverted gardener turned out to be not so shy, only cautious. Réka had fast become one of Cat's best friends, and an astute partner to bounce ideas off of about the future of MacGregor Farm. There was nothing like almost dying together to create a bond.

It had been a relief to find out that the gas leak had done no long-term damage to herself or her baby. She was able to give the doctor the exact day she'd gotten pregnant since they'd only been together once before the hospital had taken a blood sample.

She was right at six weeks now. She didn't want to be a single mom. She didn't want to be single period. Her patience for Coll's nonsense had run out days ago.

She was done letting him shut her out. From his brooding looks, it didn't look like he was happy with the separation either. "Do something about it then, you giant asshole," she mumbled to herself.

Cat was on her way to Thomas and Jo's. They were having a cookout to welcome Aileen and Mirren home. She wouldn't add Charles to that list. Yet. Her brother did a much better job at hiding his animosity towards the man than Coll did. Coll still struggled to be civil. He would either get with the Charles-Aileen program or his sister would line his ass up.

She slammed her truck door and took the path around the house to the covered back patio, where Thomas did all the grilling. There was laughter, low music, the clink of glasses, and the smell of cooking beef.

Normally, this would have been the best way to spend an afternoon and evening, but the smell of cooking meat ... Jesus, have mercy ... She felt her gorge rise the closer she got. She paused to dig a nausea sucker that Tara sold her after Cat swore her to secrecy. She crunched the sucker enough to work it off the stick. No need to announce her mama status to Josephine.

As soon as she came into view of her family, Jo noticed her and waved her over. "Come see the newest little O'Faolain. Rowan finally popped."

"I wasn't a fucking pimple, Jo. Jesus. Hey, Cat," Rowan smiled sweetly from the tablet's screen. "Want to meet Bébhinn Clarissa. Bébhinn is for my grandma, and Clarissa is Hugh's grandma's middle name, which is so close to my middle name, Clary."

The screen was then taken up with the most dainty little fairy of a girl. Black hair clipped with a tiny gold wolf barrette, clearly a one-of-a-kind baby accessory. Bébhinn had her mother's dark hair and brilliant hazel eyes. Her golden skin was all Hugh O'Faolain.

Cat felt tears prick her eyes. "She's the most beautiful wee girl I've ever seen, Row. She's stunning. Hugh must be over-the-top in love with his daughter." Out of the corner of her eye, Coll was staring at her from the sidelines. *Not for long, Mr. Barr*.

"Next to my father, Hugh is the best daddy I've ever known." Rowan's voice was full of happiness. "You're going to have to get busy and start on a wee Cat of your own," she teased.

While Thomas, The Annoying One, flipped burgers, he gave his unasked-for opinion. "Cat's too young for a boyfriend, let alone thinking about children."

Ignore him or kick him in the knee? Decisions. Decisions.

In a mock whisper, Rowan said, "Please tell me you don't let Honey Bunny anywhere near your dates."

Cat still giggled at the nickname Jo had named her brother when they first met. To be named after a fluffy blond petting zoo rabbit was the best sort of middle finger to Thomas' gruff exterior.

"I do my best to shake Thumper off my tail." A good old *Bambi* reference never failed to get a laugh. The back of her brother's neck was bright red. *Score.* He so deserved it.

Everyone signed off with Rowan, with promises to visit soon. They would be seeing all their Dublin and Oklahoma friends soon enough for Jo's baby shower. Raven had asked Cat to do the flower arrangements for it. She had a million ideas.

Cat grabbed a water bottle from one of the under-counter mini fridges, wishing her fingers could have latched onto one of the cold bottles of Guinness instead. As she took a drink, she noticed Coll staring at her. The only thing he managed with any regularity.

Thomas asked someone to go inside and grab the plate of cut vegetables from the kitchen. Unsurprisingly, Coll volunteered with alacrity. Cat was obviously too close for comfort, she thought, gritting her teeth.

Smiling at Aileen, who'd just walked up, Cat excused herself and followed Coll. She would get answers and be satisfied with them or walk away and spend the rest of her life trying to be satisfied.

When she entered the kitchen, Coll's back was to her at the open refrigerator door. He'd left the house door open, so she'd been able to enter the house without alerting him to her presence. She put her hand on the center island while Coll grabbed a cellophane-covered tray of fresh veg.

When their eyes met, she would swear she saw panic flash in his normally stoic expression. *Now or never, Cat.* "You've been avoiding me for two weeks, Coll. I deserve honesty at the least. If you no longer want to see me, or I suppose I mean, if you no longer want to have an intimate relationship with me, then I would appreciate a little fucking honesty. I deserve that, at the very least, surely."

Coll swallowed tightly, his throat bobbing in discomfort. Cat stiffened her body, preparing for an emotional blow she so didn't want to hear and certainly did not want to accept.

"Cat." His voice was beseeching as one of his hands reached, pleading toward her.

"Just admit it to me, Coll. Please. You changed your mind. You aren't attracted to me after all. You don't want us to come between you and my brother. I was an itch you scratched. You've met someone new. You've reconnected with a past girlfriend. You're embarrassed to be seen with me. You never loved me.

"Just fucking pick one and put me out of my misery. It will be awful, Coll Barr, but if you don't want me, I will survive you. I won't want to, but I will." Cat didn't realize she was crying until Coll was directly before her, wiping her tears with his rough thumbs.

He pulled her body flush to his own and crooned nonsense words into her ear. "Hush, baby, hush. There is no one I will ever want more than you. No one ever." He tenderly kissed her lips, her tears binding them both.

"But ... you pushed me away. You don't talk to me. You don't even look at me, Coll. Why?" she pleaded for an answer.

His answer was to deepen the kiss. She deserved the truth, but she wanted his mouth to own hers more. With a whimper, she gave herself over to the glory that was Coll's tongue.

He placed his hands on her ass and pulled her up his body until her legs could wrap around his waist. He fisted her curls, wrapping his knuckles in inches of red shackles.

She pulled back, though it killed her. "If this is how you feel, then what have these past few weeks been about?"

Coll was well-versed in distracting tactics. He didn't answer her question. He just kept watching her with a stony expression.

His answer was to move her hips over his viciously hard erection. The layers of their denim were stimulating and maddening.

Cat was panting and willing to take whatever he would give her with or without an explanation, which was probably his intention.

She reached her hand between them, easily slipping past his waistband, burrowing under his boxers. They both groaned as she fisted his sex and began to pump his length in time with the suck and stroke of his tongue.

"Cat. Christ, I want ..." Coll didn't finish his thought. His mouth was sealed to hers again before he could say anything else.

They were lost in each other, lost not in reconciliation but certainly lust.

Until ...

"Catriona? Coll?" The horror in Thomas' voice had them pulling apart with guilt.

"I can explain," Cat began, though Coll was still gripping her ass, and her hand, hopefully hidden, was still down his pants.

"Brother," Coll started with grim determination.

"You are no brother of mine," Thomas stated with cold detachment. "Put my sister down." And then, "You're a dead man for this."

48

How many times can a person fuck up? It must be limitless. His stupidity could easily fill an American all-you-can-eat buffet.

He was first drawn to Cat when she'd been barely twenty. That was wrong. He began a sexual relationship with Cat even though he knew he should have spoken to Thomas first. That was worse.

At least Thomas had the courtesy of asking Coll before he dated Aileen—and that had only been a kiss here and there, which Coll had hated and been pissed about, but still ... His best friend hadn't been screwing his little sister every which way he could. No ... that was all Coll.

Of course, there was the whole sleeping with the psychotic enemy in South America and speaking Catriona's sweet name in that dark hostel. She'd almost died twice because of it.

The latest bad decision—pushing away the woman he desperately loved and making her think that he wasn't interested.

And what had his streak of idiocy gotten him?

"You're a dead man for this."

He'd seen every emotion in his friend; happy, sad, disappointment, anger, rage, devastation, loss, loneliness, and everything in between. Right now, the man standing six feet away was a stone-cold, expressionless, emotionless machine.

Coll had done that to him because he'd been a selfish coward. He let Catriona slide down his body until he was sure her feet were steady beneath her. He couldn't bring himself to look at her. She loved her brother and would hate what was happening.

"Go outside, Cat. Now."

That was the first time Coll had ever heard Thomas speak to his sister that way, and it pissed him off. "You're pissed at me, Tommy. Don't take it out on her." Glancing her way, he said, "Please, Cat, go back to the others." Coll didn't dare touch her in comfort. He was sure that any contact would only set Thomas off worse.

She began to walk by her brother on her way out but paused. "I think you need to remember, brother, that I am a grown woman, a responsible grown woman. You have loved me my whole life. You have made me feel safe. You have sacrificed for all of us, and I love you. You have been a brother and a father figure. Your happiness is everything to me. I hope that goes both ways."

Thomas barely hid his wince, but Coll knew it would take more than that to make him back down.

The second the door closed, "How long?"

How long since he'd first realized he wanted her to be his? Coll doubted Thomas was asking that. "A little more than six weeks."

"You lied to me for six weeks?"

"Yes."

"Does our friendship mean nothing to you then?"

"It means everything." Coll could feel his chest start to cave in under the pressure of his regrets.

"I married your sister because I loved you both. I sacrificed. For you!" he barked. His ice was beginning to crack.

"Loved?"

"Don't bring Aileen into this."

"You're the one who did that, bro—" Coll cut himself off. "Don't let your anger at me affect your feelings for my sister."

"I would never."

"We planned on telling you. The morning of the gas leak," he explained. "We were going to tell you."

"I should have been told well before. I should have been *asked*." Thomas slammed his hand down on the marble countertop. Coll was shocked it didn't shatter.

"I know."

"Does anyone else know?"

He hesitated, but he refused to lie again. "I think Grandma knows." Coll could tell that shocked him.

"Have you ... have you ..." Thomas floundered over the question. The one question Coll was dreading.

"Yes."

Thomas' big hands were fisted at his sides, and Coll knew he was attempting to control the urge to smash his face in with them.

"Did you ... protect her?"

It was Coll's turn to wince. It was also the last straw for Thomas. With a sudden roar, he grabbed Coll by his shirt and threw him out the kitchen door. Coll's body shattered glass and splintered wood.

∾

CAT WANTED TO SAY NO, that she wouldn't go outside. She wanted to tell her brother that she loved Coll, and he loved her but ... did he still? If she had doubts, Thomas would exploit them instantly. Feeling his thick sex between her legs only moments before, and his tongue down her throat, she could say with assurance that Coll was in lust with her—somehow, she didn't think that would make her overprotective brother less lethal.

So, she walked out of the kitchen like a chastised, naughty child and rejoined the group. This was exactly what they hadn't wanted to happen, especially now that Cat was questioning the relationship.

Coll would not bow out now. He would never dishonor her in that way. He might have broken up with her if Thomas had been still in the dark, but now ...

She attempted to sip her water and smile as if the destruction of her future happiness wasn't playing out feet away.

Aileen approached her and touched her shoulder. "Cat," she said in a concerned tone, "tell me what's troubling you."

Tears instantly pricked Cat's eyes. Here Aileen was, bravely beating cancer's ass and rekindling a love she thought she'd lost over sixteen years ago, and she was trying to fix Cat's problems.

She was about to reply that she was fine when the shocking sound of glass shattering and male shouting stunned the group. Cat prayed she was hallucinating Coll and Thomas rolling across the grass not four yards from them.

"You piece of shit!" Thomas bellowed. "She's my sister!"

Cat felt her ears begin to burn as all eyes swung from the spectacle to Cat and back again. The brief flashes she'd entertained of her and Coll holding hands and smiling into one another's eyes as they told the family they were in love were now overlayed with the image of a toilet flushing.

Cat heard Jo mumble, "Oh, shit," before Aileen's, "Oh

Christ. Jo, can you grab your husband before he kills my brother?" completed by Mirren's, "This is so 1998 Jerry Springer. Can I record it?"

Punch. Grunt. Elbow to the stomach. "We were going to tell you, for fuck's sake, Tommy!"

Cat stood frozen, petrified at the exact spectacle they had hoped to avoid.

Punch to the stomach. Roll. Punch to the thigh. Twin groans. "When, you bastard? When Wee Cat was bursting at the seams with your baby because you obviously couldn't be troubled to use protection?"

Cat moaned in embarrassed agony.

Jo squeezed Cat's hand. "Let me try." Before Cat could say yea or nay, her sister-in-law was marching over to Coll and Thomas.

"Honey Bunny," she cooed, "is everything okay?"

At least her brother wasn't so far gone that he'd risk plowing into his pregnant wife's feet. Both men paused, sweat and blood dripping from foreheads and mouths. They both looked like overgrown toddlers as they stared up at Josephine.

"Go inside now, Jo." Thomas' dictatorial tone raised Jo's brows and had her brother swallowing in instant regret. "Please."

"Thomas," she said quietly, causing him to still and sit up. "I don't like seeing you so upset. What can I do?"

Jo was good. Damn good. Cat chanced a glance at Coll, who was currently straddling her brother's hips. He wasn't looking her way. If she were a betting woman, she'd say he was taking great care not to look her way. Crushed, Cat swallowed down more tears and instead stood stiffly by Mirren, who had walked up to her side.

"Coll and Cat ... they ... he ... I'm going to kill him for touching her," Thomas finally got out on a snarl.

"Answer this, babe," Jo began reasonably. "Does your sister love you?"

"Of course."

"Does Coll love you?" Thomas' face became redder, and he clenched his jaw. "Thomas," Jo chided softly.

"Yes."

"Would either of them hurt you purposefully?"

Thomas used his T-shirt to blot the blood dripping from his nose. "They wouldn't."

"You're the most honorable man I know, and I'm pretty positive you didn't call my dad or brother before we had sex."

"Not the same. They weren't my best friend."

"He's right, Jo." Coll sighed and sat back.

"Okay. Maybe you both would consider using your words now. I'm not convinced your daughter didn't video you two. If I had to guess, the Byrnes and O'Faolains will be receiving it soon."

Cat heard both men grumble, something too low for her to hear, but it seemed the worst was over. She expelled the breath she'd been holding. She kept waiting for Coll to look at her ... acknowledge her. He didn't, not even when Jo rejoined the small group by the grill.

"Let me get this straight," Mirren began. "My Auntie Cat has been secretly riding my Uncle Colly's baloney pony."

"Mirren Mòr MacGregor!" Aileen choked on her own spit when she gasped so deeply.

"What?" Mirren asked with a totally contrived innocent smile. "I mean, I have two dads. The first one married my mom even though they were brother and sister in every way except blood. My new stepmother has airplane fetishes," to which she grinned at Josephine and patted her pregnant belly, making Jo blush. "Mom and my second dad need rabbit nicknames too if you know what I mean, and my aunt and uncle have sex—am I the only one here who thinks we need a session with Dr. Phil?"

"Charles," Aileen wailed, "do something for the love of God. Thomas is too deep in his mantrum to discipline her himself!"

Cat didn't bother to tell Aileen that Charles wouldn't be disciplining anyone anytime soon since he could barely keep his laughter in. His shoulders were shaking so hard he looked like a marionette with a drunk marionettist.

"I guess this answers your question, Jo, about who was sending nude pics to Uncle Coll."

Now Cat knew that the idiom die of shame was literal. She literally might die. Coll hadn't told her Thomas had seen ... "Oh, my God." Cat whispered, scrubbing her hands over her burning cheeks.

"Mirren! For everything that is holy, stop speaking," Aileen pleaded. "How did you even know about that?"

"You had Jo on speaker, and I was in the kitchen making tea." Mirren faced Cat. "I'm sorry Aunt Cat. I shouldn't have brought it up, but seriously, I would run away and hide for the rest of my days if I sent a nudie and my dad saw it. Like ... puke."

"Thomas is not Catriona's dad," Charles attempted to interject.

"I know, it's her brother. Even worse." Mirren made gagging noises to help emphasize how gross she thought the prospect. Cat couldn't disagree.

"Not helping, Mir," Jo chided, looking at Cat with a grimace of apology. "If Thomas ever finds out..." Jo shuddered. They all shuddered.

The two most important men in her life were back to exchanging insults—fists were soon to follow.

She texted Réka as soon as the shit had hit the fan, and it

became abundantly clear that Coll was more dedicated to smoothing things over with his best friend than making sure his "girlfriend" was still ... his girlfriend.

She spied Réka's beater coming up the drive and slipped away from the trainwreck still unfolding around her. She just needed to get away and talk to a friend.

When she reached Réka's car, the woman was already out and walking toward Cat to envelop her in a big hug. Cat hadn't cried so far, but the moment she felt Réka's arms snug around her shoulders and hands patting her shoulders, the first hiccupping tears started to fall.

"Sorry, I called you. It's a mess here."

"Never be sorry for either thing. What happened? Can you tell me? Or will you tell me, I guess?" She added shyly, while stepping back.

"Thomas found Coll and I kissing."

Réka winced in commiseration. "Does that mean you guys worked out what's been bothering Coll the past few weeks?"

Cat shook her head and leaned against the car. "He wouldn't explain anything. He just stared at me and then ..."

"Kissed you?"

"Yes. Christ, I'm weak."

Cat was about to ask her friend to take her somewhere, anywhere when the women heard a man bellowing her name.

"Catriona MacGregor!" Coll was limping down the drive, fresh blood leaking from his nose and mouth.

49

Coll's body ached. Damn, Thomas, for being such a beast with his fists. At least he had the satisfaction of knowing he'd given as good as he got if his friend's groans were anything to go by.

After Jo had walked away, peace lasted all of five minutes. Only a few words of trying to make his friend understand Coll's feelings toward Catriona, and Thomas punched him in the stomach. It was on again. Coll stood unsteadily on his feet, bent slightly at the waist, attempting to catch his breath.

His damn leg was on fire. He could tell his prosthesis wasn't sitting properly against his residual limb. Thomas began to move toward him, fists raised in aggression. Coll held his hands up. "Give me a minute, brother." Damn, if he didn't feel his face burn with embarrassment when he lifted his pant leg and tried to adjust the straps more securely to his knee—not an easy task when he wasn't seated or at least leaning against a solid surface.

He saw from his peripheral vision that Thomas took another step forward. "Christ, Tommy, give me a goddamn minute." Coll's knee was really starting to hurt him. He was beyond exasperated and frustrated, and he desperately needed to speak to Cat.

"Sit, Coll." Thomas' heavy hand pressed against his shoulder until he relented and sat. "Let me help you, for fuck's sake."

Together, they adjusted his leg until it wasn't biting into his flesh. He and Tommy worked efficiently together as they had in every other aspect of their lives.

"I'm sorry I did ... something to hurt your ... your leg." Thomas hung his head as if he were ashamed to have fought a handicapped person while grasping Coll's hand to boost him up.

"Fuck you, Tom. I would have taken you with or without the leg. Cat told me that even though I may look different, I'm still me, and I can still hand you your fat ass."

"Wee Cat told you that, huh?" Thomas scrubbed his face. "Do you love her? No bullshit, Coll. Do you love her like I love Josephine?"

"There will never be anyone else. Yes."

"I guess there isn't anything left to fight about then." Thomas rubbed his bruised and bloody knuckles.

"I hope not, brother. My ribs are screaming at me, you ham-fisted prick."

"One good thing about a good brawl is that I get to have Jo dote all over me later." Thomas grinned, wagging his brows and looking ridiculous.

"Just the thought of Cat's warming massage oil makes me—"

"Too fucking soon," Thomas warned, cutting Coll off.

Coll finally let himself look toward the cooking area where the family was gathered, but Cat wasn't there. He walked toward his sister. "Where is she?" Aileen just shook her head, probably lamenting the fact that he was her brother, and pointed behind her.

Coll headed off, every step a slice of misery. He'd really screwed up his damn knee. No matter. He had to find her. Just as he took another misery-inducing step, he felt a strong arm wrap around his waist.

"I've got you. Brother."

Coll felt tears prick his eyes. Unfortunately, Coll was still close enough to hear his niece's saucy mouth.

"No, River, it was totally a real video. Yes. Yes. Oh my God, not even I could make this stuff up. Mmhmm. Yeah, like, what do I say? Hey everyone, this is my aunt and uncle twice over. I know. Seriously, my family is getting as weird as yours. If Jerry Springer steps from behind one of the trees with a polygraph test, I'll video it. Okay. Kiss, kiss. Bye."

"You're going to have your hands full with Mirren."

"I'm very aware," Thomas replied dryly.

The driveway in front of the house came into view, and finally, finally, so did Cat. "Let me walk on my own now. You know how she is, Tom. Despite how pissed she is at me, she'll insist on doctoring me up before listening to what I have to say." Without comment, which he was sure almost killed the overprotective sonofabitch, Thomas dropped his arm.

Coll hollered, "Catriona MacGregor!" He startled her, which stopped her from getting in Réka's car. Good. She was about to run, and that couldn't happen.

He limped a little closer, Thomas still at his shoulder. "Will you let me explain?"

Cat bristled. Her tiny fists planted on her hips. *God, but she was lovely.*

"Why? Have you finished smoothing things out with my brother? Did you finally remember I exist after avoiding me for two weeks?"

Damn ... "I've been an idiot." He watched Cat squeeze

Réka's hand before letting go and walking a few steps in his direction.

Crossing her arms over her chest, she looked furiously between him and her brother. "What exactly are you sorry for?"

Now or never, Coll. Taking a deep breath, Coll closed the distance between them. They were only an arm's length apart. "I'm sorry I ever thought it was a good idea to lie to our families about us. I'm sorry that I didn't tell everyone how much you mean to me. I'm sorry that ... that I did something two years ago that hurt you. When I found out that Amaru came after you because I told her that I loved you—it didn't matter that I was drugged. I compromised you. I'm furious that I was with that woman in the first place when I knew even then that you were the only woman I want—"

"That was two years ago!" Thomas angrily interjected as he stood looming over Coll's shoulder, clearly listening to every word he was saying to his sister. *Jesus.*

"I'm aware, Tommy. Now, shut the fuck up," he growled back.

"I began to question whether I deserved you. I want to deserve you, but ... you were hurt because of me and—"

"And I don't care, Coll. You could have never known what that woman was capable of. We love each other. That's all that should have mattered."

She was right. At the end of the day, that was all that should matter. He felt tremendous relief, followed by tremendous joy, capped off with terror. He dug around in his front pocket until he found the tiny, slim gold circle hidden at the bottom.

He held it out in front of him and watched as Cat's eyes went wide. "It's a lucky thing your fat-headed brother didn't squish your wedding ring."

"My wedding ring." Cat repeated in wonder, choosing to ignore her brother's squawking.

"That is, if you want to marry me. I mean, damn it ... How in the hell am I screwing this up?"

"I did too. Just keep going," Thomas added helpfully. *Ignore that your brother is a part of your marriage proposal. Ignore. Ignore. Ignore.*

"Right. Will you marry me, Catriona Elizabeth MacGregor? It's simple, I know. Just a gold band, but I wanted you to never take it off even when you have your hands deep in soil. I wanted you to have something classic and beautiful. I wanted you to look at that ring and see what I see when I look at you. A promise of forever."

"Forever." She had to blink rapidly to stop the tears, and then, "Yes." She giggled as Coll picked her up and hugged her to his chest while Thomas put his arms around them both.

Her family had moved to surround them by then. At some point, Grandma had come, and she was hugging a grinning Réka, who must have called her before she got here. Jo was trying to drag Thomas off of them—with no success. Mirren was holding her phone up, and Cat saw Raven, River, and Rowan's faces smiling and waving. Aileen was grinning at Cat, and Charles was grinning at Aileen.

"I love you, Kitty Cat" Coll spoke against her lips.

"Jesus, man, do you have to touch my wee sister in front of me?" Thomas grumbled.

"You wouldn't know he was touching me, you giant ass, if you weren't stuck to us like a damn burdock."

Thankfully, Grandma took mercy on her and Coll, and after hugging and congratulating them both, she herded everyone back to the outdoor kitchen to give them a moment of privacy. That didn't mean they were spared the family commentary as they slowly departed.

"So, Dad, do you think you'll ever be able to unsee Aunt Cat's nudie she sent Uncle Colly?" Mirren, President of the Shit Stirers.

Coll groaned right before Thomas sounded like a mortally wounded animal. "God, no. No. I'm going to kill him."

"Maybe if you hadn't been snooping on your brother's phone, you wouldn't have seen your sister's breasts," Grandma sniffed in righteous indignation.

"Is there no one here that didn't just hear that statement and throw up in their mouth?" Mirren asked.

"That's it," Aileen moaned. "Charles and I are tapping out of parenting the rest of the day, Thomas. You and Jo are up."

Before they were out of earshot, Mirren, ornery shit that she was, added, "Did Réka tell you guys that Detective Harvey is sweet on her? Reciprocation to be decided."

"Mirren," Réka choked and it sounded like someone pounded her unhelpfully on the back. "He certainly is not."

"Really? When you, Gram, and I were at the grocery store, he tried to say hello to you and ended up falling over a display of apples. I'm not a psychologist, but ..."

And then, finally, silence. "They're gone," Cat said as she wrapped her arms around Coll's waist and hugged him tight.

"And thank God and his mercy for that." He cupped her face gently, urging her to look into his eyes. "You've agreed to be my wife." The wonder in his voice made swirls of anticipation move through her breast.

"I have. And you've agreed to be my husband."

"I did." He bent and placed a firm but chaste kiss on her lips.

"And will you also promise to be a good father?" She could tell her words surprised him, but he, of course, believed she spoke in hypotheticals.

"The best of," he assured.

Cat traced a finger down one of his sculpted cheeks and across his sensual lips, scratching her blunt nail down to his chin. "Good then, because I'm pregnant."

Shocked wonder crossed his face and without a word, Coll dropped to his knees ... grimacing because he'd obviously hurt himself during the childish tussle with her brother ... and placed a reverent kiss on the flat of her stomach.

Time seemed to stand still in that moment, only broken by the clear, high voice of her niece.

"Dad. You owe River Byrne a hundred pounds."

ALSO BY ANNE GREGOR

The Scottish Lions

Josephine

Catriona

The Irish Wolves Trilogy

Raven

River

Rowan

ABOUT THE AUTHOR

Anne Gregor has a Master of Arts in History with an emphasis on the Civil War. For her thesis, she focused on Irish immigrants working the transcontinental railroad across America, specifically those who settled in Oklahoma amongst Native Americans. A love for research turned into a love for fictional writing, and soon, every old document Anne ever studied became the premise for a novel. Anne Gregor has been writing book reviews for several years and is a freelance proofreader. Oklahoma is near and dear to her heart as she lives on Grand Lake O' the Cherokees. **Anne is the author of two contemporary romance series, The Irish Wolves Trilogy and The Scottish Lions Duology.**